SAWFISH

RICK CHESLER

SEVERED PRESS
HOBART TASMANIA

SAWFISH

Copyright © 2016 Rick Chesler
Copyright © 2016 by Severed Press

WWW.SEVEREDPRESS.COM

ISBN: 978-1-925493-02-3

ACKNOWLEDGEMENTS

Special thanks to forensic death investigator and author J. Kent Holloway for his expertise on medical examiner operations. Any inaccuracies in this area are mine and mine alone.

1

Virginia Key, Florida
"Feeding time!"

Dr. Mason Rayman found it not the least bit unusual he was talking to himself. Well, not to himself, exactly, but to some animals, a group of fish. Very large fish, but fish nonetheless. He felt like he knew them, after all, what with the months of tender love and care he'd given them.

He breezed through the concrete-floored passageway, towing a large cooler on wheels between two rows of enormous round tanks, each about shoulder high. The tanks were not see-through, but made of an opaque blue plastic, open on the top. He was in the semi-outdoor portion of his laboratory, a space with a metal roof to protect the aquaria and their denizens from the rain and blistering South Florida sun, but with walls that were only corrugated metal, leaving open space top and bottom to let in air and light. Beyond the token walls of the marine lab lay the turquoise waters of Biscayne Bay. A long highway bridge, the Rickenbacker Causeway, connected this small island once shaped by hurricanes to the urban hotbed that was Miami.

Rayman heard splashes from the tanks while he walked, his charges anticipating their coming meal. He looked over to his right and saw a slash of gray carve at the water's surface.

"Hey there, number eight, how's it going today?" He stopped in front of the tank and opened the cooler. He grabbed two fistfuls of bloody fish hunks and tossed them into the tank, where the splashing grew more intense.

"Glad you like it, number eight! Bon appétit."

Rayman watched as the lab subject slashed its head back and forth in frenzied, lateral motions. The scientist chuckled to himself. "Easy boy. They're already hacked up for you, no need to slash it up yourself!" But the fish paid him no mind. It was embedded deep in its nature, buried somewhere in the very biochemicals of its genes to slash and hack and shake its guitar-shaped body back and forth. Its behavior would never change.

A sawfish.

Closely related to sharks but actually a type of ray, their most distinctive feature was the namesake appendage that was actually an extension of the head with a number of serrated teeth on each side.

Rayman heard more splashing from the other tanks as the fish sensed the commotion and knew what was coming. He looked up, eyes scanning the tanks as he addressed his charges. He'd been working with this group of a dozen sawfish for the past two years, part of a minor government grant he'd received to study electro-receptors in fish. Although the tanks and their sawfish took up a lot of space and looked impressive to visitors, they were not the main thrust of his work.

A professional researcher, Dr. Rayman had taken on extra grants in recent years, to the point he no longer even taught classes. His largest grant was, ironically, to study the smallest animals, copepods—tiny crab-like crustaceans. In his grant proposal, he had promised he would find out how gigantism—excessive growth usually due to hormonal imbalance—works in copepods. Turn little critters into big ones—sounds like fun, right?

But as the work went on, Rayman soon found out that it was anything but. Despite many different approaches, the insect-sized creatures stubbornly refused to grow. Although the purpose of his work was to discover mechanisms of gigantism, none of the methods he'd tried so far worked. Not that he expected a giant to suddenly appear overnight. Any kind of growth spurt would suffice, as these were all adult specimens from their time of acquisition, and adults did not grow in appreciable amounts over short periods of time. Yet, the last he had measured, the length, width and weight of the creatures had not been significantly different from when the study had started. He glanced over at the rack of more familiar-looking rectangular fish tanks that lined one wall. Inside them, hundreds of copepods fluttered about like aquatic insects. He shook his head while looking at them.

A disconcerting thought crept over him: *Could that be why the bean counters holding the purse strings have been grumbling lately?* Funding was tight. He and all of his colleagues had heard it over and over in recent months. Results were key. Demonstrating what did not work was not enough. And to that end, his results had been sorely lacking. All these months later, trying different things and his copepods were still normal size. He was going to have to admit that—

Something caught his eye in the far corner, Tank #12.

A head breaking the surface of the water. A head with attached saw.

Rayman did a double-take as his brain tried valiantly to process what his eyes were showing him. *No way. What is this?* Then, a second later... *How could I not have noticed this the second I walked in?*

For there in front of him, in the last tank on the right, thrashed a sawfish so large that had he been watching a video instead of standing there in person, he'd have bet his own life that it was some kind of image trickery and not real. But because he was standing here, smack dab in the middle of his own lab, he knew beyond a shadow of a doubt that this was by far the largest sawfish he had ever laid eyes on.

He mentally estimated its length as he neared the tank, his feet slowing their pace as he approached the beast. *Gotta be thirty feet long.* But that was impossible. This species of sawfish, the Atlantic Smalltooth, grew to a maximum recorded length of 21 feet in the wild, with the average adult length being closer to twelve feet. But this...

Rayman scoped out the enormous thing in Tank #12. "What happened to you, number twelve?"

His answer came in the form of a wall of water that issued over the lip of the tank and soaked him from head to toe. Rayman's first coherent thought was that a rafter or some piece of the roof had fallen into the tank. On closer inspection, though, he had to admit that he was looking at moving thing, a living thing...an animal.

Sawfish.

But that was impossible! At best, the specimen he had in Tank #12 was ten feet long, from the tip of the saw to the tip of the tail.

He eyeballed the monstrosity before him, waiting for it to momentarily cease moving while it changed directions so he could get a good look. The saw stuck way out on one side of the round tank while the tail protruded far over the other. He forced himself to stop gawking at the freakish aberration before him and make the calculation. He didn't like the number he came up with.

Thirty feet.

No sawfish has ever been recorded anywhere near that length. How on Earth...

He spun and visually checked the other tanks with sawfish, checking for more giants. But all of them were still normal size, most dozing on the bottoms of their tanks, one or two swimming in lazy circles.

"It's just you, number twelve! What happened?"

Rayman flashed on his work day yesterday. It hadn't been the best of days. He'd gotten a late start thanks to a traffic accident in Miami necessitating a labyrinthine detour, and then when he'd gotten in late and checked his e-mail there had been another all staff message about how their primary funding agency was making noises again about reviewing the current grant programs to see where cuts could be made, so to be sure and submit progress reports... *Oops, still haven't done that...* Then he'd gotten right to work on the copepods, his bread-and-butter grant. He'd scooped a batch of the little critters out of one of the aquaria...he glanced over to the wall to check on them—were they gigantic now, too?—but no, they were normal sized. Then he'd walked them— *wait! No, I remember now... I forgot the specimen box...* This was a plastic, aerated container ideal for transferring the copepods. ... *Didn't want to walk all the way back into the inside lab to get it so I just used the net and walked fast back into the indoor lab to take my measurements.* He pictured the minuscule crustaceans popping around in the open net, most of them landing back in it, but one or two falling out onto the concrete floor by the time he reached *Tank #12...*

Uh-oh.

He looked back to the rim of Tank #12, then to the floor around it. He didn't see any copepods there that he had missed. They were genetically modified organisms (GMOs), so allowing one to escape into the bay via the drain hole in the floor, for example, would be something he'd be held accountable for should anyone find out. But he'd checked very carefully yesterday and was sure he hadn't missed any. Still, he had an uneasy feeling about what must have actually happened. *One of them jumped out of the net and landed in the water of the tank, didn't it? They didn't all hit the floor.* He thought about this for a few moments, utterly transfixed, as a realization took place.

Of course!

Some types of copepods were parasites in sawfish, living in the gills. While this fact was coincidental, meaning that he hadn't deliberately chosen to work with sawfish and copepods because of this symbiotic relationship, he did not miss the irony. Here he was, struggling along with a grant to induce gigantism in one species, and he accidentally hits the jackpot with a different species unrelated to the grant.

I'll be damned. He spoke to the fish. "Number twelve, you've got a copepod in your gills, don't you?" The fish continued to thrash. Rayman's mouth tugged downward at the corners. As exciting as it was, this unexpected development was a real problem. He didn't have the facilities to care for a fish this large. He could outsource it to a local public aquarium, but that would mean explaining what happened to it, that he'd made a mistake in the lab...

No... I don't need that kind of publicity right now, what with the funding environment... He'd already had a few student protestors over the GMO aspect of his work. Just reactionary kids, really, but this... He gazed at the monster in the tank, shaking his head as he imagined the screens full of forms he'd have to fill out and submit to try and explain what happened, and then have the accident turned into accepted new protocol. It occurred to him, now that he knew how it worked, that it would be much simpler to pretend he came up with the idea of introducing the copepod to the gills of a sawfish as a result of purposeful thought rather than by accident, and apply for a new grant, the chances for approval being boosted by the fact that he already worked with both species involved. *Yes!*

But first he had to do something about this sawfish. It was wild caught from local waters by specimen collectors, but Rayman knew he couldn't just release a GMO organism of massive, head-turning proportions into the wild. He would have to destroy the fish and then he could dump the dead body into the ocean, maybe cut it up first or grind it into chum so even the body wouldn't be found.

He retreated to the indoor portion of the lab and returned to Tank #12 with a hypodermic needle full of poison. *Now how the hell am I going to do this?* The big saw was still flopping around crazily, different parts of its oversized body sticking out over the round tank. Rayman walked up to the side of the tank while the huge fish's side was there, hypo clutched tightly in his right hand, but his movements were far too tentative. By the time he brought the syringe up, the animal was mostly on the other side of the tank. Still, far be it from Dr. Mason Rayman to give up too easily. He hadn't become a professional researcher by quitting, and he wasn't about to start now.

Rayman was circling around the tank, the needle raised again for another go, when he heard the chime from his desktop computer inside the lab indicating that an email had just come in. *Hmmm, could be news on that new proposal I submitted last week. Sure could use some good news right about now...*

"Temporary reprieve, number twelve," Rayman called over his shoulder to the fish as he entered the inside portion of the lab to check his email. He woke up the dark screen by nudging his mouse. His eyes were immediately drawn to his open email program where half a dozen bold subject new messages awaited. Most of them were from his assistants, those part timers paid to carry out the leg work of his various smaller grants. The latest mail, though it wasn't a reply regarding his proposal, arrested his attention. His eyes widened as he read the subject line: Notice of grant termination #NSB92283002.

He recognized that number, all right, knew it by heart, he'd had to use it so many times by now to pay for various things, including his personnel wages. Still standing, he leaned on the desk with his left hand. He dropped the hypo onto the desk and lashed out with his right hand to click the mouse, opening the full message. It was long, about a full printed page, full of pseudo-legalese formalities, but he knew how to cut right through that crap and get to the point.

His heart clenched as he read it. Due to increasingly rare funding opportunities...competitive environment...only most critical studies...grant #NSB92283002 has not been selected for extension...

Not been selected for extension! Rayman recoiled from the screen as if it were a venomous snake. Technically, his sawfish grant expired at the end of this week, but he had applied for an extension, meaning that he would have another year to complete the work and be able to spend the remaining funds. He had done it many times before on other grants. It was a routine process, almost a formality, and the last thing he'd ever expected was to be denied the extension.

But there it was. He read the email again to make sure he wasn't imagining things, but of course he had gotten it right. The purse strings had not only tightened, but finally closed altogether. Rayman pummeled his desk in frustration. This meant the end. His other grants were not enough to support full-time work. And then he noticed his voicemail light blinking red on the desk phone. He hit the buttons to check the message, fairly certain of what he would find there. Sure enough, it was the head of the Ocean Sciences Department, the esteemed Dr. Edward Reyes, breaking the news with his characteristic "personal touch" in an attempt to soften the blow he had known was coming before Rayman did.

The marine scientist listened carefully to the message, hoping against hope the man would offer some kind of a lifeline—another grant, perhaps, or even an open teaching position he might be suitable for? Rayman cringed as he recalled his outwardly vocal stance and how real scientists did research, not teaching, but surely they would overlook that at a time like this? But as Rayman heard the rest of the message, it hit home that he would have no such luck.

He looked around at the old white walls, cracked and stained yellow in places, at the rusty filing cabinets, the shelves of science books and technical manuals. He was done. The reflection of the overhead fluorescents glared off the syringe on his desk and he considered jabbing it into his neck. Then he got sick of sitting in front of the computer, knowing the sympathy emails would start coming in next as word got around. No doubt his colleagues would be losing grants, too, but most of them also taught or had a mixture of smaller grants. He had put too much faith in those damned copepods. And the sawfish—large animals that were expensive to care for. He heard the big one splashing now as it circled its comparatively tiny tank, saw sticking over the edge like a wayward chainsaw.

2

Dr. Rayman emerged into the wet lab and stood next to Tank #12, syringe clutched in his hand. *You're going to get it now, fish. I'm in no mood to...* But then he loosened his grip on the hypo as a new train of thought settled in. Why should he worry about anything now? This giant GMO monster isn't his problem anymore. Why should he go through all the trouble of euthanizing it, properly disposing of the remains and all that, when they didn't even want him around anymore? He was done, terminated, laid off, released, shit-canned, whatever you wanted to call it. He looked around his lab at all of the tanks. None of this was his problem anymore. They'd have interns probably take care of the fish for use on other projects.

But this guy...he looked at number twelve again, still cavorting wildly in the confines of the tank. He was just too big to stay here, to stay anywhere at the university. Then Rayman caught the glint of sunlight off the ocean beneath the pier that supported the lab, and something occurred to him. Why don't I set this guy free? *They don't want to pay anyone to study sawfish anymore, well, then have fun with this thing. I'm not going the extra mile.*

Rayman walked around the tank to the side that faced the wall, which was itself near the edge of the pier. He smiled as he noticed that the gate leading outside the lab to the pier itself was adjacent to Tank #12. He unlatched the gate and swung it open. He stepped outside, delighting in the refreshing breeze that buffeted his skin. The pier was private, belonging to the university's Ocean Sciences Institute, so there wasn't usually anyone on it way out here at the end. Nevertheless, he looked around carefully to make sure no employees were present. Satisfied all was clear, Rayman turned back into the lab.

"It's your lucky day, number twelve. Governor called. Stay of execution. You're free to go." He moved to the side where a section of a kids' slide leaned against the wall. Used for moving big fish or small sea mammals such as dolphins or manatees, this sawfish was far too big to fit on it but it would have to do. He leaned the slide up against the side of the tank, one end sticking out the open door onto the pier. He quickly splashed water onto the slide to lubricate it so the fish would move along it easily, removing his hands from the tank at the earliest possible moment.

Rayman shook his head as he looked at the sawfish. He still wasn't exactly sure how he was going to do this. If moving it didn't work, he would have no choice but to kill it in place and then do the work of chopping up the dead fish until he could remove it from the tank. Attracted by Rayman's movements, the great fish jutted its saw out over the side where the slide was. This sparked an idea for Rayman, who ran to the cooler in the aisle between tank rows. He removed the largest whole fish, a small blackfin tuna, and ran back to the foot of the slide. The saw's head was still at the top of the slide. Rayman held out the tuna, aware that he could get seriously hurt indeed if this sawfish were to lunge on him. But he needed a lure. The big fish took the bait and the sawfish jumped over the side of the tank, where its massive body dwarfed the slide, which was only just large enough to guide it down like an oversized train on a track.

Rayman gave the beast a shove along its midsection to help it along, making sure he was well clear of both the head and the slapping tail. As Rayman had hoped, the sawfish slid along the edge of the concrete lab floor out through the open gate onto the pier. The wooden slats of the pier served to slow the creature's slide and it came to a stop a good six feet before the railing meant to protect from accidental falls. Rayman had thought it would clear beneath the lowest bar but was shocked at how close it came to not fitting. It would just barely make it, but not if it didn't somehow move over another six feet.

Rayman told himself what the hell and lunged at the flopping fish. It made loud percussive sounds as its tail walloped the wooden planks. Rayman put his head down like a football linebacker and barreled into the animal. He moved it forward only about a foot, but the impact had the effect of scaring the animal into an even more frenzied motion, bringing it to within two feet of the edge of the pier.

"C'mon, number twelve, you want your freedom or not?" Rayman was talking to his fish again, just like old times. "You gotta go, boy. Born free and all that…"

The huge sawfish turned sideways, and for a split second Rayman thought it was going over the side, but the upper lobe of its scythe-shaped tail hung up between the two lowest bars of the guard rail. The fish was gasping now, its gills working hard to pump oxygen, becoming more inefficient as they dried out. Rayman saw an opportunity. This was it. It wouldn't get any better than this.

He dove for the tail, snatching it with his left hand while his right stabilized his own body by grabbing onto the railing. He yanked on it, convinced that if he could just get the longer, upper lobe to clear the rail that it would come free and the fish would wriggle itself over the side. But that's not what happened at all. Instead, the oversized shark relative whipped its gargantuan head around on the pier side, toward the lab. Rayman watched the chainsaw-like appendage, the saw, arcing toward him in a rapid blur.

He rolled, feeling a splinter of wood from the pier dig into his cheek, but he was too late. The toothed blade, perhaps ten feet in length, was two inches from hitting him in the side of the face when the tip of it got caught up in the guard rail, giving Rayman time to put a hand up in defense. No sooner had he done that than he heard the sound of tooth scraping metal and the tip of the saw came loose. Now the fish's weapon completed its path toward his head, meeting his hand instead. Two of the three-inch-long triangular teeth sunk into the meaty part of Rayman's palm. He cried out in pain, reflexively coiling his body into a ball by bringing his knees toward his stomach, fast.

The motion caused his kneecaps to knock hard into the side of the big animal. With the saw and tail now free of the rail, the sawfish rolled to the left with the impact, toward the ocean. The marine biologist gave the beast another shove with both feet at the same time and the creature slid from the pier.

Number twelve twisted in midair like a powerful but ungainly high diver until its body hit the water thirty feet below and instantly transformed into an elegant, efficient swimming machine.

Rayman pulled himself up with the rail and gazed into the sea below. The water in the bay was calm and he could easily see his former charge whipping its tail back and forth in an effort to get far away from the pier as fast as it possibly could. The sawfish gave a tentative shake of its tail and then straightened out into a knife-like posture. It then disappeared into the depths, heading north, toward Miami.

When the fish was totally out of sight, Rayman turned his attention to himself. He smeared the blood off his hand until he could see the triangular, tooth shape of the wound. But something else hurt, too. The wrist on his opposite arm from the injured hand. He had a deep gash there, but it hurt severely.

He wiped the blood from that and was shocked to feel pain in the tips of his fingers that did the wiping. Something was in there. He tried again, more carefully and this time he saw something.

Jesus. Must be a thick splinter from the pier. He gritted his teeth, placed his thumb and forefinger together around the shape of the embedded object and pulled. He grunted as the foreign body slid out of his arm until it was held only by his fingers.

My God...

He was looking at a "tooth" from the sawfish's rostrum, although Rayman knew they were in fact not true teeth, but a type of scale known as dermal denticles. A big one, almost an inch across at the base and two from base to tip. Serrations along both sides. Marveling at it, he held the sawfish denticle up in front of his eyes.

"You did me in, sawfish. I couldn't figure you out in time." He couldn't keep from reminding himself that he'd lost his job. "You got me, saw."

Rayman brought the tooth to the base of his thumb on the opposite hand and sliced it deeply, until a line of dark crimson floated to the surface of his skin. He stared at it for a second and then brought it to his mouth, where he sucked the blood away while watching the sea surface in the direction the saw had gone.

He didn't know what was wrong with him to feel this way, but he'd never tasted anything so good in his life.

3

Miami

Elisa Gonzales pushed herself up from her desk chair and chugged down the last dregs of coffee from her mug that proclaimed, A GIANT CUP OF KISS MY ASS. She would need every drop for her next task. A research grant administrator for the Ocean Sciences Institute at Florida University, it was Gonzales' job to process the many grants which came in to the school's researchers. Usually the job was simple enough, being based on procedures she had been through many times now that she had been here for seven years. But today she had to break some bad news.

That kind of thing went with the territory. The institute paid her to manage the grants, and when personnel who were funded by those grants could not be supported any other way, then it became her job to formally let them know. She grabbed a copy of a letter signed by the institute head and exited her office. A small, windowless room, it wasn't much to look at but at least it was private, a rare enough thing in these days of manic cost-cutting and "collaborative" excuses for cramming people together into cube farms.

Still, this was going to suck and she knew it. *Buck up, sister. That's why they pay you the big bucks, remember?* The sarcasm worked. She actually cracked a smile as she headed out of the office and walked through the large administration building until she reached the first floor lobby. She exited onto a tiled stairway and took that down to a brick-lined path that wound its way across the sunny campus. She reached her car in the lot, a Chevy Volt electric vehicle. Leased, of course, not actually hers yet, but close enough. She plugged it in every night, it took her to work and back every day, and it never needed to stop for gas. That was good enough for her.

Gonzales got into the car and checked the rear view mirror as she was about to back out. She cringed at the bags under her big brown eyes while she did her best to tame those auburn curls with a hairbrush. *Good enough.* She eased out onto the street and made her way onto the Rickenbacker Causeway, glancing at the Port of Miami off to her left, where the industrious activity of cranes loading and unloading humongous cargo ships was nonstop.

She switched lanes at the sign for Virginia Key and exited onto the small island. She didn't come here all that often, maybe once or twice per year for a meeting, but she knew the way well enough. This was the first time she'd had to come out here for something so unpleasant. She took a deep breath as she merged off the island's main road onto the private drive for the Ocean Sciences Institute. She parked in the lot, much smaller than the one where she worked on the main campus, and got out of her car.

"Hey Elisa, your golf cart's still putting along, eh?" Despite the faux insult, Gonzales cracked a smile and turned toward the source of the voice. An elderly gentleman with thin white hair and a sparse Colonel Sanders style beard to match continued walking past as he waved.

"Afternoon, Dr. Overton. Yep, it putted me all the way over here from main campus."

"And saving the world as the wheels turn. Good for you!"

She bid him a good day and headed for the main building of the Ocean Sciences Institute. She had always found it to be an odd combination of rustic-looking wood and modern, green-tinted glass, like old meets new or past meets future. She strode up to the reception desk where one of the undergraduate students would be directing calls and visitors for a few bucks an hour that should be going to offsetting student loans but probably ended up in the local night clubs. She didn't recognize the girl presently sitting there, but that was no surprise.

"Can you direct me to Dr. Rayman's lab, please? He used to be out at the end of the pier, is that still his? I know you guys just shuffled things around over here."

The student looked up from her smartphone long enough to smile and say yes, that was still his lab. Gonzales thanked her and headed back outside where she strode out onto the pier, feeling the fresh sea breeze pick up as she went. Still, the pleasant environment couldn't keep her from thinking about what she was about to tell Dr. Rayman. Well, she knew what she was going to tell him, but *how* she was going to say it was on her mind. Should she hand him the letter first or just come right out and say it? *Pack your stuff, Rayman, you're on the next train outta here.*

She smiled a little as she walked past of couple of smaller labs near the beginning of the pier. She had never been fond of Dr. Rayman, but she would never make light of anyone's job situation, even if she didn't like the person. She trudged on, her mood returning to a more somber state by the time she reached the largest building on the pier, the lab that Dr. Rayman had called home for the last five years. She shook her head at the seeming unfairness of the situation. You'd think that if a guy had occupied the same lab for five years that he'd be pretty safe, funding-wise, but not anymore. There were all manner of researchers practically foaming at the mouth for a chance to use that facility. The building wouldn't go to waste without Dr. Rayman—Rayman would go to waste without it, was more likely. The guy didn't want to teach, so what did he expect?

While she walked up to the door, Elisa steeled herself for the imagined pushback or at least resentment she would probably get from him. But then she saw that the door had been boarded over. Wasn't that where the door had been? She wasn't sure, it'd been years since she'd been out to this building. She shrugged and proceeded to walk around the side of the building facing the ocean, figuring there'd be a door on that side. She heard the sound of a hose being sprayed as she walked along. *Good, at least there's somebody here.* It occurred to her that maybe Rayman took his cue from the grant agency email and decided to jump ship early. It occasionally happened when people were so upset over the situation that they didn't want to see anyone. Somehow Rayman didn't strike her as being that type, though. He seemed more like a fighter who would demand she jump through all sorts of red-tape hoops to make it as difficult as possible for everyone involved because they should know better than to get rid of him.

But as she neared the end of the lab building and prepared to turn the corner, she lost this train of thought completely. There was a man wrestling a gigantic fish by the side of the pier. Looked like he was losing too, judging by his curses and the way he was getting walloped by the gigantic fish. She'd never seen such a giant fish in her life. She was about to shout and ask the man if he needed help when she recognized two things: one, the man was Dr. Mason Rayman, and two—the fish was a sawfish, the same type of fish she'd processed a grant for Rayman to work with.

Elisa took out her smartphone and activated the video camera. She pointed the lens at Rayman and watched the struggle play out, knowing it was being recorded. She had assumed that he was trying to get the fish away from the side of the pier, but as she watched, it became clear that the opposite was true. She crouched behind a car to keep from being seen by Rayman, and not long after that he pushed the sawfish over the edge. Rayman peered over the edge for a minute, then he pulled something from his hand. After that, he jogged back into his lab.

Elisa stopped the video and then continued walking until she reached the open door to the outdoor section of the lab. She called out, not wanting to spook anyone.

"Dr. Rayman? Hello?" She heard the hose stop. She yelled again and this time heard the sound of wet footsteps on concrete.

"Yes?"

She recognized the male voice. "It's Elisa Gonzales, from Contracts and Grants."

"Oh, come in."

She stepped over the threshold, aware that a visit from a grant officer could be either a very positive or a negative thing. She felt bad that right now he still had hope for the former, a false hope that she would soon dash. Inside the lab, she looked around but still didn't see anyone. Only the rows of those big round tanks. Ah, the sawfish. She remembered submitting that grant. She wondered what would happen to all those fish now, but it wasn't her problem. She needed to stay focused. But wait a minute...there used to be a sawfish in each of the dozen tanks. She was sure of it.

She knew this because it was stated in the grant application that Rayman need access to a facility that could house twelve sawfish. But the tank nearest to her was empty. The water still sloshed around heavily inside of it. And what was that big plastic thing on the floor...a slide? Was the sawfish she had just witnessed Rayman tossing over the pier the same one that used to reside in that tank? Couldn't be, though, it was much too large to fit in this tank.

Suddenly, a man exited the inside lab space and walked toward her. "Hi there." Dr. Rayman walked over to her and extended a hand.

Gonzales looked away quickly from the empty tank and forced herself to keep her demeanor professional yet subdued. The fish thing was weird, but none of that really mattered anymore. The semi-fake smiles she usually offered him would work against her here by giving him the impression that everything was okay. "Good afternoon, Mason." She glanced down at the paperwork in her hand. Rayman's gaze followed hers.

She cleared her throat and looked up at Rayman, whose gaze still lingered on the paper. "As you know from the emails..." She hesitated while she searched for just the right words...until Rayman filled in the blanks for her.

"...my main grant has been denied an extension."

She nodded. "That's right. I'm very sorry, Dr. Rayman. I double-checked everything to make certain there's nothing we're overlooking that could be done. But the agency isn't budging on this." An uncomfortable silence settled over the two of them. The hum of pumps and bubbling water filled the air.

"So what do I need to sign?" Rayman tipped his head toward the papers.

"Oh, it's the form that formally notifies you of your grant termination and then another one that severs your employment with the university since you will no longer be funded for full-time research and teach no classes. I'm sorry, Dr. Rayman. I really am."

He pursed his lips flat but reached for the papers. "Lemme take a look."

As he reached out to take them, Gonzales couldn't help but notice that his hand had blood on it. A lot of it. "You okay, Mason?"

The scientist looked up from his paperwork, distracted. "Huh? Yeah, sure. As fine as anyone who just lost their job, I guess."

"No, I mean your hand." She pointed at his left hand, where a three-inch gouge oozed blood. No doubt as the result of his battle with that huge fish.

He followed her point. "Oh that. Cut it on the edge of a tank I was positioning." He withdrew the pen from the paper, where he'd been about to sign. "Last chance for worker's comp, right?" He grinned at her.

Gonzales did her best to return the smile out of courtesy but clearly her heart was not in it. "Go see a doctor if you need to, while you're still covered."

Rayman narrowed his eyes ever so slightly and then grabbed a clipboard with water data from a post that supported the roof. He put the form on the clipboard and put his signature to it. He shook his head while handing the paper back to Gonzales.

"I'm sorry, Mason," she said again. "Truly."

Rayman's expression suddenly changed. His eyes bulged slightly from their sockets, his face reddened, his carotid arteries grew more prominent. "Will you please stop saying that? What do you care, anyway? You're funded by the department, not a grant. Your job is secure."

Gonzales took a reflexive step back at the change in attitude and personal direction. "Excuse me? My job?"

Rayman shrugged. "Yeah. Your job. It's secure. It must be easy for you to walk around and get paid to tell other people they don't have a job anymore."

Gonzales put her hands on her hips. "Look, Dr. Rayman, you've made more money in the last year than I've made doing my full-time job here for the last five, if that makes you feel any better. You're only shooting the messenger. Good bye, and good luck." *Asshole.*

She turned and breezed out of the lab onto the pier. Rayman followed her out there after waiting a few seconds. He watched her walk toward the road at the foot of the pier. Then, satisfied she was actually leaving, he stared out over the sparkling blue bay.

4

Crandon Park Beach, Key Biscayne

"It's one mile, Harry, we can do it. We've been doing the half-mile runs for months now. Let's give it a chance." Mrs. Harry Olivera glanced at her husband of thirty-five years as he pulled on his white swim cap. Around them, about a dozen other seniors, the most avid members of the Key Biscayne Senior Swim Club, began trotting into the water that lapped against the dry sand.

At sixty-five years old, the Oliveras were healthy and in good physical shape for their age. Having retired to Florida last year from Ohio after 9-5 desk-bound careers, they'd made a pact with each other to get in shape and stay in shape once they moved to Florida. To this end they'd joined the swim club, which also offered the benefit of a social scene. But part of that social scene involved peer pressure to participate in the swims. Most of it was good-spirited camaraderie, but Harry in particular felt that there was actual pressure that made him feel like he was somehow less of a man were he not to participate in the longer swims. It didn't help matters that his wife was all for it, seeming to take to the water like a fish from the get-go and enthusiastically signing up for each new swim.

So here they were, standing on the beach at 4:30pm, ready to enter the water at the south end, swim to the buoy line about a hundred feet from shore, and then head north just inside the line until they reached the parking lot at the end of the beach a mile away. It was twice as far as they'd gone so far. But the day was beautiful, the sun still up and glittering across the water, the sky blue with a smattering of puffy white clouds. The ocean was calm as could be, with a glassy smooth surface to the horizon.

The leader for today's swim, a punchy 79-year-old by the name of Chancy McCray, waved his arms to gain the club's attention. "All right, everybody... Swimmers ready!"

There were hoots and hollers as the oldsters stepped into the shallow water and began to walk out along the firm sandy bottom. "Stop yer lip flappin' and let's get to it, Chancy!" one of the men called out.

"First one to the finish gets a martini on me at the club." He held an arm up and yelled, "Three...two...one... Swimmers go!"

The shallow water churned into foam and sand with the passage of dozens of stomping legs. "Nice and warm," one of them commented. Those who had been fastest to run in were now pushing off the bottom into a shallow dive to kick-start into swimming mode. Each participant started to swim with a splash into the ocean, most of them employing crawl strokes. Soon the water's surface was pockmarked with whitewater displaced by legs and arms.

Chancy and two others reached the swim line first and made the left turn to the north. Harry and his wife followed suit a couple of minutes later. As was his habit, Harry reached out and touched one of the swim line buoys, his fingers slapping the smooth wet plastic, before following the prescribed course. Normally, he swam with his eyes closed, forgoing the use of goggles, but he liked to open them once when he reached the line to see how clear the water was, and he did that now. Even though they were a little ways from shore, the water here was only about eight feet deep.

Harry put his head down in the water and opened his eyes. What he saw was blurry, but he still thought that something was off. *It shouldn't be this shallow here.* It looked as though the bottom was only three feet or so below him, like if he put his feet down he could stand. He was about to try just that when suddenly the bottom appeared lighter in color and also deeper down. *What the...am I in a sand cloud or something?*

Then he caught movement and the bottom was once again darker colored and closer. He lifted his head out of the water. Heard the splashy sounds of the swimmers both in front of and behind him. He turned and saw his wife, kicking off down the swim line. She wore goggles and he wanted to ask her to take a look down there. As he opened his mouth to call her name, he felt a surge of water rushing against his body, and then something hard and sharp hit him in the head.

He didn't know what is was, but he knew it was bad. He could feel his warm blood sliding down his face, a lot of it. His thoughts automatically turned to what had happened. His first thought was that one of the swim-line buoys had knocked him in the head. Sometimes if there were swells, they could move up and down with some force and he did make a point to maintain some distance from them. But still, they were just little plastic balls, they might hurt a bit, but gash his head open?

He brought a hand to his neck and held it in front of his eyes. Blood poured from his fingers. He took his other, blood free hand and swiped it across his forehead and it, too, came away smeared with crimson.

That's when he heard the first cries. "Shark!"

His skin began to crawl, his limbs felt paralyzed but he knew he must not be because he was still keeping himself afloat in a swimming position. He also knew his blood would attract sharks. He opened his mouth to call for his wife again. He saw her, only a few strokes ahead. She was calling his name now, and looking terrified beyond belief.

"Harry, look out! It's behind you!"

Shock was setting in for the elderly man, and he was slow to react. By the time he turned around, he saw a massive shape that he mistook for a small boat (*did I get hit by the propeller?*). But even to his unsettled mind, it seemed strange that this boat came up from the depths rather than plowed along on the surface. *Maybe it's sinking after it hit me?* These strange semi-logical thoughts plagued him until it was too late.

Harry was turning around when he was hit again. This time, the force was greater than before and, again, focused on his head. He didn't see what hit him. One second, he was in full panic mode, wondering what was happening, what to do. The next, he was dead.

About a half dozen swimmers who hadn't yet reached the swim line turned around and headed back to the beach at the sight of the attack. Those at the front of the pack, including Chancy, stopped and treaded water, but were too far away to help. Harry's wife and two men who had been not far in front of her swam back to help. She got there first, was the first to reach the body, although she didn't yet know he was dead.

"Harry! Harry, I've got you, c'mon, let's get you back to the beach." Concerned he was face down in the water for who knew how long, she scooped an arm under his left shoulder and flipped him over. Suddenly, she felt her husband's body move sharply away from her. She gripped him by the arm but it continued to pull away, like she was in a tug of war with an unseen force. The man who had been right in front of her while swimming now reached her and grabbed onto Harry's other arm. "Flip over, this way!" He indicated Harry's right side.

"Something's pulling on him."

"Three, two, one, now!" Harry's wife pushed and the newcomer pulled, and together they felt the body pull free of whatever had been holding it. A fresh cloud of blood stained the water as it flipped over.

"He's got some bad gashes along his side," the male swimmer said. "We've got to get him to—"

Harry's wife shrieked, a bloodcurdling vent of emotions that had people turning heads on the beach.

Harry had no head.

5

Coconut Grove, Miami

Dr. Mason Rayman stared listlessly at his TV while he sat on his couch with a microwave dinner untouched on the coffee table. A bachelor in his mid-thirties who'd never married, with no kids, he'd given his life to his career, which had now come to a screeching halt. He took another pull from his imported European microbrew (*going to have to switch to domestic cans soon*) as the local news started up with its hyper theme music.

Breaking news: loser scientist gets funding cut, has no job, no family, he thought sourly.

He drifted off into unpleasant thoughts about all the things he'd have to do in the near future—find a new job, transfer his 401k, maybe apply for unemployment, while he ate his dinner without tasting it. Maybe he'd even have to move somewhere else and apply to a school that would let him teach. *Jesus.* He'd always been a researcher and didn't know how he would think of himself if he did something else. It just didn't seem right.

Lost in these unpleasant thoughts while crushing his bland food into submission, it was some time before Rayman glanced up at the TV. When he did, the screen was filled with a beach scene, where a crowd stood on the wet sand by water's edge. An elderly woman sobbed with her face in her hands, the hands of those consoling her on her shoulders while men wearing jackets emblazed with Medical Examiner on the back loaded a sheeted corpse into an official vehicle. On screen, the live shot peeled away to a studio reporter, a Hispanic brunette with shoulder-length wavy hair and the fashion-conscious outfits common to Miami television news.

"Let's break away now from that live scene on Crandon Park Beach, where a Miami-area resident is confirmed dead from a suspected shark attack. A warning to younger or sensitive viewers, the footage you're about to see, shot earlier today on Key Biscayne, is graphic in nature."

Rayman set down his fork and focused on the screen. *Look at this, someone's having a worse day than me, who would have thought?*

The tape ran on screen and Rayman actually reared back in his seat as he processed what he was looking at. *Wow, TV stations are really pushing the limits of what they'll show in the name of ratings. Never would have seen this level of detail when I was a kid.* The point of view was from a shoulder-camera, shaky while the cameraman moved to frame his shot. The pale, thin body lay in the wet sand on its stomach, still within reach of the water lapping onto shore. Rayman squinted as he looked at the figure. Something about it just wasn't right, it was as though the head were buried in the sand...

Then the camera angle shifted and it became clear the victim no longer possessed a head. It was missing altogether. *What the—* Rayman stood and walked closer to the TV. He never was much of a TV watcher and the screen was small. *Won't be upgrading to a larger one anytime sooner, either.* He stood a couple of feet in front of the set and studied the body while a male reporter provided a voice-over from off camera.

"The victim, Harry Olivera of Miami Heights, was pulled from the water this afternoon while participating in an ocean distance swim as part of a Miami Beach Silver Swim Club event. His wife reported that he was swimming along without problems shortly after the swim began, but suddenly called for help. Soon after that, he disappeared below the water for a short time, and then blood was seen in the water along with a large shark. The type of shark has not yet been identified."

The camera zoomed in on the corpse and panned along its bloody length. Rayman sucked in his breath as he realized that, in addition to completely missing the head, the body featured a series of long and deep slash-like wounds along the torso. He unconsciously stroked the stubble on his chin—he liked to keep himself smooth shaven to avoid showing his gray hairs—he had enough on his head already, didn't need them on his face, too—while he studied the injuries.

Shark? His face took on a doubting expression while he gazed at the macabre scene of death. Those wounds didn't look like the shark attack bites he'd seen in person, although even on his little HD TV, the level of detail offered by the live shot was simply not there. There were triangular cuts, but the teeth would have to be ridiculously massive for it to be a shark, and the distance between tooth tips was all wrong. No, this was more like...chainsaw injuries. Maybe this guy fell asleep on the beach and was run over by a sand grader? It had been known to happen. Yet the eyewitness testimony from several persons attests that he was definitely in the water and was attacked there, in a shallow, sandy area just off the beach, by a creature thought to be a shark.

So what caused those injuries? Rayman rubbed his face as he considered it while the camera angle expanded to show the entire corpse. The news footage didn't offer any real detail, but it looked at least superficially like a chainsaw type bite... Not a *bite*, per se, though, but a series of slashing wounds. With a saw. But not a chainsaw... a *sawfish*. And then he had to kneel on the floor when the possibility hit him.

To Rayman's considerable knowledge, sawfish were not known to attack humans. Not a single documented attack existed so far as he knew. A sawfish caught fishing and hauled into a boat was known to pose a danger as it thrashed around, certainly, but an in-water attack on a human, like a shark attack? Unheard of. Nevertheless, sawfish *could* cause wounds like that, couldn't they? Theoretically, they were capable of it. He nodded to himself and stared down at his wounded hand. The news broadcast cut away from the tape of the victim back to the newscaster in the studio, but Rayman was no longer listening.

What if the experimental procedures had somehow modified its behavior? He doubted it. Even if it were true, a normal adult sawfish of the Atlantic Smalltooth variety wouldn't leave such massive, gaping wounds. It was highly likely that this man would have died from the slash wounds to his torso alone, even if his head hadn't been removed.

The marine biologist mentally pictured a dead whale being attacked by a sawfish that he had witnessed while scuba diving. The way it slashed and tore at the thick hide with that natural weapon, the saw. The ragged but orderly gashes it left...like a chainsaw. The jagged ripping pattern was similar to what he'd seen on the news video, but he'd have to get a closer view to be certain.

He flashed on his struggles with his recently released specimen, number twelve. He watched it in his mind as it slithered over the edge of the pier into the water of Biscayne Bay and swam away. Was it large enough to produce these kinds of wounds? Perhaps. And then, as the news story ended altogether, switching to a piece about a drug-crazed homeless man biting another's face on the side of the road in Miami, Rayman had a most disturbing thought indeed.

Maybe it wasn't large enough the last time I saw it. But what if it kept growing after I released it? What if it's still growing? It's not like I had ample time to study the effects of this gigantism.

He thought about going to city authorities with what he knew, so they could at least consider looking for a sawfish instead of a shark, but that wouldn't exactly be good for him, would it? He was the one who had not only created the sawfish, if that's what was responsible for this, but had released it, too. Besides, he mused, now turning off the TV altogether before sitting down to the rest of his cold dinner.

It's not my job anymore.

6

Surfcasting. It was a type of saltwater fishing where practitioners waded into the ocean surf in order to cast their lines far out into the waves hoping for a big fish. Paul Matheson had been doing it when he could for the better span of four decades. Now retired after a successful career as a long-haul trucker, he and his wife had settled in South Florida to enjoy their golden years in a retirement community populated with fellow seniors. A couple of them were Paul's on-again, off-again fishing buddies, but if he couldn't find anyone to go with him, he would go alone. He couldn't even count the hours he'd spent dreaming about fishing from the confines of his cab on some lonely Midwestern highway, and now that he finally had the chance to go pretty much whenever he wanted, he was going to go, alone or not.

Especially on a weekday, which he now preferred to weekends when it was more crowded. At this early hour, he was the only soul on the beach. He tried the odd Saturday or Sunday and found it over-crowded with a litany of other fisherman vying for the best spots, while swimmers, beach exercisers and even scuba divers all used the beach in their own way. The fishermen always got the dirtiest looks. No one wanted to get hooked in the water, no one wanted the fearsome ocean predators they imagined were attracted to the bait cast into the sea. So he concentrated on weekdays, when, if he went early enough, he might have this scenic stretch of beach with only the automated lighthouse on the point to keep him company.

Paul bent down and scooped a live baitfish from a five-gallon bucket fitted with an aerator to supply oxygen. He hooked the mullet, a large one about a foot long, through the mouth, knowing that most predators attacked their prey head on. Then he waded out into the gentle surf. The water was clear and it was high tide, which he preferred to low tide because it meant he had a shorter distance to walk to get into deep water, and also that the fish would be brought in by the currents.

The hip waders he wore prevented the water from coming into contact with his skin, but he knew it was warm. He waded out further, shuffling his feet to prevent stepping on a stingray. Better to nudge them out of the way than to come right down on them and get the stinger as it whipped up in fear and surprise.

By the time he was waist deep, he was past the churning surf and the water was nice and clear. He grinned at a school of baitfish flitting about, some of their number jumping out of the water a few feet from him. *Always a good sign to see signs of life like that. Where there are little fish, there are big fish.*

Paul cast his line further out into the sea. Although he couldn't see it, he imagined his hooked mullet sinking slowly to the bottom, stunned from flying through the air during the cast and slapping the water, and probably only just now starting to swim, a few inches above the sandy bottom. Slowly at first, he began turning the crank on his reel, feeling the tension as the line took up on the spool. Then he got into a rhythm, smoothly winding in monofilament at a faster pace, visualizing his bait thrashing around on the hook.

He had that feeling again, the one where his inner sense told him something was about to hit the line. He didn't know what that sense was, how to define it, really, but it was almost always right. After decades of fishing, he'd learned to recognize it. Sure enough, not three seconds later, he felt that familiar tug—tentative at first while the fish picked at the bait, before switching to a full-on tug of war as the fish swallowed the offering and ran with it.

Paul jerked back on the rod hard, setting the hook. As he did, he got his first look at what he hoped would be his first catch of the morning, as a large silver fish launched itself into the air about fifty feet from him.

Tarpon!

He hadn't really been expecting to hook one of those, but they were one of the most famous sport fish in South Florida waters, well respected not for their value on the dinner plate but for the incredible aerial fight they put up when hooked. Also known as the Silver King, a tarpon preferred shallow, sandy water such as sandbars. Paul knew right away that this fish was something special. Very large, even for a tarpon, when he saw it leap from the water for the first time it took his breath away. Had to be pushing 100 pounds. A monster fish, nearly six feet long. The retired trucker knew he was in for one hell of a fight.

You're too old for this thing... Come on, you can do it. This'd be your biggest Silver King yet. Wait till the guys back at the club see this trophy...

He settled in to the battle, letting out some more line, giving the fish room to run while it still had all of its stores of raw energy. Paul walked a little further out to sea, until the water reached his waist. *That's enough. Any deeper and the reel will be underwater.*

The tarpon leapt again, a low dash just over the surface of the water this time, straight out in front of him. And then, only a few seconds later, a grand vertical jump, water cascading of the fish's body in the morning sunlight as it reached for the sky. *Wow, he's really going crazy, never seen one do—*

Suddenly, the water darkened in front of Paul, like a shadow blanketing the day, only the sun was still visible on its morning rise. A massive shape rose from the water. Paul had trouble processing what he was looking at, but saw teeth, lots of them, an expanse of grey, and then his tarpon falling back to the water only to disappear into the goliath form, which itself fell back into the water, still moving fast.

Paul felt his fishing line snap and go limp in his hands. It wasn't the first time he'd had a bigger fish eat a fish that had been on his line. One time, he was reeling in a yellowtail snapper only to have a small hammerhead shark rip the fish off the hook. But this...it was unimaginable, he'd never seen anything like it. So immense, he had a hard time making sense of it, but there was no time to reflect on it because suddenly it was coming at him, preceded by a sizable swell of water being pushed ahead of it as it moved.

Paul dropped his rod, turned and "ran" towards shore, but one couldn't really run in waist deep water wearing hip waders. He just sort of hopped along as fast as he could, the water becoming shallower at a frustratingly slow rate. He was looking up onto the beach to see if anyone was there who saw what was unfolding, but there was only a lone figure practicing yoga almost a hundred yards away. Then his right foot landed in a depression in the sand and he went down, his floppy fishing hat coming off and floating away when his head splashed into the water.

Get up, you old fool! Paul pushed hard off the bottom with both hands until he could spring to his feet. He knew he should keep moving toward the beach, but he could feel water raining down on him from above, and a large wave pushing against him. He spun to look behind him and an enormous flat-bladed club slammed into the side of his face, severing his left ear. He felt the warmth of his blood for a split second before it was washed away when he fell sideways into the water again.

His eyes were still open but everything grew dark and then he felt himself being lifted up, thrown into the air like some kind of toy, until he splashed back into the waves again. Something closed over him, it was all happening so fast that he couldn't get it to gel in his mind what it meant, but then he felt horrible pain as multiple flat molar-like teeth crushed his body in myriad places.

Paul Matheson had lured his last fish.

7

Virginia Key

Rayman parked his red Ferrari 308, the vanity plate reading ICHTHY, in the space outside the lab, the one that was usually never available. He wondered if that was because today was his last day and they wanted him to be able to carry out his stuff quickly. Bastards. He left the trunk open as a show of goodwill to anyone who might be watching that he was indeed preparing to clear out, grabbed a couple of empty cardboard boxes, and then stepped into the lab building. *Last time I'll be going through this door.*

Inside, he went straight to his office rather than the actual lab, since that's where he had most of his personal effects. He sighed heavily as he looked around at the well-used room. It was an old building, and he could practically feel the toil that had gone on here, not just from his own years, but from the decades of those who had come before him. And the room would go on supporting more work, he knew. Someone would be moving in here shortly after he left, he didn't know who, but they'd find somebody.

He started with the obvious, the personal photos on the desk and wall. A shot of him scuba diving to collect samples, another of him with an old girlfriend in front of some pyramid in Mexico. His framed diplomas. He stashed those in a box and moved onto the desk itself (*all these pens are mine, damn it*)... My old Swingline stapler—*metal, not the cheap plastic crap they hand out these days—that's coming with me.* So on and so forth it went. He was surprised at how much stuff he had accumulated over the years, and by how hard it was to walk away from it all. He could just leave it for them to deal with, but he actually wanted some of this stuff. He busied himself with filling his boxes, and a few minutes later failed to hear the footsteps approaching his door until he heard the voice.

#

"Excuse me? Dr. Rayman?" Elisa Gonzales rapped softly on the closed office door, the one that led from the lab, not from the outside. She'd heard Rayman come in and considered that he may be pretending not to hear her. It was his last day, after all, and so who knows what he might do. But probably he would just be trying to slink out of here. Or, maybe he was trashing the place, who knew? She saw him chuck that big fish right into the ocean, got it on cell-phone video, even—*oh my God! and then the attacks started!* Her hand froze in midair over the door as the realization consumed her: those news reports—first one yesterday and then one this morning already. She hadn't paid all that much attention to them, but knew they involved people dying at the local beaches after being attacked by some kind of sea creature, probably a shark. But what if it wasn't a shark? *Could it be?*

She called his name again and this time heard him walk to the door. He opened it and smiled that thin, fake grin of his he seemed to reserve for anyone who hadn't won a Nobel Prize, but especially for a lowly admin worker like herself. She usually enjoyed working for the university, helping professors and researchers with the non-science aspects of their work so they could focus, but Rayman was always a condescending jerk. It was for that reason Elisa didn't feel quite as bad as she normally would when someone unexpectedly lost their job.

Suddenly, the door opened and she had to go from thinking about Rayman to talking to him.

"Hi, Elisa. Clearing my stuff out. Almost done." Rayman turned his back on her and resumed rifling through the desk drawers.

She cleared her throat as she walked into the room. "Dr. Rayman..." He still didn't look up from what he was doing. The bastard wouldn't even give her the courtesy of eye contact on his last damn day. Figured. *What comes around, Dr. Rayman, what comes around...*

He paused suddenly and looked up at her. "Do you need something? I signed the exit papers already, right?"

34

Wow. True to form right 'til the end. She sighed, making no effort to hide her exasperation. In fact, she made no effort to even be friendly anymore. Why should she? It was his last day. She didn't like him. He was an ass. *Let him have it.* "They want me to take this office after you leave, so I was just checking to see how much longer it's going to be. Also, I need you to turn in your keys and sign here." She handed him a form saying that he had relinquished his keys.

The narrowing of Rayman's eyes was short lived yet immensely satisfying to Elisa. He pulled the keys out of a drawer—clearly he'd already separated them from his personal ones—and handed them to her.

"*You're* going to be working in here?" He signed the form without reading it and shoved it back to her.

She nodded. "That's what the powers that be tell me." Meaning the Institute. Deal with it.

Rayman shrugged and glanced around the smallish space. "Where? I don't see how there's room for two desks in here."

"There isn't going to be two desks in here."

"Well then where—?"

She understood. All of a sudden, she put herself in the mindset of this pompous bastard and there it was... *He thinks I meant that they're going to cram me in here to share space with whichever researcher moves in next. Try not to gloat too hard.* "They're not putting me in here with someone else. Just me by myself."

Rayman appeared confused. He tossed some books into one of his boxes and then straightened, finally giving her his undivided attention. "You mean this is going to be your office now—all yours?"

She nodded. "Space is short and they have me taking care of more and more people all the time." *Thankfully, not you anymore.*

Rayman wagged his head back and forth. "Premium research space with direct ocean access going to admin staff. Makes a lot of sense. Looks like I'm getting out at the right time." He went back to packing.

Elisa felt the fury well up inside her and knew she was going to lose this battle with her inner Zen. She supposed that part of the reason he was mad was that he was partially right. Who was she but a pawn to be moved around by the Institute as they saw fit? The truth was that they had already told her this would be a temporary location for her, until the search for Rayman's replacement was completed. That could take a few months, but still. And it wasn't like she was making lots of money, like Rayman and some of these guys. Miami wasn't a cheap place to live, and her modest salary didn't go very far at all as a single mom. Rayman had only himself to worry about. Sure, he had earned his degrees and worked his way up, she understood that, but to be so callous and rude about it just rubbed her the wrong way. Today, especially.

She pulled the phone from her pocket, swiped up the video she'd taken and held the phone out toward him with it playing. "So I saw on the news last night that a swimmer was killed by a big fish."

He nodded without turning around. "Shark is what they think, yeah."

"And then this morning there was another suspected *shark* attack, also in Biscayne Bay."

At this, Rayman turned around. "This morning, you say?"

She nodded and took a step closer to him, holding the phone out. His eyes narrowed for a second but he stepped closer. "That the news report from this morning?"

"Take a look." She knew if she said no that he'd turn away. Only cares about himself. The fact that he approached her to see the video set off an alarm bell in her. *It's true. He's worried about it. Why else would he give a crap about a random shark attack? But it wasn't random was it? And it wasn't a shark...*

She observed Rayman's face go through stages while he watched the video unfolding frame by frame on her smartphone screen. First, he was merely trying to focus, then his brain was processing what his eyes saw, registering the fact that he was looking at himself on the tiny screen. That's when his eyes narrowed and his skin turned reddish. He looked up from the screen just long enough to glare at Elisa and ask, "What is this?"

"It's just what it looks like, Dr. Rayman. It's you dumping that giant sawfish you had over the pier and into Biscayne Bay." She let that sink in while he concentrated on the screen for a few seconds longer, probably now in the *Is this real?* phase of trying to verify the authenticity of what he was seeing. That stage apparently complete, his right hand swiped out and tried to grab the phone from her hand. He missed and the tips of his fingers brushed against her lower chin. She backed away a step, still holding the phone, which still played the video.

"What are you doing, Dr. Rayman? Get away from me. Do I have to call security?"

He appeared indignant, puffing out his chest in response. "What are *you* doing, videoing me in my own lab without my knowledge?"

Elisa pocketed her phone now that Rayman was no longer looking at it. "It's not your lab anymore."

"It was when you filmed me."

"You were acting suspicious. I came in simply to give you the paperwork to sign and saw you wrestling that huge fish out of the tank. I didn't even know you were doing anything wrong at that point, I just thought it would make an interesting video, you know, Our Scientists In Action kind of thing—something I could use for the website."

"Oh, bullshit!"

"But then when I saw you drag it out to the pier and push it over, I did think it was a little strange. And now people are being killed on the beaches by some kind of marine animal, Mason."

He cocked his head to one side as he made the connection. Stammered out a reply. "Wait...wait a minute...Y-you think..." Then he erupted into obnoxious, bellowing laughter.

"You think it's so funny? It's so hilarious that you let loose some...*genetically modified organism*...into the wild without a permit, and now it's preying on the local population? I don't know why I even showed you the video. I should just send it in to the local news, let them interpret your actions."

Rayman took a step toward her. "Give me that phone, Elisa."

"Fuck off! I will not!"

"Just let me delete the video and I'll hand it right back to you. The public can easily misconstrue this kind of thing, and it's actually against the Non-Disclosure Agreements I signed with the funding agency to reveal aspects of the research before it's published. You of all people should know that."

She was tired of this guy thinking he could have whatever he wanted. The arrogance. The sense of entitlement...the fact that even on unemployment he would still be making more than her paychecks, based on what he had been making. Meanwhile, she worked full time and struggled to pay normal bills for a one-room apartment on the not-so-good side of town. All of it conspired to muddle her thoughts, to conflict her emotions until she uttered a phrase that would change her life forever.

"What's it worth to you?" *Whoa.* There it was, an ugly, evil thought, formed in her brain and now floated out there on the air for someone else to hear. But before she could try to take it back or to play it off as a joke or something, Rayman said, "To delete the video? How much do you want?"

A beat. Silence, a pause from both of them while she contemplated this new turn of events, much like Alice looking around after falling down that rabbit hole. This was it. A fork in the road, a turning point, whatever you wanted to call it, but the decision was hers. The sound of seagulls squawking out on the pier broke the silence until she replied, "Ten thousand dollars."

She had no idea where she got that figure. It just seemed like a nice round amount, and not so astronomically high as to seem like a joke. Someone like Rayman would probably be able to pay it if they really wanted to. The terminated scientist stared at her without saying anything, his expression completely serious, just making eye contact with her as if to gauge how committed she was to this.

He's going to tell you to fuck off and die, he's been let go, what does he care... After all, releasing a fish into the wild isn't exactly the worst thing someone can do these days, is it?

"Where else is the video besides your phone? Has it been uploaded anywhere yet?"

Whoa... The fact that his answer was not an immediate and outright rejection was in and of itself...something. She wasn't sure what. But it wasn't what she expected. She didn't know what else to do at this point, so she answered the question.

"This is the only copy. No one else has seen it besides you and me."

"I guess I just have to take your word on that, don't I?"

The thought of actually having an unexpected ten thousand dollars made itself known in her head. Suddenly, she didn't want to say anything to change his mind about the direction this little exit interview was taking. "You have my word that this is the only copy and that it's never been viewed, nor its very existence even mentioned, to anyone except us."

"Okay. So delete it, and then I'll get your money."

Elisa took a step back, almost subconsciously, as if she was somehow alert to the possibility of Rayman making another lunge for the phone. It wouldn't take much. All he would have to do is grab it and chuck it into one of the tanks in the adjoining wet lab and the files on the phone would likely be irretrievable. Had she known she was going to pull this reckless stunt, she'd have uploaded the video to the cloud before coming here, but she hadn't known. This was just another patented Elisa Gonzales Impulsive Moment, like that time she had too much wine at home and went on an online shopping spree that took a year to pay off. Packages piling up at the door for days. *I owe, I owe, it's off to work I go...* That's all this was, right, just a little impetuous behavior that would work itself out. But right now she knew she had to respond.

"Sorry, Charlie. You're a fish guy, you remember Charlie the Tuna, right? Anyway, that's not how it works. You pay first, then you get the item. It's like eBay. Nobody sends the person their item and then waits for the money. It's the other way around, silly."

Rayman rolled his eyes. "It's not like I walk around with that kind of cash on me. I'm about to be collecting unemployment, for Christ's sake!"

Elisa frowned. "Boo-fucking-hoo, Dr. Rayman. Your unemployment checks are going to be higher than my regular paychecks. Cry me a goddamn river. I'm sure you've got something saved up. You're smart, right? If not, sell that ridiculous car you drive, or the boat."

"What's so ridiculous about my car?"

"A Ferrari? Really? What academic drives a freakin' Ferrari to work every day?"

Rayman shrugged. "I'm a Magnum PI fan, so what? How about your ridiculous car, that electric thing you think makes you environmentally conscious, I suppose."

"At least I'm not polluting the atmosphere like your high-performance gas hog."

"You don't have the faintest clue about the environment, do you? Where do you think the electricity comes from to charge your battery every night? From burning coal and oil at the power plants, that's where. And at the end of its life cycle, when that battery is no good anymore, where does it end up? In the landfill, leaching heavy metals and toxins into the groundwater supply. But keep on being 'good to the environment' if your ignorance makes you feel better. Scary to think there are probably other areas of your life where you make the same kind of stupid mistakes."

If Elisa had been harboring any thoughts of changing her mind about going through with her blackmail scheme, Rayman had just erased them. "Let's get back to business."

Rayman made eye contact with her for a moment and then said, "I assume you're not going to want a personal check, and I guess you don't take American Express, right?"

"You're right, it has to be cash."

"That's a lot of cash."

"This is a lot of incrimination." She patted the phone in her pocket, afraid to take it out lest he make a move for it. Come to think of it, she wasn't even sure how safe she was now, alone in his presence. What if he freaked out and decided to physically take it from her, or worse? This was all such a bad idea, she really ought to leave now and—

"Look, I'm not admitting any guilt here when it comes to those deaths on the beach. They haven't been connected to a sawfish. But I shouldn't have let that animal go in that manner, I admit that. Seeing as I'll be looking for a job and I don't need any negative publicity right now, I'm willing to give you a little something if it will help you out—I know admins don't make a lot—in return for deleting that video and forgetting you ever saw anything. Okay?"

Looking at him, Elisa almost felt bad at this point. He sounded so reasonable, so…normal. Not a bad guy at all, just a professional who fell on hard times and is doing what he can to turn things around. Was *she* really the bad person, here? *Oh my God, no, what am I doing?*

"Give me a couple of days, I'll have that money for you. Where do you want to meet?"

Elisa thought about this. The logistics were rapidly making what had seemed like a mere revenge fantasy all too real. *Where do you want to meet? Uh, I guess your place is out…Let's see…*

"I'll text you a location," she came up with.

"You have my cell number?"

"If it's the same one on file with the Institute, yes."

Rayman's eyes narrowed ever so slightly. "I'm trusting you not to leak that video in the meantime. I'll be monitoring the Internet for signs of it. If I get so much of a whiff that it's been released into the wild, the deal is off and I will sue you."

"I'll be in touch, Dr. Rayman." Elisa turned to leave. "Oh, just one more thing." He glared at her and she continued, "Don't leave the place a mess. I need to get right to work."

8

Dr. Rayman left the office and walked into the main lab. He slammed his fist into the side of one of the big round tanks. *That bitch! Blackmailing my sorry ass!* He gripped the edge of the tank and forced himself to calm down, taking deep, measured breaths while closing his eyes and imagining a tranquil coral reef scene. *There...better. Now think rationally.*

He thought about whether it was his sawfish that committed the attacks. Because if it wasn't, then that dumbass secretary could go to hell, couldn't she? *$10,000 my ass.* But if it wasn't a gigantic sawfish, then what was it? A shark, right? But the victims' wounds, from what he saw on TV and Elisa's miniature phone screen, didn't appear consistent with those caused by shark attack. But he really needed a much closer look to be sure. *If I could only get an in-person look at one of the victims...* But that would entail a visit to the Medical Examiner's office at this point. No doubt the bodies were there already, being prepared for autopsy. Normally, he could use his university position as reason to warrant getting a look at the victims, in order to help the City of Miami by identifying the type of animal responsible for the attacks. He looked around at the lab. Come to think of it, he was technically still employed for one more day—today—wasn't he? So if he went down there today, he would not be lying if he said, "I'm an ichthyologist—I study fish—with Florida University, based at the Ocean Sciences Institute out on Virginia Key..."

A few minutes later, Rayman found himself saying those very words into the phone.

#

Dade County Medical Examiner's Office, 2 hours later

"Welcome, Dr. Rayman. Through those double doors there, down the hall, last door on your right. Dr. Villanueva is expecting you." The Cuban-American female directed a bubbly smile at Mason. He thanked her, put his university ID away, and headed through the indicated doors.

Rayman tried to recall the last time he was here while he walked down the hallway. Once he had been called in to confirm a shark attack and to identify the species if possible. That was what, about five years ago? Six? Not something that happened often, that was for sure, but one of those interesting career moments when it did. The kind of moment he wouldn't be having after today, he reflected sternly. This would be a profitable visit, though, if he could prove that it was a shark, no doubt about that. If he could confirm those people had been killed by a shark beyond a shadow of a doubt, he could tell what's-her-face to shove it, right? Because if his sawfish weren't responsible for killing those people, then what did she really have on him? Proof he dumped some fish over the pier? That wasn't worth ten grand. More like a slap on the wrist. If they had killed people, though...

He came to the door and saw the Medical Examiner through the embedded windows. She was standing over a cart with a nude cadaver laid out, and talking to a female assistant. Rayman pushed his way inside, glancing at his watch as he did so. "Excuse me, Dr. Villanueva?" The M.E. nodded while the assistant looked on expectantly and he said, "Mason Rayman, I'm the ichthyologist from Florida University. Sorry I'm a bit late, traffic on the bridge..."

Villanueva smiled warmly. "Not a problem. Dr. Rayman. We were hoping you might be able to shed some light. This is my autopsy tech, Robin Consuela, and she'll take you to get a gown on, then you'll join me back here. This is not a pretty corpse, by the way, so I hope you're not feeling too queasy."

"That the man from the beach this morning?" Rayman asked, peering at the cadaver as he followed Robin into a small adjoining room. The M.E. nodded. "Yes, the second victim. The first is in the cooler. I'll pull him out while you get suited up."

A couple of minutes later, Rayman returned to the autopsy suite with Robin to find Villanueva standing over a second wheeled cart supporting a second cadaver, missing the head. The M.E. pointed to the headless corpse. "Besides the obvious beheading, this one also has the slash wounds to the torso, similar to the other. Let's start with the other one first."

Rayman tore his gaze from the ragged neck stump like a rubbernecker driving past a fiery wreck. He joined Villanueva and Consuela at the other deceased. "Male Caucasian, sixty-five years of age," she read from a clipboard before pointing to areas on the cadaver. "Found deceased with severe trauma to the torso, minor trauma to lower extremities. Major trauma thought to be from a shark bite or multiple bites—although no shark was sighted—at 7:03 this morning at Bill Baggs Cape. Bystanders say he was fishing, wading in the surf."

She looked up from her report to watch Rayman staring at the deceased. She continued, "Now I'm no marine biologist, Dr. Rayman, but having worked at the Miami M.E. for over twenty years, I have seen a couple of shark attack victims, and this..." She stepped over to the corpse, eyeing the chunks of open wounds on the right side. "...this looks like it *could* be that, but my findings at this point are inconclusive. On first glance I almost thought it was a boat propeller strike, but I'm not so sure about that, either."

She paused to let Rayman have an uninterrupted period of concentration while he viewed the corpse up close. He wrinkled his nose behind the surgical mask he wore as he took in the gory details. The entire right torso was gashed apart, with three long and deep jagged slits. It was a savage attack, whatever had caused it.

The M.E. pointed deep inside one of the gashes. "I didn't remove it yet, because I wanted you to see it *in situ*, but you see that glint of white...back there?" She aimed a red laser pointer into the open gash, where a white object was just barely visible.

"That's not bone?" Rayman leaned in closer. Villanueva shook her head. "It's not. Not human, anyway."

He turned around to look at her. "So it could be a tooth?" *Oh shit.* Hard evidence. There would be no getting around it if it wasn't a shark's tooth—if it was a sawfish tooth. He wasn't sure what other kind of tooth it could be if not shark or sawfish. Orca? Barracuda? *Don't be ridiculous.*

"Do you mind if I...?" Rayman nodded toward a long pair of plastic forceps with rubber tips.

The M.E. nodded. "Go ahead. We usually use those for removing bullets—the soft tips prevent the metal from being damaged—but I figured it should be suitable for an animal tooth as well."

Rayman picked up the instrument from a tray and moved toward the deceased.

Villanueva and her tech moved to either side of Rayman, out of the way but close enough to watch his every move.

"I'll just tease this piece of...flesh of some kind, out of the way..."

"Go for it," the M.E. said. Rayman continued with the forceps. He clenched the tips around the hard, white object. He pulled ever so gently, but the big tweezers slipped off the bony substance.

"Maybe slice that tendon there out of the way," the assistant offered, pointing deep into the open cavity. Then she turned to her supervisor.

"We already photographed and measured this wound, correct?"

Villanueva nodded, clearing the way for Rayman, who appeared concerned, to move in with the scalpel. He cut the tendon out of the way and then gripped the target of his extraction again with the forceps. Lifted... "Got it!"

Despite the situation, he was excited at the prospect of seeing whatever this thing was that had found its way so deep into the deceased fisherman's body. He removed the forceps from the body cavity and held the object up to the surgical lights.

A tooth.

No doubt about that. A large, spear-like tooth with serrated edges. Rayman's thrill of discovery soon gave way to disappointment, though, and something else...fear. *Because this isn't a shark tooth, is it? In fact, it technically isn't even a tooth at all. You know damn well what it is. Even they will probably know it's not from a shark...*

The tooth was gigantic, which was probably why no one in the room had said anything yet. They all just stood there gawking at the ridiculously large spear of bone-like material that had been extracted from deep within the dead man's side. It was longer than Rayman's hand, and wider at the base. But to Rayman, it was clear right away that this was not from a shark. He forced himself to remain objective while he studied the specimen. *Spear-type tooth, way longer than it is wide, not really triangular at all...* But he couldn't deny it.

Sawfish rostrum tooth, a dermal denticle.

He was holding one of the modified, tooth-like scales that had broken off the saw from a very, very large adult smalltooth sawfish. In fact, the "smalltooth" species name was more laughable now than ever, wasn't it? Rayman imagined the size of the fish this "tooth" must have belonged to, the long blade-like saw appendage it would have been attached to before it was ripped off during the violent, blunt-force trauma that ensued with the deceased.

"It does appear to be a tooth of some kind," Dr. Villanueva remarked at length.

"Is it...is that from a shark?" Consuela asked.

Rayman told himself to be convincing before he answered. "Actually, although a bit unusual, I do believe this could be from a shark." *Christ, could you sound any more ridiculous?*

"What species?" Villanueva asked, irritating him by using the correct terminology of species, rather than the generic "kind," as in "What kind of shark is it?" as most laypersons would ask. She wasn't leaving him any wiggle room.

And look at the damn thing, Rayman thought, turning it over in his hand, as if he had to examine it some more to be sure of what species it was. It looked absolutely nothing like a shark tooth, had absolutely no business being in a shark's mouth. Way too long, not really suited for chewing or tearing by working jaws up and down. But when fixed to the edge of a sword...well then, it became quite the slashing, hacking weapon, didn't it? He looked back down at the victim, shuddering involuntarily as he imagined all too clearly the struggle that must have played out as the fisherman met his gruesome end.

And the other guy didn't even have his head! That was how much power was behind this saw, and this extremely large fish it belonged to. That was the other thing, Rayman thought: It wasn't just a sawfish rostrum tooth, it was an oversized, greatly exaggerated sawfish rostrum tooth. A tooth that could only come from an unusually large sawfish, far bigger than those previously thought to exist in nature.

He was aware that Villanueva's question still hung in the air, but he had no idea how he should answer it. He couldn't very well come right out and say it was from a sawfish, now could he? That would mean incriminating himself in the release of genetically engineered animals. He would be known as a creator of monsters! A mad scientist unleashing terrible beasts on the unsuspecting populace. So he was glad to hear Consuela pipe up with some amateur conjecture of her own.

"You know, it almost looks like an alligator tooth."

Rayman looked up and raised his head in a conspicuous gesture of contemplative interest, his eyes widening as he took the bait. Alligators were common enough in South Florida...why not? "I was thinking the same thing," he said, trying not to sound overly dramatic. "The length, the shape..." He shook his head as if viewing a gigantic reptile in his mind's eye. "Although maybe not an alligator, but a saltwater crocodile."

"A croc?" Villanueva asked.

Rayman nodded. "A huge one." All in the room were aware that crocodiles were occasionally sighted off the beach in Miami. Unlike alligators, they preferred brackish or saltwater to freshwater. They were also known to be more aggressive.

The M.E. looked over to the other deceased victim. "What about him, though? Croc bit off his entire head?"

Rayman's gaze travelled to the ragged neck stump. "Looks that way, doc." Then he glanced at his watch. "Listen, I've got to get over to another appointment. I'm going to take this tooth with me for precise identification—I need to compare it to a species identification key—but for now I'd say we've got a large saltwater crocodile loose on the beaches of Miami, and I'd go ahead and put that in the reports for now. I'll be in touch."

He started to walk out with the tooth and Villanueva raised a hand. "Just one moment, Dr. Rayman. I suppose we can let you take the tooth so you can make a formal ID, but you will need to fill out a chain of evidence log first." She frowned slightly, as though disappointed Rayman was unaware of this procedure, before continuing. "Also, we'll need to photograph and measure the tooth."

She nodded to Consuela, who approached Rayman for the specimen. He stood there, not actually offering it to her, but allowing her to take it from his limp hand. Consuela went to work immediately, placing the tooth on a black cloth and photographing it next to a ruler while Villanueva walked up to a computer station and began printing out the forms.

This is not good! Rayman's brain screamed at him. *Not good at all!* He had been naively hoping that by taking the tooth he would be preventing it from being properly identified by other experts later on. But the evidence protocol Villanueva had outlined would keep him from quickly "wrapping" the case file. He would get to take the specimen, which would help a little bit, but with the quality photographs and measurements, any fish expert would be able to say what it was with a high degree of certainty at any time. The uncharacteristic size of the rostrum "tooth" would tend to throw them off, but Rayman knew they would eventually peg it for what it was.

He stewed quietly in these thoughts for a couple of minutes until he was interrupted by the M.E. handing him a set of papers. "Just sign here…here…and here, and you'll be good to go."

Good to go to jail, Rayman thought. He had no idea how he was going to get out of this one, but when the tech handed him the tooth, he took it, thanked her and walked out of the room.

9

Rayman fumed behind the wheel of his Ferrari as he drove back toward the campus from the coroner's. He'd put the sawfish tooth in his front jeans pocket, but when he sat down it ripped through the fabric so he put it up on the dash instead. Now he couldn't help but stare at it.

He'd straight up lied to the coroner, saying he thought it was a crocodile tooth. Any crocodile expert in the world would take about five seconds (after finishing laughing) to explain how there is no way it could have come from a crocodile or an alligator or a *T. rex*, or any reptile at all. And now they were now waiting on him to get back to them with some kind of formal analysis. What a crock. *Oh, sorry, forgot to tell you that was my last day!*

The fact that he was now heading over to the university after withdrawing $10,000 in cash from his bank ("hundreds is fine, thanks") wasn't making matters any easier on his psyche, either. *Ten fucking grand!* But if it would make her disappear so that he could get on with his job search without having to be worried about being blackballed from ever working again due to unprofessional and unsafe conduct...

Rayman wasn't a stupid guy, though. He asked himself as he turned into the long street that led up to the university's main campus, which was some distance away from his lab on Virginia Key: What if she refused to let up after he pays her this money? There was no way to confirm the deletion of a digital file, after all. Even if she really did delete the only copy, as she insisted she would do, it was likely the phone carrier itself would still have it somewhere on their servers, waiting to get hacked by some teenage kid or group of misguided do-gooders who would spread it around the net. Or even subpoenaed by a judge if he ever got sued for creating and unleashing killer fish. So what the hell would he do if she reared her ugly-ass head again, after this, demanding even more money?

Then he went over a speed bump as he drove onto university property and the tooth slid off the dash onto the seat beside him. He glanced at it, shaking his head. Thing was, even if it was one of his sawfish, which it pretty much had to be, something still wasn't right. *How'd it get so damn big?* He mentally pictured the saw on the fish when he'd dumped it over the pier. This tooth was much longer than those he had at that point, which could mean only one, scary thing.

It was still growing.

It had to have grown measurably since it was released only days ago! But how?

Then he reached the faculty parking lot and had to end his speculation for the time being. He parked and sat there looking around for a minute to make sure he didn't see anyone he knew. But there were only a few backpack-wearing students walking to and from classes. *Study hard, kids, it's a big, mean world out there...*

Then he grabbed his messenger bag containing the cash and stepped out of the car. He was looking for a park bench set "next to the dedication plaque from the Class of 1963." There was a cluster of shrubbery behind the bench, Gonzales had texted him, and that's where he should leave the money. Then the obligatory no funny stuff or the video file hits social media. Rayman shook his head in disgust as he walked onto a narrow paved path that wound through a sculpture-lined lawn. *How the hell did I get myself into this mess?* But with each step he took, the answer became increasingly clear.

He pictured the computer screens depicting the various genes of the sawfish he had worked with and manipulated. The fish in their tanks, clinically cared for with the precise amount of protein feed and water characteristics—temperature, salinity, dissolved oxygen, pH, etc.... He had single-handedly raised them into...*killing machines*? It appeared so. At least the one that had been released so far. Was it behavior or simply a consequence of how huge the fish was? *Got to do some more research on that...* But for now, he forced himself to stay on task. *Find that damn bench and get this over with so you can get on with your miserable life.*

He continued strolling along the path, passing buildings, some of which he was familiar with due to occasional business over the years. The building housing the prestigious Institute for Molecular Research and Biotechnology, for example. He'd worked a few times with Dr. Jennifer Asura, that Japanese scientist who worked what, thirty-five hours per week?, while he was putting in sixty-five. But she was Asian and female, a minority, so people gave her the benefit of the doubt. That's what he liked to think, anyway.

He passed a sculpture of some kind of weird abstract art installation (*what a waste of money*), and then a kiosk plastered with flyers advertising cheap student housing before he spotted a bench a little ways off the main path, with a smaller walkway leading to it. A group of bushes was carefully arranged in a semi-circle around it. He hurried his pace a little, but not too much as he approached it. Looked around. No one on the bench. No one hiding in the bushes that he could see. Only the normal university daytime foot traffic in the near distance.

He walked up to the bench and sat, setting his bag down next to him. He took out his cell-phone and held it in his hand so as to seem like he was just a professor or staff of some kind taking a little break. Every few seconds, though, he glanced around, looking for signs of Gonzales. Was she lurking somewhere nearby, watching him to see if he would try anything "funny?" If so, Rayman thought, then she was really good at hiding, because he didn't see how she could be anywhere on the ground... Unless...

He shifted his gaze upward, first to the trees (*Ridiculous! imagine that fat slob climbing a tree, and how much attention would that attract!*), but then to what really was a more legitimate concern—the windows of nearby buildings. Most of these were only two- or three-story affairs, but there were a good number of windows from which someone *could* be observing this very spot. He looked closely at a few of them with the most direct line of sight and couldn't see anyone. In fact, most of them had closed blinds in front of them. But at the same time he couldn't rule out the fact that it wouldn't be impossible for Gonzales to be up there somewhere observing him, like a sniper. Or worse, someone else.

He imagined some adjunct professor here for a few months on an H1-B visa from Mongolia watching him hide a bag under some bushes and then walk away...

Which brought up yet another uncomfortable thought—never mind someone else taking the money bag—what if Gonzales herself takes it but then claims she never got it? What could he do? Nothing, that's what. Jack shit nothing. He let his head loll back on the top of the bench as he exhaled in a rush of vented frustration. This whole thing was so fraught with pitfalls as to be almost worse than simply taking the fall for releasing the sawfish. Most people didn't know anything about fish, they wouldn't even understand how or why what he had done was wrong. Then he shook his head to himself. That might have been true up to the point that his fish killed two people. And it was still on the loose, out there somewhere in Biscayne Bay, ready to strike again. As big as it was, and apparently still growing with each passing hour, it would have to consume a lot of calories in order to sustain that kind of energetic metabolism.

What if it gets even worse? More dead. The fish, the saw, growing larger and larger with each passing week? How powerful was the effect of the parasitic copepod he'd tweaked? He didn't yet know the answer to these questions, but as he stood from the bench, gripping his bag, he had an uneasy feeling he was going to find out.

Hold on a minute... He looked over to the Institute for Molecular Research and Biotechnology building again. Asura's lab was in there. She had those mass spectrometers and other machines that would help to figure out the technical reasons for the excessive growth in the sawfish. He experienced a powerful jolt of adrenaline as he walked up to the bushes and slipped his hand into his messenger bag. If he could figure out what makes the gigantism work, he could use that knowledge not only to stop the freakish growth, but *to make more of them!*

Head on a swivel, he took in his surroundings one last time before committing to the drop. He saw no one, though was aware that he was none too skilled in this line of "work." Still, he had made up his mind to go ahead with it, so here goes. He slipped the Ziploc gallon bag with the bundled C-notes in an envelope from the messenger bag and chucked it deep into the bushes. *Let that bitch crawl in there to get it. I'm not going to take the risk that someone casually strolling by looks over and sees it...*

He backed away from the foliage and plucked a small flower from the shrub, as if that was the reason for his walking up to them in case anyone was watching. *Just a little token of love for my non-existent babe.* He turned around and walked back to the path. Done. He could now wash his hands of this filthy business. But as he strode away from the drop site without looking back, he was struck with that new thought as he passed the Institute for Molecular Research and Biotechnology. *Make more of them...*

Gonzales might not simply go away. If he could make more giant saws, well then...maybe he could figure out a way for her to meet up with one of them. To anyone watching him walk along the university path, he was just a middle-aged man, probably a professor, smiling to himself at the end of a long, hard work day about a job well done.

10

Florida University main campus, 10:30 P.M.

Rayman parked within easy walking distance of the Institute for Molecular Research and Biotechnology's main building, the same one he'd noticed earlier that day during the drop. He was in it to win it, now, that's all he could think. After this there would be no backing down, no changing his mind. If it worked, that is. He was pretty sure he could elucidate the molecular biomechanism responsible for the sawfish's gigantism, but only time would tell, and hopefully not that much time.

The ichthyologist hefted his messenger bag. It was full of the bio-samples he'd taken from his lab this morning. No way was he going to leave that stuff for someone else to pick up and continue his work where he left off. Let them figure it out for themselves; he was the one who'd done the heavy lifting. And right now, he was glad that he decided to grab that stuff, because then—only a few hours ago but what seemed like a long time—he hadn't had any idea that he would want to continue his gigantism research on his own. Or had he?... Did his subconscious relay the idea to him this morning, well before he "thought" of it when he left the cash in the shrubs? He was no psychologist but supposed it was possible.

Forget about it now, though, he told himself as he neared the rear stairwell of the biotechnology building. He had work to do, not the least of which was getting inside the lab without being seen by anyone. Well, he thought, climbing the stairs at a relaxed pace, not really *anyone*. Colleges had higher than usual activity at night—students studying, partying, scientists burning the midnight oil to run an experiment. It wasn't as if simply being seen walking around here at night was out of the question. But the fact that it was Dr. Mason Rayman—the "fish guy" who'd had his funding terminated and whose last day was *today*—might raise a few eyebrows. And were that same Dr. Rayman to be seen in the laboratory of Dr. Asura, when the two were not known to be close friends or even work associates for that matter, genuine alarm bells would be raised. Literally. Sure, technically it was still his last day, giving him the right, he supposed, to be on the property in general until midnight. But try explaining that to some campus security guard or college police officer. It was tenuous at best and no way did it extend to another person's lab.

He stepped off the stairs onto the third floor and entered the hallway where Asura's lab was located. Far down on the other end of the hall, where another exit sign glowed green above a door, a backpack-wearing person walked away from him, not bothering to turn around at the sound of the opposite door opening. Probably a grad student lab rat, Rayman guessed, and probably an Asian female judging by both the appearance—long black hair—and the work ethic.

He knew Asura's lab was on the right-hand side about halfway down. He went to it at a normal walking pace. A bulletin board next to the door featured a presentation of Asura's recently published work: protein inhibitors, biochemical uptake, blah blah blah; it was all boring to Rayman, who wanted only to do something very specific: control the growth of his sawfish. He reached out and turned the door handle, but as expected, it was locked at this late hour. With tens of thousands of dollars' worth of equipment inside, not to mention sensitive experiments in progress, a little security was to be expected.

But Rayman had come prepared. He fished his keys out from his pocket. Although he'd handed over the keys to Gonzales when asked without a fuss, what she didn't know is that he'd had the foresight to make copies the day before. He wasn't sure why he'd done that. Something about the sawfish, he guessed, when he learned it had grown, told him that he might want to be able to have access to the lab. Asura's lab key was on his ring because of a brief collaboration three years ago, where she'd given him a key. He still had it on the ring, so it got copied. Hopefully the locks hadn't been changed since then. He wasn't even sure which one it was, so he tried a couple before one slotted in and turned the lock.

He knocked on the now open door a couple times and even called out, "Hello?" in case someone, probably an intern or lab assistant (he was sure it wouldn't be Asura herself), was working quietly deep in the bowels of the lab. But all lights were off save for a few incubators and LEDs on various pieces of equipment. He walked inside, keeping the main lights off, closed and locked the door behind him.

He looked around the lab, allowing his eyes to adjust to the dim light. He hefted his bag, reminding him of the contents inside, the bio-samples he needed to run through various tests in order to figure out what exactly is causing the sawfish to grow so big, so fast. He moved to a lab bench and set down the bag. Then he proceeded to walk around and identify the various machines he would need to use. He considered turning on the main lights because it would speed things up considerably, but the bank of windows to the outside on the right wall made him nix that idea. It would be painfully obvious from the ground below that someone was in here, which wasn't in and of itself all that unusual, but it would be much better if no one was around later to say, "Yeah, I did see the lights on up there last night..."

So he moved around in the semi-darkness, using his cell-phone to illuminate equipment labels and specifics. Twenty minutes later, he had one of his samples loaded into a PCR machine connected to a computer. While he ran that sample, he set about setting up the next step. He was working again, doing what he did best.

#

Elisa Gonzales took a seat on the bench next to the plaque, as Rayman had done a few hours before her. She pretended to be engrossed in her smartphone screen, also as Rayman had done. Yet another similarity to what Rayman had gone through was her thought process: *I can't believe I'm going through with this!* She could feel the presence of the clump of bushes behind her. *I wonder if it's in there?*

She considered what she would do if it wasn't. Give Rayman another chance? She didn't really want to become involved in any kind of university scandal, even as a whistleblower. Who had time for that? It's not like they would give her a promotion for going the extra mile to look out for the Institute's best interests. But something else was eating at her, something even more serious. Was it a coincidence that people were being killed by a "shark" on the local beaches right after Rayman loosed his monster sawfish? She wasn't so sure. But if it was his fish, then by not coming forward—by taking money in return for her silence—wasn't she complicit in the act?

It's not too late, she contemplated. You could get up, forget about what's in the bushes, walk back to your car and drive home. Tell Rayman to forget it, go pick up your cash. *I was just trying to make a point.* Which was true, wasn't it? She *was* simply trying to make a point, a point that...that what? That you were always a rude, arrogant prick and now that you've done something wrong, I'm more than happy to hold it over you? And to make some much needed cash in the process. That was pretty much it, wasn't it?

Yep. She got up from the bench and looked around. A young couple embraced almost a football field away, and she could hear laughter coming from somewhere beyond that, but that was it for human presence. She looked up at the surrounding buildings, where most lights were now off, including in the Biotech lab, but there were one or two here and there still on. She couldn't see anyone looking down on her, though, and so she moved quickly to the bushes and crawled underneath and out of sight. It was dark underneath the foliage but she didn't dare use a light unless she couldn't find what she was looking for.

How far did you put it back in here, Rayman, geez. What a jerk. His idea of making her work for it, she guessed. But for ten grand, she could handle that. She wriggled deeper into the bramble of greenery, feeling about on the ground with her palms. *Ouch!* Caught her finger on a thorn or something, but she kept going, inching her way back. She thought about what she would say if she was by chance to be stopped by a security patrol. *Fell off my bike earlier today and lost my ring, thought maybe it bounced back in here...?*

She was shaking her head at how screwed she'd really be if that conversation came to pass when her left hand brushed across something smooth, soft and unnatural. Trash? Definitely a plastic bag of some sort... She lit up her smartphone and illuminated the object. Saw the envelope inside and snatched it up. Couldn't help it, had to look now, so she opened the back, pulled out the envelope and opened it to reveal the green inside. Even took a bill out to see if it looked real enough. She'd check it more carefully back home with a UV light to detect any counterfeiting, but for now it sure seemed like the real deal.

Elisa Gonzales was ten thousand dollars richer.

11

Miami Beach, next morning

Divemaster Kelly Jacobson counted his students as they all settled in a circle on the sandy bottom. *...Four...five...and where's Tatiana, she's always lagging—maybe her weight belt is light again—ah, there she is...six.* Satisfied he had not lost any of his charges yet, Kelly began conducting the "skills and drills" portion of his class, known as a "check-out" dive that, accompanied by a written exam, would bestow SCUBA certification on his students.

Once his divers, a mix of locals and vacationers ranging in age from early twenties to mid-fifties, had taken a couple of minutes to get accustomed to kneeling on the flat sandy bottom, adjusting their gear, Kelly got down to business. He pointed to the diver immediately on his right side, Eric Anderson, an M.D. from Coral Gables. This guy was sharp, top of the class, and he knew he wouldn't be likely to have any trouble, so he decided to kick things off with him. Get the rhythm going, let the other students watch him go through the drills, get the butterflies out.

Kelly pointed at Eric's mask. The student nodded and proceeded to tilt his head back and lift the mask off his face, flooding it with water so that he could no longer see clearly. This skill was known as "mask clearing" and was to make sure that a diver would know what to do in the event their mask was flooded or even knocked completely off their face. The doctor, after waiting about five seconds to be sure the instructor had seen that the mask was completely flooded, proceeded to exhale sharply through his nose. This blew air into the mask, which forced the water out of it. The dive student lowered his head, once again looking out through a dry mask, and gave his instructor the okay signal, thumb and pointer finger in a circle. Kelly nodded and returned the gesture.

Next, he put his hand on his own regulator, or breathing mouthpiece, and removed it from his mouth. He tossed the regulator over his shoulder, to simulate that he had accidentally had it knocked out of his mouth, and then traced the length of hose back until he put it back in his mouth. He exhaled first to clear the water out of it, then resumed breathing normally. Then he pointed to the doctor, indicating that he should perform the "regulator retrieval" skill now.

In this manner—one student at a time running down a list of several skills—Kelly went about the business of conducting his checkout dive. He hoped to run smoothly through the drills without problems so that they had some time left over to swim around and do a little actual diving—this site was known as Jose Cuervo, so named for an underwater bar that created a sort of artificial reef-- but they had to get through the skills first.

Kelly frowned as he saw one of his students—that surfer kid, Pascual—fiddling with a GoPro camera. He had specifically asked all students to refrain from bringing along accessory items like cameras and any other gadgets beyond the core set of scuba gear necessary for safe diving, since it distracted from the skills they were supposed to be learning. "Get certified first, then you can branch out into your various interests," he liked to say. But it seemed like there was always one in every crowd who just had to break the rules, especially with cameras. Kelly pointed to Pascual and shook his head. The kid nodded and shoved the camera into his BC pocket. Kelly got back to conducting his class, demonstrating the skill set.

When Eric completed all of his skills, Kelly pointed to the diver on his right, Eric's wife, Gloria. She was competent as well, and so Kelly anticipated little in the way of problems as she flooded her mask. The other students watched while maintaining their position in the circle, constantly adjusting their buoyancy and checking their air pressure gauges, as was common among new divers.

This was probably why no one other than Kelly took notice when a large shape of some sort passed swiftly above their heads, temporarily blotting out the sunlight.

The group was only twenty feet underwater, making it quite bright on this sunny day, and so the sudden shadow was noticeable to an experienced diver like Kelly.

What was that?

He glanced up quickly but received only a stab of sunlight in the eyes for his trouble. Meanwhile, the doctor's wife was waiting for him to acknowledge yet another completed skill. Kelly went back to focusing on his work, shepherding his class through their last dive before being certified as scuba divers, able to dive on their own anywhere in the world, to buy their own equipment and get their air tanks filled at dive shops everywhere.

As the next diver in line was about to start his skills test, Kelly watched in surprise, which quickly morphed into outright alarm, as an enormous shape erupted from the sandy bottom not ten feet from the opposite edge of the circle, across from Kelly. As any experienced diver knows, a sandy bottom is home to some large creatures, especially stingrays. At first, that's what Kelly thought he was looking at, but then as the form grew larger—so much larger than even a giant ray would be—he wasn't so sure. He wanted to point out the animal to his class, since sitting in place on the sand for most of a whole dive wasn't very exciting. If he could show them something interesting, well that's what diving was all about, and it would buoy their spirits.

But this apparition before them was no confidence builder, no mere point of interest on an otherwise dull dive. On the contrary, Kelly had never seen anything like it. He began to think it might be some kind of submarine, or sinking boat (*but it was moving so fast—a jet ski crashed and going down?*) it was so large. But he knew it was a fish, the way it moved, with such effortless, graceful motion. A fish moving incredibly fast.

Shark?

That's the only thing he knew about that was both that large and could move with such speed and agility. The diver three to his right—Melissa, he felt a little sorry for her because she had told him she was only doing this for her husband who really wanted to dive, and Eric had told her that was not a good reason to dive but she had insisted anyway—was in the middle of retrieving her regulator when the great fish swooped down on her. Something long and flat, like a shovel but at least twice as long, ripped into her head.

Kelly saw the blood in the water, with still a hint of reddish in color at this shallow, sunlit depth, but mostly dark. He heard the muffled grunts and shouts of the others vocalizing through their regulators in shock and surprise, trying to communicate despite the lack of ability to speak down here. For all his experience and preparation as a scuba instructor, where inaction was almost always the least of his options, he found himself utterly transfixed by the brutal spectacle playing out before him, unable to do anything but sit and stare as the woman's regulator hose was severed by the shovel-like appendage and a torrent of air bubbles spewed out into the water around them with a gurgling rush.

But when she opened her mouth and let loose a bloodcurdling scream, audible even across six feet of water to his ears, realizing that she had lost it and was in full panic mode and would probably drown if she didn't bleed to death first from her sudden wounds, Kelly was galvanized to action as the rest of his divers began to scatter, breaking out of the circle formation.

He reached down and grabbed his "octopus," a second regulator mouthpiece attached to his tank to be used in any situation where either his own primary regulator was malfunctioning, or if another diver was out of air, to avoid having to share a primary regulator. He kicked off the bottom and swam toward Melissa, waving at her with his left hand while extending the octopus in his right. *Come on, this is what you need, see me, see me!*

But she didn't see him, blinded by a white hot panic that even an experienced diver would be lucky to emerge from with a modicum of rational thought, much less a brand new diver not even yet certified. Her lack of self-control grew along with the spreading blood cloud in the water. She began flailing her arms uselessly. To his credit, Kelly saw her husband (Thomas, some kind of accountant at a bank), attempt to drag her close to him, one hand on his own octopus. But his actions were those of a newbie, much too tentative and not at all decisive enough in the face of such a sudden onslaught of unexpected activity.

The divemaster reached Melissa and shoved his spare regulator mouthpiece into her open, screaming mouth. *Breathe out first, breathe out!* When first taking air from a regulator that has been underwater, it is necessary to exhale first to expel water from the mouthpiece, then a normal breath can be taken. It was a common pitfall for new divers to forget to blow out the water first and then suck in a mouthful of water when they went to take their first breath. As it was, though, Kelly needn't have worried about this scenario simply because Melissa was already so far gone panic-wise, that she didn't even attempt to breathe. She spit the regulator right back out, too out of her mind to even attempt to hold it in her mouth.

Got to get her to the surface, now!

At that moment, he felt a powerful swirling of water around his midsection and knew that the big—fish?, whatever it was—had to be very close to him. But he didn't dare turn around. He gave his class a quick thumbs up signal with both hands to increase the chances that as many as possible would see it, meaning, *Let's go up to the surface.* If Melissa was in trouble, what if the others weren't far behind? These were brand new divers, after all, prone to spooking and not at all tested in situations where things don't go as planned.

He circled an arm around Melissa's waist while trying to make eye contact to calm her down. Looking into her mask, he could see that her eyes weren't even open. She had mentally checked out, was no longer even trying to survive. In deep water, this situation could likely be fatal. But here, less than twenty feet down, he knew he could save her. He kicked hard toward the surface, his long fins providing strong propulsion, lifting both him and his student toward the sunlit world above. He tried looking into her eyes again but now there was a blood cloud obscuring his view. She was still bleeding, heavily, and in the back of his mind, the single word SHARK patrolled around his mind. Shark attacks at South Florida beaches in shallow, sandy water were not uncommon. Add copious amounts of blood to the mix, and well...he didn't want to be around for that, so he kicked even harder, aware that he had five other divers to worry about as soon as he got her to the surface and made sure she wasn't dying.

He glanced around to see if he had any visibility in any other direction, but the blood cloud seemed to be all-encompassing. A little alarm bell went off in Kelly's head. *This is bad! How the hell did this happen! Crazy shark attacking my class, why me?* In five straight years of full-time scuba instructing, Kelly had never had a serious incident of any kind (unless you count the time one of his female students had asked him out to lunch in front of his girlfriend), a fact he took great pride in.

But now here it was. A Serious Incident that swam up out of the blue and chewed up his perfect safety record. And then he looked up and could see the water lightening. He was close to the surface. Glanced at his depth gauge to confirm it: yep, under ten feet now. He could still hear Melissa gurgling and screaming. Good. It meant she was still alive, for one thing, and that she wasn't holding her breath, which in turn meant she wasn't likely to suffer an air embolism—a potentially deadly condition caused by the rapid expansion of air in the lungs due to lessening pressure during an ascent.

He began mentally preparing himself for the steps he would take as soon as they broke the surface—*grab her BC inflator and put air in it, get her buoyant…be ready to do in-water CPR if*—

His thoughts were interrupted by an all-consuming physical force. Suddenly he felt himself—and Melissa, since he refused to let go of her—being lifted rapidly the remaining few feet to the surface. He felt *something* close around his legs, making it impossible for him to kick, and yet he was still rising, even faster than before.

Water washed from his mask and he was staring at a kaleidoscopic whirl of blue sky, sun and waves as he—and Melissa, mouth agape in utter bewilderment—were thrust into the air. Into the sky, it seemed—how high were they going? It seemed like forever, but then he was aware that he was falling back, to one side. He saw a tremendous expanse of rough, gray hide below him.

12

Dr. Asura's lab

Rayman took a chance and activated his cell-phone flashlight application. He knew it was risky but had reached a crucial stage of his experimentation and needed desperately to read an instruction manual about a piece of technical equipment. He'd used them before but Asura had a newer model. He had already done some gene-sequencing work from sawfish tissue samples, and had moved on to the parasitic copepods—how to produce as many of the modified gigantism-inducers as possible? It looked like he'd figured out a way, but he had to see what he was doing here...

The first time he worked with these critters, he'd modified them by accident in his lab, so his work here tonight was to figure out what he had actually done to change their DNA, and second, to make more of them. That is, to alter the batch of live sawfish to have the gene variant that caused the sawfish gigantism when the tiny crustaceans were introduced to their fish host.

Rayman watched the slender, wriggling, bug-like creatures crawl about in their Petri dish. He needed to wait a prescribed amount of time, fifteen minutes or so, to allow for uptake of a certain genetic marker. There was a lot of waiting around for processes to finish, and he wondered if he would be able to get it all done tonight. If not, he supposed he could come back tomorrow night, but that was really pushing it. He would do everything he could to wrap it up tonight. Still, for right now there was nothing to do but watch the clock so, noticing the open door at the rear of the lab that opened into a small, windowless room, he decided to poke around in the office part of Asura's lab.

Inside, he decided it was safe enough to shut the door so that he could flip on the lights. He raided the mini-fridge in here and found a can of Coke there that he now guzzled, needing the caffeine to stay focused. He looked around the cluttered room, overflowing with bookshelves and most of the rest of the space being taken up by a simple but overflowing desk. A desktop PC occupied the desk and Rayman was surprised to see that it was on, no screen saver or power save mode or anything. He was staring right at Dr. Asura's open email Inbox.

What the heck, let's have a look... He moved behind the desk and took a seat. Scanned the subject lines for something of interest... Plenty of the usual stuff, work emails between colleagues regarding ongoing projects, mails from students about classes, administrative stuff...but *hmmm, what's this? No subject.* Could be interesting, Rayman thought, so he took hold of the mouse, opened the message and began to read:

With all the cuts around here, we'll be lucky to hold on to this lab at all. Some of this equipment might have to go. How often is it used, really?

Rayman noted that the reply was from a well-known Professor of Molecular Biology, no one he knew personally or had worked with before, but of solid reputation.

While some of it is rather infrequently used, when it is used, it is absolutely essential in that there is no other way to accomplish what it can do. Yet the administration insists that something has to go, so what do you recommend?

Rayman's features took on a distasteful expression as he read the reply and saw the name of the exact machine he was using right now at the top of the list. *That means I need to finish up tonight. The penny pinchers are coming for the machines, along with me, too. Asura's head isn't on the chopping block, though. Wonder whose dick she sucked—*
Rayman heard a beep from the lab machine indicating his procedure was almost done. He clicked out of the open email so

that it was just the inbox again as he had found it, then he exited the office, leaving the door open, also as he had found it.

Back to work...

* * *

Rayman carefully snapped the lid on the small box containing his new copepods. He had done it. He was confident that he had recreated the genetic manipulation that had caused the copepods to induce gigantism when introduced to the sawfish. He made no effort to stop and think if he *should* do this, only that it looked like he could. He made certain that everything in the room was exactly as he had left it, and then he left Dr. Asura's lab. No one in the hallway, good. He moved at a decent clip, not fast enough to attract attention at this late hour but not dilly-dallying, either.

He wasn't sure at what point it had entered his brain he was going to do this, but as he got into his Ferrari and started the ignition, he knew there was only one course of action to take. He got on the expressway, light of traffic at this hour, and drove the speed limit to the Rickenbacker Causeway. He was well aware that red cars, especially sports cars, tended to be pulled over most often, and he didn't want to get stopped and have to explain what the hell those things were crawling around in the box. He crossed onto Virginia Key, quashing the wave of uneasiness that washed over him when he passed the Ocean Sciences Institute sign at the entrance to his lab's property. His *former* lab, he mentally corrected himself.

Checking his watch (one of those Casio waterproof digital jobs with a zillion functions, though he never used most of them), he had to shake his head. After midnight. It was officially the day after his last day of employment. He was trespassing now, beyond a shadow of a doubt. He knew that the Institute didn't have their own security guard on premises, but that the campus police had one officer patrolling the whole of Virginia Key, including the pier labs. Hopefully he wouldn't run into old Herman, who he knew liked to hang out a lot in the guard booth watching sports on the little TV in there. If he did run into him...well, he hoped it wouldn't come to that, because light acquaintances or not, the man had a job to do and would have received notice of Rayman's termination. He'd ask to see his ID and when scanned, it would come up no good.

Rayman parked in a guest lot about a five minute walk from his lab. Didn't need his ostentatious car to be recognized sitting right outside the lab. If everything went well, this shouldn't take long and he'd be out of here soon, a job well done, another mystery of the universe solved. Or so he hoped.

He carried the small box of water containing the modified copepods in both hands as he walked up to the lab. No cars in the lot. Perfect. No inside lights on, only the usual outdoor security lighting. Also optimal. He walked up to the rear lab entrance, facing the water on the pier and fished out his keys. Hopefully they hadn't changed the locks yet, if they ever would. He put the key into the rusty old lock and turned it, smiling as it opened.

Rayman moved through his old office, noting it was still in the same state in which he'd left it, the bitch Gonzales hadn't moved her stuff in yet. He passed through the door into the wet lab, pausing to check for sure that no one was out there. Coast clear, he walked into his old lab, the subtle tang of saltwater bubbling in the tanks reaching his nostrils, the soft hum of the pumps and filters creating a familiar blanket of white noise.

He looked into the empty tank that his now ginormous sawfish used to call home. He quickly passed by the other eleven tanks. Each still contained a normal-sized adult smalltooth sawfish. Three of them lay motionless on the bottom, resting, while the others swam in lazy circles, moving counterclockwise around the edges of their circular tanks. He grinned as he looked at his charges. *Good to see you guys again.*

He set his high-tech copepods on a lab bench and opened the lid of their container. He grabbed a pair of forceps and isolated one of the arthropods, gripping it softly between rubberized tips. Then he closed the lid and moved over to Tank #5 with his copepod in hand. From a nearby bait bucket which he deliberately hadn't cleaned up (might as well leave a little smelly present for the new inhabitants) and was now glad for, he scooped out a hunk of rotting fish and held it just over the lip of the tank so that it dangled into the water. He needed the sawfish, a big (but normally grown) adult at six feet in length, to expose its gills in order for him to embed the parasitic copepod.

Rayman shook the bait in the water, distributing the scent. Normally, he just tossed the food in and left, but he had also fed them in this manner before. Immediately, the sawfish came to life, whipping around from its resting position on the bottom of the tank. It rose to the surface toward the rotten fish. Rayman angled the forceps held in his right hand so that they were ready but wouldn't get knocked by the fish's long rostrum as it broke the surface to collect its meal.

The big animal thrust its entire head out of the water as it shoveled the meat into its waiting gullet. Rayman craned his neck to move his own head well clear of the elongated saw that protruded beyond the lip of the tank. It was a practiced motion he'd done many times before, so he was not frightened at all. To the contrary, he felt a pang of sadness that this minor ritual in his professional career was about to be relegated to that of nostalgia.

Focus. The sawfish (specimen #7) slid the base of its saw along the edge of the tank, slowing its body, while it swallowed the bait. Rayman saw his chance. He saw the sawfish's gill slits opening and closing with the exertion of its feeding efforts, and he thrust the clenched forceps deep into the gills. Then he released his grip on the big tweezers and withdrew the implement just as the big saw retreated beneath the water of the pool. The copepod was no longer on the tweezers, having been released deep inside the sawfish's gills, where it would in all likelihood become parasitic on its new host.

Rayman watched for a few moments to make sure the copepod hadn't fallen out and was now loose in the tank, but in his experience there was little chance of that, and he didn't see it. Time to move on. He proceeded to repeat the process on four more sawfish, implanting each of them with one of his special copepods. That would leave six saws remaining that had not received the parasite, in case he had made a mistake with this batch that didn't make itself known until later. Not to mention, he was breaking and entering and so time was of the utmost essence. When he was finished, he stood in the middle of the lab (no longer his), and looked out over the sawfish (still very much his).

"You guys remember number twelve?" he said aloud to the fish. "You're going to get your chance to go meet him. In the ocean!"

His only reply was the sound of sloshing water caused by the motion from the recent feeding activity. Rayman thought about it. He could toss the sawfish over the pier now, like he had the first one, and it would be much easier while they were still normal size. But he wanted to know for certain that his copepod procedure worked, which would mean waiting until tomorrow night. Because if it was successful, that was certainly worth knowing about. Who knows, it might even help him find a decent job, doing a formal write-up on it, repeating it with other species.

Rayman left the lab and headed to his car while the fish churned around in their tanks, something new awakening inside them.

13

Biscayne Bay, early next morning

Reynaldo Gutierez grinned as he paddled his kayak away from the mangrove-lined shore. He loved being out here—the quiet, with only the sound of birds and the splashing of his paddles as they dipped into the water—the solitude, just him out alone on the ocean. It was a rare break from work at the supermarket, where he managed the meat department. Even better, today was a weekday, meaning there was less boat traffic than a weekend; he had this little stretch of coast all to himself.

He turned his small craft north about fifty yards from the mangrove forest along the coast. Looking into the water, he could see that it was crystal clear today. He could easily make out the colorful sponges and green patches of turtle grass on the sandy bottom. He lowered the brim of his hat against the strong reflection of sunlight off the water. Hot day, he thought, gotta be pushing ninety. *Might have to take a dip in a while to cool off.* But for now, he continued to dip his paddle into the water, wanting to put some distance between himself and his launch point, to get this little excursion truly underway.

He recalled from a previous outing that there was an inlet in the mangroves about a mile north of here. He'd marked the spot on his GPS so that he could come back and explore it later, and he decided that today was the day to do that. He eyeballed the small screen on his handheld device and adjusted his course slightly. Another fifteen minutes of paddling and he'd be there. Gutierez settled back into a paddling rhythm, his sleek craft slicing across the water's surface. When he found his thoughts turning to work related things (*I wonder how Carlos is handling it today by himself, I hope he remembers that repair on the slicer...*), he deliberately forced it from his mind by checking his progress toward the waypoint on his GPS. *You'll be at work all day tomorrow, worry about it then. Right now, your job is to have some fun.*

A small fish leapt from the water a few feet off to the starboard side of his kayak and he grinned at it. *Out here in nature, that's the place to be...* He lined up his gaze according to the GPS and now had a visual on his destination. He turned his kayak left, pointing the prow toward the barely visible opening into the mangroves. Glancing over the side, he saw that the bottom was about four feet of gin-clear water beneath his hull, and mostly white sand. Knowing that this was an excellent place to get in and cool off, compared with closer to the mangroves where the nice sandy, firm bottom could transition to soft muck, he stopped paddling and let himself coast. Maybe he should take that dip now? He looked over the side again for a suitable spot, making sure he wasn't about to step on a sponge or something sharp.

Then Gutierez saw the bottom *move.* He didn't know how else to describe it; as if the entire seafloor suddenly shifted. Earthquake? In South Florida? Think again... Silt cloud? Must be some kind of underwater current stirring up the bottom, a riptide, maybe? But as he stared at the motion some more, he couldn't deny that it had a certain definition to it that stirred up mud wouldn't have. Defined lines, true form. Trying to get his bearings now, he turned around and looked behind him to see what things looked like back there. *Okay, normal bottom, there's the sand, some sponges, turtle grass...*

He whipped his head back around and looked forward, off his bow. A wave was rushing toward his kayak now from that direction. Not a wake from a passing boat or a little wind ripple, either, but a full-on wave, rising higher than his head from his sitting position in the kayak. *Tsunami?* Maybe there *was* an earthquake...

Suddenly, a massive shape lifted from the water. It rushed toward his little boat. He saw a long lance of some kind with teeth on the sides.

Oh. My. God! Shark! Ray! Something huge!

He should have been reacting, taking action to move out of the way, but the sheer size of the thing caused him to gawk at it for a moment too long. Easily four times the length of his twelve-foot kayak, he didn't see how this moving thing could be a mere animal. A whale? But the teeth…and then he got a glimpse of the underside of the beast's head as it began to fall out of the sky. Guitar-shaped, a funny cookie-cutter smiley face carved into the doughy white ventral surface… Gutierez was reminded of a stingray—a colossal, alien ray that appeared out of nowhere on this semi-isolated tidal flat area on a calm, sunny day.

Then the great behemoth's saw-like appendage came slicing down on Gutierrez's right shoulder, hacking the meat deeply while breaking his collarbone. Worse, it knocked him from his little boat into the water, flipping the kayak over in the process, bonking him on the skull in a way that was not serious in and of itself, yet was the last thing he needed at this moment. It just added to the confusion and panic. Where was the big ray now?

Gutierez stamped his feet on the seafloor, seeking solid purchase with which to launch himself into a shallow water run, but he had the bad luck to bring his right foot down on a large vase sponge. The cup-shaped invertebrate easily allowed him to place his entire leg inside it up to the knee, but the bottom was soft and springy and when he moved to leap, the contrast between that and the firm bottom under his left foot threw him off, sending him sprawling headlong back into the water.

Waves sloshed over his head as the sawfish churned the water while moving into a wide turn. The ocean was reddish now with the meat manager's blood, the sight of it making him queasy and lightheaded, further diminishing his capacity to mount an effective defense against this marauding uber-predator. Still, he struggled to his feet yet again, this time testing his purchase before attempting to push himself off the bottom and into a run for the shore. There were only mangroves here, but he would gladly scramble up onto those exposed roots and take his chances with the spiders and snakes and anything else that might be in there. Absolutely anything had to be better than this.

He made a run for the carpet of tangled greenery that represented salvation a mere sixty feet away. His mind was a tapestry of shrieking numbness, completely unable to process the incredible magnitude with which an ordinary fun afternoon had so swiftly gone so horribly, horribly wrong. He knew only to stagger forward, one splashy stomp after the next, and that with each footfall great gouts of blood—his lifeblood—spilled into the ocean.

He didn't fall again, though, and as the water became shallower, a shoot of hope burst through the numbness like a sprouting seed. He could make it! He could reach the mangroves and climb out of the water to safety. *Keep going...it hurts, but keep going just a little farther, you can do it...*

It took all of his self-restraint not to turn and look behind him to see where the sea monster was, this strangely huge beast that had knocked him from his craft, which now drifted south, overturned and flooded. He kept on, stumbling at times, even going down onto one knee once, but nothing was going to stop him from reaching those watery trees. The roots were hardwood, exposed in the air beneath thin but hard branches that looked as though they would support his weight, especially if he could spread his body mass out among several of them.

He could hear the rush of water close behind him as the monster fish pursued him into the shallows. He summoned a reserve of strength he knew he would need in order to make the jump up into the trees. He eyeballed the tangled root system—the step-ladder from which he would launch himself to safety in the canopy of salt-laden foliage. *Put your right foot on that big one there, then left foot on that one, there...*

His shoulder exploded in a burning wave of agony as he made the leap. But his footing was true, and he propelled himself upward until his hands and arms clawed and grasped and clutched their way to a desperate hold on three different branches at once. His face was raked against a tree trunk in the process but he cared not a whit about that. All he knew was that he needed to get higher, get up away from the water as fast as humanly possible. Everything else was a distant second.

Except for the sawfish, which had steadily been gaining on its prey, rising steadily at an angle, its back now visible above the surface of the shallow water. Some rays were known to make acrobatic leaps out of the water in pursuit of prey, and while this one was too large for anything resembling grace, it did manage to launch the lower third of its body out of the water as it approached the trees.

For an animal of this size, it meant that its elongated, toothy saw, nearly a dozen feet in length, was raking the tops of the trees, actually higher than where Gutierez cowered in fear on his precarious perch. The mouth was level with the human, but passed a mere foot away, unable to make contact with its potential food source. On its fall back down, the big fish whipped its head in a convulsive manner, hacking its tremendous saw blade into the thigh of Gutierrez.

Giant teeth hooked into his leg, dragging him from his perch. He tried to push the saw off of him, but it cut his hands to ribbons as soon as they came into contact with it. He was pulled from the tree, a thin waterfall of blood in his wake. He fell six feet into a few inches of water at the base of the mangrove. He nailed his head on the roots, nearly knocking him unconscious, which would have been a good thing, since now he had to watch the mega-fish's grand maw open in anticipation of a meal.

14

Virginia Key

Rayman had already downed a pot of coffee by the time he pulled up to the same parking spot on the pier nearby his lab. He'd stayed up late and gotten up early, probably about three hours of sleep. *Screw it. It's called work ethic, these losers around this place should get one.* He looked around, immune to the beauty of the sun rising over the Atlantic beyond the pier and looking only for other people. He saw none at this hour, but knew he didn't have long before the "early bird crew," as he called them, showed up. They were a contingent of scientists and lab workers who prided themselves on showing up very early to work, 7am, sometimes even 6:30, as if the earlier you arrived, the more dedicated you were. Rayman was pretty sure, for a few of them, anyway, that they just wanted less people watching them do nothing while they were at work. He'd always been more of a night owl himself, figuring that in the world of academic research, which should be results based if anything was, no one would care if he got to work at 10am, but over time it became clear to him that they did care. If you weren't seen at your desk working, then you must not be working at all.

How's this for some early bird shit? Rayman thought as he keyed into the lab. He entered directly into the wet lab itself, bypassing the office, since he didn't need anything in there. *The early bird gets the damn worm, isn't that how it—*

Oh my...

...God.

The sight before him was so stunning as to leave him stupidly standing there with the door still open. After a few seconds, he snapped out of it enough to be able to lock it behind him, magnifying the sound of the intense splashing that reverberated throughout the concrete and metal lab.

The sawfish—all five of the ones he'd implanted only a few hours ago with the parasitic copepods—were huge! Bigger than the first one he'd released. He must have really perfected the copepod modification. *Wow!* Five of the tanks had a massive fish tail dangling ten or so feet over its edge. They were far too big for their tanks already, and had to position themselves with their heads down on the bottom in order to have water to breathe. He checked the other six saws which had not received the copepods, what he thought of as his control group. They were still normal sized.

Rayman knew he needed to get to work right away if he was going to have these colossal animals out of the lab before anyone showed up here and, one: asked him what the hell he was doing here, and two: got a look at his freakish science experiment. A chill overtook him before he set himself into motion. If the first sawfish killed those two people like that...*imagine what these five will do.*

But that was the point, wasn't it? The fish scientist was moving now, gathering up the slide for the makeshift ramp he'd used on the first sawfish that was thankfully still here, stacked up against the wall where he'd left it. These five new marauders would wreak absolute havoc on Biscayne Bay and probably even beyond. These mega-predators would need to spread out in order to maintain habitats with sufficient prey stocks on which to feed and sustain such massive body mass and intensive growth. The City of Miami, and possibly even the State of Florida, would be desperate for a solution to this fishy problem. Tourism was a staple of the state's economy, after all, and who'd want to swim with killer fish in the waters waiting to hack up the tourists? During summer season, no less. And Rayman would be only too happy to put forth a solution, wouldn't he, because he *was* the solution!

A grin ebbed over his features like a rising tide as he moved to the giant sawfish nearest the door. Might as well start with the easiest trip first, get things rolling. In spite of the fact that he could plainly see this was going to be anything but easy, Rayman continued to fantasize about coming forward with the "solution" to the sawfish scourge. Like a firefighter who deliberately set fires in order to give himself a chance to be the hero by putting them out, Dr. Mason Rayman, sawfish expert of record, would once again become a world renowned scientist after he told the city and the state exactly what they were dealing with, and precisely how to go about neutralizing the threat. After that, they'd be tripping over themselves to hire him as their resident ocean scientist! He would field lucrative offers from the world over...the speaking engagement fees alone...

Saltwater landing on his face broke him out of his trance. *Better get a move on if you want to have a shot at pulling this off...*

He pulled a length of stout rope used for docking boats from a hook on the wall and uncoiled it. Getting it around the sawfish's massive caudal peduncle—the area where the tail joined the main body—was easy enough. He cinched it down tight so that he had a hold on the animal. But that alone would be far from enough. He grabbed a mass of netting—a throw net normally used for cast netting fish samples from the beach, and unraveled that into a pile on the floor of the tank next to the creature's unwieldy head. Then he grabbed the makeshift ramp and positioned it up against the tank so that he would hopefully be able to slide the gigantic sawfish out.

When he got the slide in place, he realized how small it was compared to the fish. This sawfish had to be half again as large as the first one he'd released, good ole number twelve. Then there was the "small" matter of how to handle things once it slid to the floor. A flopping, desperate fish out of water, as any fisherman could tell you, was nothing to be taken lightly, particularly not one...*forty*?! ...feet in length. Studying the concrete floor, slick with water spilling over from the tanks full of thrashing monsters, he decided to set up an impromptu barricade the funnel the fish toward the exit. Once he got it out the door, he thought he could use the tail rope to drag it to the edge of the pier. He wasn't positive about that, but there was only one way to find out.

Rayman unreeled a hose and took it out onto the pier to flood it with water to lower the friction for when he dragged it across. He looked around carefully for signs of people—no one yet, but the sun was now wholly visible in the lower part of the sky. He'd better get moving. He left the hose on, knowing it was a bit of a risk since someone might come to investigate running water if they saw it, but at the same time he was going to need all the help he could get to move not one, but five forty-foot sawfish by himself from the lab to the side of the pier.

Back inside the lab, Rayman took a deep breath. He gathered up the other end of the rope tied to the sawfish's tail and took up the slack. The fish was not all that active, laying with its saw on the bottom of the tank on the side away from where he now stood. Rayman began to walk toward the door, tugging at the line attached to the huge fish. The long tail easily slid over the edge of the tank, but when the bulk of the body hit the side, the animal grew more lively. It began thrashing side to side and Rayman received a rope burn as the line passed quickly between his fingers. He held on, though, and began pulling the fish in earnest.

He didn't know if he got lucky or if his timing was absolutely perfect, but as he pulled he was surprised to see the fish do a 180 degree turn, flap its "wings" and slither over the side of the tank, landing face down on the floor, where it slid some distance toward the exit. Then it wiggled back and forth, probably trying to bury itself in the non-existent sand or mud as rays liked to do. Rayman grabbed the ramp slide. He held it out in front of him and used it to wedge the sawfish toward the door. It whipped its huge saw wildly back and forth, narrowly missing Rayman's head on the first pass when he lifted it over the top edge of the board in order to see the animal.

The water slick on the floor worked as intended and the giant beast was actually able to propel itself forward somewhat as it endeavored to swim out of water, its prehistoric evolutionary design only knowing how to move to one advantage—in water. Rayman pushed after the freak of nature with his slide, cajoling it to the exit doorway. It was barely wide enough, and had Rayman been legitimately employed here and doing this as part of sanctioned work, he'd have gone out the wide rollup door on the other end of the lab, but that side was too far from the edge of the pier for him to be able to drag the fish there. The last thing he needed was for the sawfish to expire right in the middle of the research pier. So he wedged the creature through, pausing a couple of times to unstick a fin here or the body there, the rough sandpaper hide chafing his skin raw.

Once through the door onto the pier itself, Rayman again glanced all around the area, head on a swivel. This was absolutely the worst time to be seen by anyone. No one would be able to simply pass this off as "not my business." The curiosity factor alone was simply way too high. No one was present, though, the sun still not risen fully in the sky. But it had taken longer than he'd allowed to get the fish out of the lab, since it had grown much larger than he'd anticipated. Knowing he still had four more to go after this one, Rayman grabbed hold of the line and swung the massive fish around in a circle until it pointed tail first toward the edge of the pier, which was some fifty feet away.

Then he began to pull. The hose still flooded the pier, providing lubrication as he slid the thrashing animal along foot by excruciating foot. At one point, the sawfish flipped over onto its side and the tip of the saw wedged between two of the pier boards, snapping the tip of the saw off as the fish rolled to free itself. Rayman felt bad for the animal; this was normally a serious injury that would affect its ability to hunt and procure food—the broken saw would not regenerate. But in this case, he was looking at about a four-inch chunk missing from a ten-foot saw blade, so he wasn't concerned for the animal's welfare in that way. In fact, Rayman thought, eyeballing the ragged edge of the saw, it looked pretty nasty as is. He sure wouldn't want to get cut by it, seemed like it would be like being slashed by a broken edge of thin but rigid fiberglass.

Rayman kept on dragging the fish until he reached the edge of the pier, where he realized the extent of his next major issue. A four-foot high railing ran the length of the pier, wrapping around the end and along the other side. Two wooden rails were spaced at even intervals between the top rail and the pier floorboards, such that sliding a fish this size underneath the railing was not possible. He thought back to how he'd dumped the first sawfish over the top rail, but of course that one was substantially smaller in overall size and weight. He sighed in frustration as the reality of the situation hit home. He just wasn't going to be able to do it. He laughed to himself as he imagine holding the rope tied to the tail and jumping of the pier, so that his weight would pull the fish up when he reached the end of the line...but screw that. He wasn't about to end up in the water with this thing. Plus there were five of them and he didn't have time for that. He estimated people would begin showing up in about a half an hour, maybe less.

He looked around the pier while the fish started to gasp, working its gills in an attempted to wring oxygen from the salty air. What was he going to do? Then his eyes lit on an L-shaped metal structure not twenty feet to his right on the same edge of the pier, towering over the rail. *Of course, why didn't I think of that in the first place!* It was a crane used for launching and retrieving small boats. The sawfish was actually more like a medium boat, but the crane would be far better than attempting to lift it by hand.

Rayman bent to the task of dragging the colossal beast over to the crane. It was slow going, especially as soon as he left the floodplain of water from the hose, but he got it there. He became concerned about the fish needing to breathe, though—this was taking longer than he'd hoped—and so he ran back to the lab to grab a bucket of seawater. Ran it back out to dump on the fish but froze when he saw a car turn onto the pier.

Shit. Rayman froze as the car, headlights on, rolled at a slow pace onto the wooden pier. He could hear the planks rattling and creaking from here. He didn't know what he was going to do if the vehicle drove all the way down here. Hide in the lab? Jump over the pier and swim to the beach—abort mission? But it was a moot point as the car turned into a parking spot in front of one of the admin buildings at the foot of the pier and turned off its lights. It was a warning, though, that was for sure. Time to get this rodeo underway and get 'er done.

He dumped the bucket of water directly into the open gill slots on the sawfish's right side. The fish seemed to settle down a little with the infusion of oxygen. "That's gonna have to hold you over, buddy, 'til we get you in the water." He dragged the sawfish the rest of the way to the foot of the crane. Fortunately, he'd used it before to launch a boat, so was familiar with its operation. He pressed the control to lower the harness of canvas webbing down to the fish. Then he pulled it beneath the body, wary of the tail which thrashed out every now and then. When he had the harness in place, Rayman ran to the button to raise the crane arm and punched it.

He heard a mechanical whine and the arm began to slowly raise the webbing until it drew taut around the sawfish. "Hang in there, buddy, almost there." When the fish dangled above the rail, Rayman hit a different button to swing the arm out over the edge of the pier. Normally at this point, the crane would be used to slowly lower the payload, usually a boat, to the water's surface, about twenty feet below. But Rayman had no time for that. With four more to go after this one, he had to get this show on the road. Besides, he thought, eyeing the immobilized mega-fish, this big boy's not going to be hurt be dropping a few feet into water. It would just have to deal with it. Rayman was confident it would survive the drop.

He stepped up onto the base of the crane and unlatched the hooks that held the net in place. The sawfish's saw protruded well beyond the webbing, so he didn't have to worry about it getting snagged in the harness. He watched as the massive aquatic animal rolled out of the harness and dropped through the air to splash into the ocean below. It lay still for a moment, no doubt dazed as a result of its experience, and then gave a couple tentative shakes of its powerful tail. It angled its head down, submerging itself, and then, just like that, the beast swam quickly out of sight, down into the gloom.

Rayman smiled and ran back to the lab, glancing down to where he'd seen the car. No further activity. Good. Only four more sawfish to go.

15

Miami Beach

Parasailing. Probably the very last activity Jim Long wanted to do on vacation, but like his friends told him, it was his fault for marrying a wife twelve years his junior. She wanted to go, and so he was going, too. End of story. So here they were, on an airbrushed speedboat boat not far off the golden sands of Miami Beach, which was the same stretch of sand as the more well-known South Beach, but on the northern end.

"Tandem, right?" the boat captain, a Cuban-American kid in his twenties asked from behind yellow-tinted sunglasses and an infectious smile. Standing beside him, an assistant, also Cuban-American, who appeared even younger than the captain, nodded in enthusiastic agreement. Mr. and Mrs. Long said yes, they want to sit side by side on the same flight rather than go individually, and the captain gave them a hearty thumbs up.

"Hold on, enjoy the boat ride while we get out to the launch site. Five minutes!" He turned and went back to the helm where he put the boat's powerful engine, idling at a throaty rumble, into gear. The Longs sat in bucket seats with their arms around one another while the boat accelerated sharply until it was "on plane," hydroplaning along the water's surface at cruising speed. The water was calm today and so it was a relatively smooth ride, but still, at forty miles per hour, there were plenty of bumps and jolts. Jim was starting to regret that breakfast of Cuban sausages when the boat slowed and settled down in the water. They were about a mile off Miami Beach. The parasailing assistant was already clipping lines into place, setting up the rig. The captain placed the engine in neutral and walked back to his passengers, the only two on the boat, which was licensed to carry up to six passengers. He clapped his hands together as he addressed the Longs.

"All right! How you feeling? Are you ready to fly?"

Shana Long nodded, her nose ring flashing in the sun. "Yes! How 'bout you, hubby?"

Jim took a deep breath and watched the assistant unravel a length of rope. "Ready as I'll ever be, I guess."

"Let's get you strapped in, then!" The captain looked back to his assistant, who by now had the parachute in the air, tied to a T-bar on the boat, with the harness seats lying on the stern deck behind the seats. The captain stepped back over to the helm and turned down the marine radio where an excited fisherman reported unusually high catch activity somewhere nearby, while the assistant helped the Longs into the tandem harness. They faced forward in the boat, Shana on the left and Jim on the right, while the assistant clipped them in.

"So like we talked about before, I'm going to let the line out and you're going to go up, up, and away, okay?" Shana flashed an excited smile while Jim nodded, all business. "Just sit back and enjoy the view. First we'll take you up high for a scenic look, then after that, if you're lucky, we'll dip you! Okay, here we go!"

He turned back to the captain and gave him the thumbs up signal, indicating they were ready. The captain returned the gesture and then the assistant began letting out the harness line that was attached to the chute. A minute later and the Longs' feet separated from the deck and they were lifted into the air above and behind the boat, which started moving forward as soon as they were airborne. The assistant heard Shana say, "It's okay, honey!" as they lifted off and then their words were lost to the wind and distance behind the boat's engines. His job now was to watch the parasailors for signs of any problems and to direct the boat driver if need be.

In the air, Shana was having the time of her life, and even Jim seemed to be coming around. The view from their lofty vantage point was intoxicating. The narrow barrier island that divided Biscayne Bay from the Atlantic Ocean, and which hosted Miami Beach and South Beach on the Atlantic side, was sprawled out beneath them, stretching for miles along a carpet of blue water.

Shana pointed out various sights to Jim, who nodded at each but she could tell he wasn't really concentrating. Simply being aloft was more than enough of a thrill for him, and after a few minutes, she simply let him enjoy the ride. The sun, the breeze, looking down on the world for a change...she found it all to be so intoxicating. She felt comfortable to the point that she brought out her cell-phone and snapped off a few pictures. She stopped short of uploading one to her social media page, figuring she should enjoy the moment. She put her phone away and gazed straight down at the water, about five hundred feet below.

She squinted behind her designer sunglasses as she spotted a dark shape marring the blue. A boat? Looked like it was underwater, though. A rock? She could have sworn she saw it move. She tapped her husband on the shoulder. He glanced over from where he'd been looking at the city beyond the beach, to see her pointing almost straight down. He looked but didn't immediately see anything for her to get excited over. He turned to her and shrugged.

"Right there!" she yelled, pointing again.

Then on the boat, the assistant was gesturing up to them. What did he say that signal was, again? But before Shana could recall, their parasail was dropping sharply, the ocean surface rushing up to meet them. She squeezed Jim's hand tightly. They were going down, to be splashed into the water and lifted back out again. It was supposed to be fun, but she was distracted. *What was that thing?* She didn't want to land on a rock or anything that wasn't water. But these guys running this tourist operation had to know what they were doing, right? They wouldn't dip them in an area they weren't familiar with...*right?*

She hoped not, but there was no more time to think about it as her toes sliced into the ocean and Jim was shouting like a kid on a roller-coaster. She felt the water reach a little over her knees, and then felt a jerk as the chute was pulled up by the boat operator, lifting the parasailors out of the water again.

The assistant cupped his hands and shouted to the thrill-seekers. "Cool you off a bit? Back up for one more!"

But no sooner had he finished his sentence than a gargantuan...structure—to the assistant it looked like some kind of structure, it was so large—broke the surface of the water perhaps fifteen feet away from the parasailors.

"Up! Take them up!" the captain yelled from his position at the wheel, where he'd been watching the dip maneuver, waiting for the opportune moment to accelerate. The assistant frantically let out more line, wishing the breeze was stronger. He yelled back for the captain to go.

The boat rocketed forward just as the long, flat saw blade attached to a leviathan of a sawfish sliced through the parasail cord—

—and Shana Long's legs below the knees.

Her severed feet dropped into the ocean even as her harnessed body, along with her husband, continued to be lofted upwards by the sail. The parasail rig was no longer attached to the speedboat, however, and after an initial upward burst of momentum left over from the boat's acceleration, the chute began to drift back down to the water.

The assistant went slack with disbelief, shock, and the general surreal feeling of the moment. He could not believe what he was a witness to. A steady stream of blood fell from the woman, who clutched at her husband, but quietly, not screaming. Meanwhile, what he had come to recognize was not an object gone astray—a wayward boat, perhaps—was in fact a living thing—a creature that had attacked his clients. He pulled at the line until he understood the futility of his actions—he was yanking on a rope that was no longer connected to anything on the other end. That thing! That thing cut the line! Somehow he managed to verbalize this thought to his captain, who promptly put the boat into a turn and headed back around for the parasailors.

They chased after the now drifting 'chuters, praying they could reach them before the marauding mega-beast got to them again. The copious volumes of blood pouring into the water were stirring the animal's hunger drive, stimulating its senses and spurring it on to do one thing and one thing only: feed.

The assistant shouted and pointed, but the captain was screaming MAYDAY MAYDAY MAYDAY into the marine radio, even as he turned the boat around. When they were pointed at the parasail, which now drifted only about ten feet above the ocean's surface, the captain dropped the radio mic and hit the throttle.

"It's almost to them!" The assistant followed the progress of the sawfish with a pointing finger. Rather than slowing down or veering off to one side, the captain increased his speed as he came up to the rampaging predator. In his experience, almost all animals would move out of the way once they heard the whine of the engine and felt its vibration. The manatee was sometimes an exception, but he found it to be true for most creatures, and right now he could think of no other options.

As he neared the sawfish, he began to wonder if this was a mistake. The fish was longer than the boat, and wider too, at least where the pectoral fins flared out like wings. But at the same time, he had clients whose lives were at risk. He was duty bound to do something. Help should be on the way after his radio call, but life-saving action was needed right this second.

Against his better judgment, the captain slammed the throttle up to full, calling out "Hold on!" to his assistant, who had the foresight to immediately grab hold of the nearest support rail. The boat leapt out of the water toward the attacking ray. The problem for the captain, besides the fish itself, was that he could easily overshoot the animal and plow into the parasailors since they were now so low to the water. But seeing what had happened to the woman already, he figured she'd rather take that chance than have him abandon her to the giant beast due to an overabundance of caution.

Then he felt the boat's sleek hull bump into something—something he knew must be the sawfish. They were in deep water by Florida coastal standards—twenty feet; there were no sandbars or shallow reefs to hit, which was why this area was popular with parasailing in the first place. The collision caused the boat to shift course to the right, away from the beach, as it deflected off the sawfish's smooth dorsal surface.

It also caused the great sawfish to change course: toward the boat. Good, the captain thought. Lead it away from the clients. Follow me over here, fish. The monster saw jutted from the water next to the boat, a cascade of water dripping from the long teeth on the sides of the blade. The splash made when its body fell back into the ocean drenched both men in the boat.

Meanwhile, the Longs dropped back into the water, Jim shouting for help. The captain noted with great unease the spreading blood in the water as soon as the woman hit. Also of concern was the fact that the parachute was now landing on top of them. It wasn't nearly as large as a skydiving parachute, which would be a real problem—the parasail was a crescent shaped sliver of chute, designed for being towed behind a boat, and falling from relatively low heights over water. Nevertheless, with everything happening now, the Longs didn't need any further complications. But they would have to deal with the fact that the chute was draped over both of them, crumpling into the water as it began to slowly sink, threatening to take both of them with it.

Muffled screams reached the boat crews' ears. "Grab the boat hook! We gotta get 'em out of there!" The captain began motoring to them as fast as possible without going too fast, while the assistant grabbed a metal pole with telescoping sections that extended to full length. It was normally used for grabbing ropes, but the intent here was to use it to pull the chute off of the downed parasailors before it dragged them underwater.

The sawfish had gone back underwater, a roiling, swirling footprint left on the surface in its wake. The captain watched for it nervously as he nosed up to the chute and put the boat's engine into idle mode. Seeing they were approaching front first, the assistant ran up onto the bow and stuck the hook out over the rail. He saw a section of sail cord trailing off the chute and reached out with the boat hook, snagging it.

"Jim, Shana—I'm pulling the chute off of you, then I want you to swim to the boat, we're right here." He received a bloodcurdling scream in response. The assistant began pulling on the cord with the hook, dragging the chute off of the two swimmers.

"Jim!" Shana screamed, still shrouded behind the parachute. The assistant pulled the cute up to the boat. At first he was confused, because it seemed like the chute—which was red and white in color—was still near the people in the water, but then the sickening realization hit him that they were swimming in blood. Shana was spinning in a circle, screaming over and over.

"He's gone! Jim—he's gone!"

The captain expertly maneuvered the craft until it was right next to the stricken swimmer. The assistant leaned over and pulled her from the water, shocked at the sight of her bloody stumps streaming blood onto the boat's white deck. In the distance, they saw a boat approaching them, fast.

"Coast guard's coming," the captain said, pointing.

"Need a tourniquet." The assistant looked around the deck. Neither he nor the captain wore a belt. The captain grabbed a rope used to dock the boat and tossed it to the assistant, who used it to tie around Shana's legs, stemming the blood flow.

The Coast Guard boat, small and fast, was hailing them over the radio now, informing them they were preparing to board.

Meanwhile, the captain scanned the water for signs of Jim and the sawfish. He saw neither.

#

Miami Shores

The Vasquez family was enjoying the sunny day outside in their backyard, located on a saltwater canal lined with houses all featuring boat docks, and which led to Biscayne Bay. Benito and his wife, Marissa, watched their three children, aged six to fourteen, use a garden hose to shoot water into the canal, hoping it would attract a manatee to drink. The gentle mammals were known to swim up canals and drink fresh water from hoses. Many a time, when Benito washed down his boat after an outing, there would be a visit by a manatee or two.

"See any yet?" he called over to his kids. They called back that none had showed up yet.

"Watch the water bill!" Marissa admonished. "Turn it off for now."

Benito picked up the cold bottle of beer from the table next to his chaise lounge. "Maybe we should let them have some fun. You and me could slip into the house for a little while, and I wouldn't have any problem paying the higher water bill." He gave her a wink that she'd seen many times before. She laughed and picked up her own drink. "Oh, so as long as something's in it for—"

"He's here!" The shrill voice of their youngest cut through all conversation, making them turn to look over at the canal, where one of the kids sprayed the hose with a trigger nozzle out into the middle of the canal. About thirty feet wide, the waterway separated the Vasquez home from their neighbors directly facing them on the other side. That house was owned by New Yorkers who bought it as a second home, and they rarely even used the place, nor did they rent it out. Which was just fine with the Vasquez's.

"Tell him I said hi!" Marissa went back to her drink, and her husband.

On the dock, the kid with the hose adjusted his aim as a manatee came to the surface with a breathy gasp. Also known as sea cows, the fat and slow-moving marine mammals ate only plants. Gentle by nature, they had a grace about them that belied their size and shape.

"Can you believe sailors used to think they were mermaids?" Marissa asked Benito.

He raised his eyebrows while looking over at the whisker-encircled mouth, the fat pink tongue lolling around inside as the manatee positioned itself to catch the water shooting from the hose.

Benito took another sip from his beer. "Sure, I can believe it. Out there at sea for months at a time, no women..."

Marissa laughed. "I forgot who I was talking to." She pointed to his drink. "A few more of those, and I'd bet you—"

"Hey, where are you going?" the kid with the hose yelled as the manatee moved away from the stream of fresh water.

"Maybe he's not thirsty anymore," the youngest child offered.

The eldest sibling shook his head in response. "No way. They usually drink way, way more than this. Remember the time Mom told us to stop because she said it was drinking too much and it might be bad for it?"

The daughter chuckled. "Yeah, he was drinking for like an hour that time!"

"So where's he going?" the child with the hose asked again.

"Looks like he's coming to the dock." The kids moved over to the stretch of concrete not taken up by the family boat, a twenty-foot speedboat. The manatee shot toward them like a barreling, legless hippo.

"I've never seen one move that fast before!" Benito remarked, indicating for his wife to look at the canal.

The hustling sea cow reached the edge of the dock and crashed into it, rolling back into the water. It was like an oversized seal attempting to slide up out of the water, but without the speed and agility of a seal.

"It's trying to get up on the dock!" the kids all shouted at once.

Benito and Marissa stood from their chairs. Benito pointed further down the canal, about halfway to where it met with a larger canal that led to the bay off to the right. "Hey, what's that?"

The kids were still laughing at the wayward sea cow.

"What's what?" Marissa asked, also watching the manatee try to get up onto the dock again.

Benito raised his tone sharply, wagging his finger while still pointing. "That!"

Everyone looked down the canal, where a strange sight indeed awaited them. A sizable wake was making its way down the canal, rocking the boats tied to their docks on either side as it passed. That alone could possibly be explained rationally—a large boat could have started up further down the canal and throttled up too fast—people were sometimes reckless. But the thing is, Benito thought, scratching his head, to generate a wake like that would take a lot of power, and he hadn't heard any motors at all. So then...

He squinted through his polarized sunglasses which supposedly made it easier to see down into the water when there was glare from the sun. He concentrated on the area just behind the forward moving wave, where there ought to be something pushing that water ahead of itself...

There! Something splashed out of the water about forty or so feet behind the wake. He tried to stay focused on that area as the wave moved toward their end of the canal. The sound of clanging sailboat rigging and boats knocking against their docks became louder as the moving wave approached.

Now the kids were pulling on the manatee as it flopped its comically small head up onto the dock, trying in vain to help it gain sufficient traction to pull its half-ton body up onto dry land.

"Dad, help us!" one of them called. "Get the net!"

Benito shook his head, bellowing, "All of you let go of him and get back from there. Now!"

A couple of them did, but the oldest one still tried to help the struggling creature in its endeavor. "I said *now!*" His voice was tinged with a certain fear, causing his wife to look at him.

"What's wrong?"

He pointed to the spot behind the wake, where once again, he saw something thrash out of the water for a just a moment before submerging again. "Something's there. Something's causing that wave, under the water. I don't know what it is, but… I think it's an animal of some sort… That manatee…it's scared, that's why it's trying to get out of the water. Manatees don't usually haul out. I've never seen one do that, have you?"

She shook her head slowly while watching the wave approach. Then she cupped her hands to her mouth and yelled toward the children. "Kids! Up here, now!" One of them was looking down the canal and pointing toward the wave travelling at them. The others looked up from the struggling manatee to see where their sibling was pointing.

"Mama! Something's coming. " The youngest turned and ran toward the house.

"Everybody, up here—come on!" Benito urged. The other two kids turned and followed the youngest away from the edge of the dock to their parents. The manatee chuffed and wheezed after another failed attempt to beach itself on the dock.

And then they saw it: Long. Grey. Sinister. The sleek shape moved effortlessly toward their section of canal, veering toward the manatee.

"It's some kind of fish," Marissa said. "A shark?"

The surge of water pushed ahead of the sleek predator enabled the corpulent manatee to tumble onto the dock. But that didn't mean it was safe.

"Look, a sword!" One of the kids tugged at his father's sleeve, as if he wasn't already staring open-mouthed at the incredible sight. Indeed, a mighty staff rimmed with six-inch-long, conical teeth, like some kind of medieval Viking weapon, erupted from the canal. Marissa began to scream, triggering the youngest to wail also.

The manatee dug its front flippers into the concrete as it fought to gain traction against the water receding from the dock. It had sensed the sawfish's presence early, and so had swam into the manmade canal system, hoping to evade the super-predator, to venture far into the upper tributaries of the artificial system of waterways. Its speed was hopeless against the gigantic ray, a true tortoise and hare comparison, so it had fled early.

The tactic had almost worked. The marine mammal was rolling itself toward the house, having given up on dragging its hulking body with its flippers and deciding that rolling would be faster, like an infant first learning to move itself from a stationary position. It had just reached the point where it was clearly beached up on the dock, no longer in danger of sliding back into the canal, when the towering saw blade slammed into its ample, blubbery flesh. The side of the mammal split apart about midway from head to rounded tail. A dark river of blood snaked out across the dock, dripping over the edge in a macabre waterfall, the doomed manatee's blood returning to the water it had sought to escape.

Mortally wounded, the warm-blooded creature lay still, except for a rapid opening and closing of its mouth. The sawfish fell back into the canal, unable to drag its weighty meal back into the water.

"Call somebody!" Marissa was shouting to her husband.

"Who?"

"I don't know! The police?"

"What are they gonna do?"

"Just call somebody!"

He dug for his phone in his pocket without looking away from the bloody spectacle unfolding in his backyard. Dialed 911 and told the operator about a monster fish attacking a manatee. She didn't sound very alarmed but said she would send someone to the address. Benito pocketed the phone and looked up in time to see the colossal sawfish leap from the water and come down on the hapless manatee yet again, hacking its saw firmly into the prey's side. This time the saw established purchase deep in the flesh, allowing the fish to drag the sea cow off the dock and into the water, where a thick cloud of blood marked the disturbance.

"Is the manatee dead?" one of the kids asked.

"Yes, he is," Benito said.

"We don't know that for sure," Marissa countered, wanting to spare her youngest of the reality of death. "He was hurt, but maybe he swam away after he was dragged back into the water."

Benito eyed the swirling blood cloud doubtfully, unable to see the sawfish ripping its prey apart because of the cloudy, red water. "I guess I don't know for sure, but I do know one thing." He looked over at his family. "None of us will ever swim in this canal again."

#

South Beach

Wall-to-wall people. That's how many would describe this day on the famous stretch of sugary-white sand fronting the legendary Ocean Drive strip of world class restaurants, clubs and hotels. The sound of Cuban salsa music wafted over the beach from the outdoor dining areas across the street. A patchwork of towels, blankets and bodies sprawled across the wide, sandy beach, becoming denser closer to the water.

For lifeguard Alyson Friar, it was just another day. From her vantage point on the lifeguard tower, she dropped the binoculars around her neck after scanning the water for signs of trouble. The surf had picked up somewhat from its usual calm state, to the point it was just large enough to be cause for concern. Especially for the little kids who waded in the shallows, which were pocked with depressions in the sand where they could suddenly find themselves in over their heads. Combine that event with a rush of whitewash from a wave steamrolling over them as they struggled to tread water, and you had a recipe for potential disaster.

But that's why Alyson was here. She knew what to look for, what to anticipate, and when to act. Unfortunately, a fair amount of her on-duty hours consisted not of water rescues, but more police-type actions, warning people not to consume alcohol, to leash their dog, to turn down their loud music or pick up their trash. That was on a good day. On a bad day, she'd break up fights and call the actual police for assistance. She'd been called names, spit at, even assaulted by drunk beachgoers spilling over from downtown looking for trouble.

That's why she came to look forward to the core aspect of her job, water safety. The ocean was what had attracted her to the job in the first place. Growing up on the South Florida coast, she'd learned to scuba dive as a teen, surf, and sail. One day, she even hoped to transition from the community college where she now attended to a four year school to study marine biology; the lifeguard position was a means to support that end. Sure, the job would be open to her for quite some time, but she had no desire to make a career out of it. While she admired the competence of her coworkers who'd been guarding for decades and risen to managerial roles, she truly loved the sea and wanted to center her life around it, not around paperwork or law enforcement or even saving people from drowning in it over and over again.

All that was in the future, though. For right now, she was faced with a whole slew of people on this beach, coming and going in and out of the water, running around, making noise...*what was that?*

Her ears had become attuned long ago to the sounds of struggle. She was adept at isolating individual voices from the greater cacophony and homing in on them.

I'm not kidding!

Somehow her brain isolated the phrase from hundreds of others being spoken within audible range. She glanced left, to the north along the beach, all the way up to the next lifeguard tower. Maybe it was Alfonso's turf, if it even was a "situation" and not random silliness, children playing. She spotted Alfonso walking the sand in front of his station, holding the red lifeguard can, swinging it slowly back and forth in order to maintain high visibility. He didn't seem worried about anything at the moment. Surely he would be able to hear what she heard if it had originated right in front of his tower.

Alyson began tracing her gaze back down the beach from Alfonso's station to hers, a little ways out into the water. She didn't think the voice had been farther out than that. If it was—

"Excuse me, can you tell us where the La Paloma Club is?" The lifeguard frowned, annoyed that her train of thought and search process were interrupted for such a petty matter. She flicked her wrist toward the street, saying, "Two blocks that way, green awning out front."

The European couple thanked her and walked off toward the main drag. Alyson quickly scanned her immediate surroundings to make sure no one was in need of assistance, then went back to her more difficult search for a possible situation.

—right there!

There it was again! She compensated for the new information, brushing her windblown hair out of her eyes. About three quarters of the way to Alfonso's station, a cluster of teenaged kids had been tossing a football around in the shallows. After an errant throw the ball had ended up floating beyond the surf. The voice she heard was from the kid standing on the little sandbar, calling out to his friend. She saw the ball, but she didn't see the friend.

Alyson took off at a run toward the sandbar. She still wasn't sure if this would be an actual rescue but something told her to check it out. Beachgoers stared at her as she passed, then looked out to sea to try and see what she was responding to. She reached the water's edge and began to step higher. Continued diagonally toward the group of ball players standing in the shallow water of the sandbar, which was separated from the beach by a bowl of deeper water. She dove into that and breast stroked across it until she reached the sand bar, where she stood and ran across it to where the water became deep again, leading out to the true ocean.

On the edge of the sandbar, a young woman stood facing out to sea, hands cupped around her mouth.

"Is someone in trouble?" Alyson walked over to the girl, who turned to face her.

"My friend is out there, a little past those people." She pointed some distance out into the ocean, where a group of people stood in water up to their chests. Alyson squinted into the sun from behind her Oakleys as she scanned the water. She spotted a young man a few yards out from those standing on the bottom. He was treading water comfortably with a ball in one hand, and did not appear to be in trouble. She turned to the beachgoer.

"Was he hurt?"

"No, but I saw something in the water and was trying to get him to look at it."

"What did you see?" Alyson continued searching the waves around the man, but saw nothing out of the ordinary.

"I'm not sure. I... I thought I saw... I thought it was a dolphin at first, but then it lifted this...thing...out of the water and I was like, no, this can't be a dolphin."

"What kind of thing?" In Alyson's experience, people visiting the beach were prone to all sorts of sightings, everything from mysterious sea monsters to pirate ships to drug-and-alcohol-induced apparitions. Usually it amounted to nothing. Usually.

"A spiky-looking thing."

"Spiky?"

"Yeah. At first I thought it was like a narwhal's tusk, but of course there's no narwhals here, right?" She laughed.

"Right, they're Arctic." Alyson caught movement in her peripheral vision about fifty feet to the left of the young man treading water. *Shark?* She put her fingers on the whistle around her neck. *Don't make a fool of yourself. Be sure.* The last thing she wanted was to call everyone out of the water, yelling shark, and it turned out to be a school of baitfish running from a mackerel. Sure, it was better to err on the side of caution, since if someone was attacked and she was the lifeguard on duty, she'd be questioned about what she saw—oh, someone told you they saw something but you didn't do anything? That would be even worse. But she didn't yet *see* anything that was a threat. She couldn't just scare the crap out of hundreds of people without being certain of what she herself saw.

"Did you see any fins?"

"Not really."

Not really. What is that supposed to mean? She was about to ask for an elaboration when the man in the water was thrown into the air. It reminded her of a seal being lobbed out of the water by an orca. At once, she saw the person gyrating in mid-air and a gray behemoth surging out of the ocean. Immediately, she understood what the "spiky" thing was that the young woman next to her had reported seeing.

A sawfish? But it was much too large. Alyson knew that sawfish were rays, and about the same size as rays but with a different body shape. Yet, as she watched the creature erupt from the water, shaking its head to and fro in a classic attack behavior— as if slaying a school of fish—she could think of no other animal that fit the bill. *That's a giant sawfish.*

The young man splashing into the water only a few feet in front of the edge of the sandbar spurred her to action. She grabbed the young woman next to her and pointed to the beach. "Get out of the water! Go!" Then she waved toward the beach while shouting for others to do the same. "Sawfish! Get out!" Many of them were still standing around. She figured *sawfish* wasn't something that many people would be scared of, or had even heard of before, so she changed tactics. *The hell with it. I've got to get these people out of harm's way.* So she yelled something she knew would get results.

"Shark! Everybody out!"

That did the trick. First one person, then two, began splashing through the surf to reach the sand. A few seconds later, a full-on stampede broke out. Alyson and the young woman stepped aside as the people swimming out in front of the sandbar headed straight for them with chaotic, splashy crawl strokes.

"That's it—head for the beach," she encouraged. She turned to the woman. "You too." Then she dove into the water heading straight for the young man who'd been tossed by the sawfish. Was she frightened? Absolutely. But this was her job, and the sawfish was not in sight. The man was a very quick swim away after being thrown. Quick for her, at least. She would do what she could to bring him to safety.

Eyes open underwater, she took in the familiar seascape—the sun-dappled striations of sandy bottom dotted with bits of seashells and the occasional seaweed. Arms pulling in front of her, she knew that the surface was mere feet above her head right now, but getting deeper the farther out to sea she went. She followed the bottom contour down until she was perhaps ten feet underwater. Having the bottom right beneath her made her feel safer because it meant a predator, usually a shark, couldn't attack her from below, which was their preferred method.

She looked up and to the right, where she saw the blurry form of the swimmer's kicking legs. She looked left, didn't see anything. The water clarity wasn't terrible, she could see maybe twenty feet ahead of her, but she'd seen it much clearer than that.

The small surf was kicking up the sand a bit, clouding the water. The predator was somewhere out there in that gloom, hopefully retreating but Alyson doubted that. She saw the way it flipped that swimmer. That was a classic predatory move, probably an opening strike rather than a one-and-run. The likelihood was decent that it would be back to finish what it started.

Knowing that it was lurking out there scared Alyson, she couldn't deny that. But nevertheless, she kicked hard off the bottom with her arms extended in front of her, fingertips together in a point, a hydrodynamic ally efficient posture. She was halfway to the stricken swimmer before she had to use her limbs to propel herself. Employing a scissor-kick, she pulled with her arms up toward the kicking man, feeling the void of eight feet or so of water below her now.

When her head broke the surface, she heard screaming. Multiple voices.

"Hurry!"

"Go, go, go!"

"Look out!"

Out of her peripheral vision, she saw people gathered on the sandbar. Whether they took refuge from deeper water or waded out to it from the beach in order to get a better view of what was happening, she didn't know, but probably some of both. Though he was very close to the sandbar now, the man struggled, coughing, flailing his arms. Alyson couldn't blame him. She wasn't sure what her composure would be after being tossed through the air like a ragdoll by a giant sawfish. Hoping she wouldn't have to find out, she kicked faster toward the victim.

When she was within a few feet of him, she called out, "Lifeguard here. Can you swim?"

The young man spun about wildly, eyes lighting on her but still continuing to spin around in uncoordinated, splashy circles. She shouted at him again, "I'm here to help. Try to relax, okay?"

With this, he stopped most of the extraneous movements, now treading water in a more normal fashion as he turned to look at her. "What happened?" he asked.

"You got flipped out of the water by a big fish. The sandbar is right behind you. I'll take you to it, okay?"

He said nothing, just stared at her. Alyson wanted to hear the acknowledgement that he was complicit in this rescue. As many a lifeguard had experienced too often, approaching a panicky swimmer was a risky proposition. They were known to cling to a rescuer or actively fight them off, placing both of them at risk.

"*Okay*? Talk to me."

"Okay." He turned and looked back at the sandbar, probably not realizing how close he was to it.

"Great, you see how close we are? I'm going to come up behind you, grab a hold of your arm and we're going to swim up onto the sandbar together, okay?"

She wasn't sure if he had been injured or not. It seemed like he might be able to make it the rest of the way himself, but the nature of her profession was not to take those kinds of chances. She kicked over to the man. Put an arm under one of his shoulders as she had been trained, and maneuvered into the rescue tow swim, setting off toward the sandbar. To his credit, the guy was relatively calm once she started towing him. Didn't thrash around, creating counter-productive motion or scream or try to grab her. Pretty much a textbook under-shoulder support tow.

When she saw the legs of the crowd gathered on the sandbar, she stopped swimming and put her own feet down. She carried the man up onto the sandbar, where he was able to stand on his own. He was in the process of thanking her when an onlooker pointed and then turned and ran toward the beach.

"Something's coming!" More people turned and ran. Alyson was confused. They were standing on dry sand in some spots, ankle-deep at the deepest. They were safe from any predatory fish here. So what was everyone worried about? She turned around to look back out to sea, where a massive sawfish was launching itself from the water up onto the sandbar.

It seemed like a semi-truck driving up over them, or maybe a yacht. But there it was, and Alyson had time only to duck, pulling the man she'd just rescued down with her. He was the only one within her reach. She shouted for the rest to move out of the way, and they did just that. Most of them.

Those on the left side of the sandbar facing the beach weren't so lucky. The sawfish sailed through the air—part of its white underbelly passing a few inches over Alyson and the rescuee—and landed on the sand to the left of them, where it skidded across the submerged land, plowing into a clutch of teens. The gigantic ray hooked its saw back and forth as it hydroplaned across the sandbar, catching a young woman in the upper thigh.

It gouged a large chunk of flesh from her body but luckily for her, the saw didn't hold in her leg or she would have been dragged and crushed...the way the man a few feet ahead of her was. Wearing baggy shorts, the ladder-sized saw's teeth became entangled in the fabric. The sawfish shook back and forth even harder, attempting to dislodge its stunned prey so that it could come back around and eat it. But polyester wasn't something the animal was used to encountering. Unable to free its appendage, the fish wagged its shovel-nosed head to and fro, a furious series of movements that whipped the man this way and that across the sand.

Another man nearby tried to pull the victim away. He gripped his arm with two hands while yelling for others to help him, but the gigantic animals was far too strong. The fish's prey was ripped from the rescuer's grasp and flung into the sawfish's body itself. Then the flat, shovel-like head seemed to ride over the body. This wasn't readily visible to the onlookers, but when the sawfish had moved, they saw that the man was gone. Like a vacuum, the sawfish had inhaled the man into its maw.

It must not have preferred the taste, or found his clothing otherwise indigestible, because a few seconds later, the man was disgorged from the ray's mega-gullet. The unconscious man lolled about in the surf, bleeding from multiple places. If he was still alive, it wasn't readily apparent.

Pandemonium reigned on the sandbar as people screamed and began running en masse to the beach. The sawfish herded them in, skirting alongside the crowd. When the first of the runners started to splash up onto the beach, the oversized ray plowed through their midst, severing Achilles tendons and body slamming people into one another. One elderly man was pummeled into the wet sand by the fish, which rode up onto the prostrate body and ingested the head and shoulders into its gaping mouth.

Alyson, who had just deposited the young man she'd rescued onto the beach, was on the ray's back, pummeling it with her fists. Two men joined her in her efforts, and after a minute, the fish slid away into deeper water.

Alyson and the men dragged the man up onto the dry sand where she could perform CPR, but it was too late. His throat had been crushed, pulverized—not by the saw's modified scale teeth— but by the sawfish's flat, grinding teeth in the mouth.

Another lifeguard drove up to Alyson on a quad-runner vehicle and asked her what kind of help she needed. She looked out over the water before answering, the sawfish not visible.

"No swimming signs. We've got to keep people out of the water."

16

Miami City Hall

Miami Mayor Pablo Cristobal paced his office while looking out at the city view. A single news van was parked down below. Not exactly a media hell storm yet, but combined with the light but steady stream of calls, emails and text messages he'd been receiving, it didn't bode well at all. His third year in office, and he had a feeling for these things. With all the crap going on now—a workplace shooting that happened yesterday in Pembroke Pines, the district-wide teacher's strike, the uproar over recent Cubans who washed ashore on a makeshift raft who were allowed to stay per the controversial wet foot, dry foot policy—he didn't need another meeting.

But as he glanced at the blinking red light on his desk phone and heard the beeps emanating from the smartphone in his pocket, he knew that another meeting was exactly what he was looking at. This one didn't seem to be critical, though he hadn't heard the details yet. Something about a big fish? Whatever. He was sure it could wait. He sat down at his desk to answer as many emails as he could before that lunch meeting with the Cuban developers. He'd just gathered his train of thought and was typing out a rapid reply like one of those monkeys bashing on a typewriter when there came a knock at the door.

Frowning, he tipped his head back and called, "Come in, Estrella." He recognized his executive assistant's knock. Whenever she knocked instead of using the phone, it meant something urgent was happening and that she wouldn't be put off. The door opened and a sixty-something, overweight Hispanic woman waddled into the room. Her extra weight belied her energetic demeanor as she bounced over to the end table where the

TV remote control was, snatching it up and flicking it on to a local news channel.

"Some sort of big animal is reportedly killing people on our beaches. So far I've heard shark, I've heard crocodile, but now they're saying it's a sawfish. Seems like they aren't sure yet, but whatever it is you're going to have to do something about it. Here, just watch, the latest attack happened this morning." She thumbed up the volume as a reporter interviewed a young female lifeguard on South Beach.

"...have been a terrifying moment for you as well. Can you tell us what was going through your mind, Alyson?"

The lifeguard took on a faraway look as she mentally relived the traumatic events. "Just...do what I can to help people. Get them out of harm's way. That's it, really. I..." She trailed off, overcome by emotions. A crawl at the bottom of the screen read MONSTER FISH ATTACKS SOUTH BEACH SWIMMERS.

The mayor turned to his assistant. "What is this, a shark attack? Someone we know? Why is it important?"

The assistant muted the television. "They're saying it's something called a *sawfish*. Sort of like a shark but with a really long, well, *saw*, that sticks out from its snout..."

"I know what a sawfish is. Friend of mine caught one when we were fishing once from his flats boat in the Keys back country. Had to cut the line, no way did we want it in our little boat. But still, it was only maybe four feet long. Not something that could tear up a whole beach."

His assistant had been working for him long enough to know she need not be offended by his lack of agreement. He was a to-the-point kind of guy, extremely protective of his time. She knew she wouldn't have lasted as long as she did if she didn't save him time on the whole, so she wasn't worried.

"This is apparently a very large sawfish. *Jaws*-size, I'm afraid. Killed four people today on South Beach, injured five more. Other deaths in the last couple days might also be attributed to this same fish, including a parasailor."

The mayor screwed up his face in disgust. "Seriously? You're telling me we've got a killer fish roaming our beaches?"

She shrugged. "It appears that way, Pablo. The lifeguards are closing all of Miami Beach until they can be sure the threat has passed. They want to send up spotter planes, and then hire spotters on the beach and in boats after that."

"They don't need my permission for that."

"They say their budget is strapped, and they want a meeting to discuss augmenting it based on emergency need."

The mayor sighed. "Meeting when?"

"Today, anytime you can make it, sooner the better."

Pablo eyed the email he'd been composing and shook his head. "Fine."

17

Miami, Intracoastal Waterway

Water Taxi Captain David Grosch glanced at his watch as he entered the final stretch of his two-and-a-half hour scheduled run from Fort Lauderdale to South Beach with a full load of thirty-two paying passengers. *Right on schedule.* Not that most of the people aboard cared much about punctuality. The water taxi was more fun than necessity—overland routes existed and there were cheaper options—but the experience was one-of-a-kind and wholly pleasant as long as the weather cooperated, which in South Florida was often enough, today included.

Until now, the highlight of the trip had been sighting a pair of large alligators on a mud bank near Port Everglades, but as they threaded their way toward South Beach between the glitzy, mirrored high-rises of Miami, the smartphones came out again for videos and pictures. Grosch heard his crewman, a twenty-something kid named Jairo Rojas who hadn't known squat about boats when he'd hired him, field a question from a passenger about what time the last taxi headed back to Fort Lauderdale from South Beach. Plenty of time to get your margaritas on, the kid finished with. He was getting the hang of it, learning how to wring out those tips.

The captain pushed the banter out of his mind as he concentrated on navigating the waterway, which grew increasingly congested the deeper into Miami they went. A mixture of pleasure and work boats plied the water on all sides of him. Everything from sleek speedboats forced to restrain themselves like a Lamborghini in traffic, to plodding barges loaded with construction materials, to jet-skis, and even a smattering of paddlers vied for position in the water. The radio was rife with chatter from boats stating their navigational intentions and reporting possible situations of concern.

Captain Grosch maneuvered his way through the organized chaos with practiced skill, and a few minutes later, he picked up the radio transmitter and let his dock workers know to prepare for his arrival. None too soon, he thought, as a little kid started to bawl, something about wanting an ice cream cone. *Sorry kid, this ain't a Carnival Cruise, you're gonna have to wait a few minutes.* Jairo moved to the starboard side of the boat, where they'd be pulling up to the dock. He reminded the passengers to remain seated with their hands inside the boat until they were told it was safe to deboard, and then uncoiled a line to have it ready to throw to the dock crew.

The South Beach terminus was a floating dock beneath a bridge, with docking access on two sides to allow for multiple water taxis at once. Grosch eyed the crowd already waiting there to board for the return trip to Lauderdale. He eased back on the throttle as he put the craft into a slow turn that would bring it alongside the dock. He had lost count of how many times he'd performed this exact same maneuver, so ingrained into his muscle memory it was. The currents varied somewhat depending on wind and tide, but he'd been doing it so long he was familiar with those combinations, too.

So it was that Captain David Grosch was confused for the first time he could remember when his boat didn't respond as expected to his throttle commands. Poised to toss the dock line to the dock worker, Jairo turned around to look at the captain, not saying anything yet, but clearly wondering what was going on. That alone was unusual enough on Grosch's water taxi. He worked his hands furiously over the console controls, coaxing movement out of his boat, but it was still not responding as it should.

"Need it a little closer," the crewman called back, now eyeballing the gap between the dock and the boat.

Grosch gunned the throttle but again, when the boat should have glided right over to the dock, instead it refused to budge. If anything, the captain noted with distaste, they appeared to be drifting away from the dock. He was forced to admit something was wrong. Though he prided himself on careful preventative maintenance of his boat's engine and had never needed to be towed or rescued while at sea, something was definitely wrong now.

Suspecting a stray rope from the dock may have gotten wrapped around his boat's propeller, he moved aft to check it out, leaving his crewman to focus on getting a line over to the dockworker, should that be possible. Grosch leaned over the transom and looked closely for signs of obstructions in the propeller, but he saw none. Monofilament fishing line could foul a prop and be very difficult to see, so he braced himself against the motor and the transom and leaned out even farther for a closer look.

"Line wrapped around the prop?" Jairo called over. The captain squinted into the water, even removing his sunglasses to see if that gave him a better look, but no, there was nothing there. So what was the problem? He was pulling himself back into the boat when he caught subtle movement out of his right eye. At first, he thought his eyes were playing tricks on him. The motion was so slow he thought it was sand swirling over the bottom at first. But then he realized that he shouldn't be able to see the bottom here, it was plenty deep. So what—

He never completed his thought, for at that very moment a shape so large he had mistaken it for the bottom of the waterway floated out from under his boat—just wafted away, gently, like a sheet blowing in a breeze. He eyeballed it, casting his gaze from his boat's bow and back along to where he stood in the stern, and then out some distance over the water, seeking to establish the dimensions of whatever this thing was. That's when he saw a ripple of movement along one edge of it, an undulation of sorts that triggered a spark of recognition in him so strong he was paralyzed in fear, unable to move.

This thing is alive. It's an animal...a fish or maybe even a whale!

"Captain, what's up? You okay?" Grosch snapped out of it and looked over at his crewman, who still hadn't thrown the dock line.

"Something's over there. Can you see that?" He pointed toward the larger than life entity in the water, but Jairo was preoccupied.

"Hey, whatever you did, Captain, it worked. We're close enough now... Hey Tony, yo!" He whistled toward the dock and then tossed the rope. As it sailed through the air, the dockworker suddenly froze and pointed out into the water. The thrown line hit him in the face and he let it drop.

"Tony, what are you doin'?" Jairo received no response from the slack-jawed worker, so he turned around to see what he was gawking at. The entire middle section of the waterway was dark in color, as if the bottom was much shallower than usual. He too became transfixed by the odd sight. Then Grosch's gravelly voice woke him from his stupor.

"It's movin', whatever it is!"

Indeed, a groundswell of water rose up and travelled outwards in all directions, including toward the boat and the dock. Other onlookers on the dock also started to point and shout.

"Where'd it go?" Grosch yelled.

"Went deep!" his crewman returned.

And then the water taxi was lifted from below, not so much a hard slam as a gradual raising of the vessel from the water. It was enough to put the captain off-kilter, though, and he was knocked down. Fortunately, he landed inside the boat, hitting the deck where he landed hard on an elbow. His cursing nearly drowned out the roar from the onlookers.

Unbelievably, the boat continued to rise out of the water. A thick, elongated structure festooned with long teeth broke the surface for a few seconds before receding beneath the waves. An enormous tail fin was visible ten feet past the bow of the boat. Then a shiny, wet hide became visible as the water taxi was lifted out of the water by the oversized fish. The captain heard someone yell the word *sawfish*, but he didn't even care what this animal was. It was so big, so strong, he only wanted to get away from it, and wanted the others to get away, too.

"Get everyone off the dock!" he bellowed. But the warning came too late. The strength of the sawfish was enough to fling the boat off its back as it dove back beneath the surface, leaving the vessel to careen toward the dock while canted sharply to its port side. Jairo was forced to jump overboard or be crushed by the boat if it overturned. He tried to make the dock but came up short, landing in the water within arm's reach of it.

The man he'd thrown the rope to had already turned and ran, yelling for others to do the same but not stopping to make sure they complied. Now Jairo faced a decision: try to claw his way up onto the dock in time, or dive down, before the boat bashed him into oblivion. And if that didn't get him, there was the creature itself lurking somewhere below.

He wasn't much of a swimmer, so he opted to try and climb out on the dock. He put his wet hands up on the planks and kicked, doing a pull-up to try and drag himself out of the water. He didn't know if it was the fear, the panic, the rush of adrenaline causing him to lose coordination, or if he was simply out of shape, but he could not pull himself out onto the dock. He hung there, one leg up, holding onto the edge with two hands, but unable to lift himself any higher.

The boat continued to roll, and Grosch climbed onto the rail as the deck went past vertical, the boat's hull now out of the water. He yelled to his crewman, "Move, Jairo! Boat's rolling, get outta the way!"

Jairo whipped his head around in time to see the barnacle-encrusted hull topple onto his face. His neck snapped as it was crushed between the dock and the three-ton vessel, and his limp body slowly sunk into the water.

The boat turtled over, the captain somehow managing to move on top of the upturned bottom, balancing on all fours like some kind of hapless monkey. In the water, the great sawfish circled around, its incredible saw visible as it propelled itself toward the overturned boat and the dock behind it, where a few people still stood watching the mayhem.

The rush of water ahead of the sawfish pushed against the boat and the captain had no choice but to abandon ship. It was either leap into the water or onto the dock. He chose the dock, already being elevated a few feet above it, confident he could make the jump. His arms windmilled as he sailed through the air. His lead foot slid out from under him as it hit the dock, which had been flooded by the water thrust ahead of the sawfish. He felt his ankle snap and went down, grabbing onto a dock line to keep himself from washing off the other side and back into the water where he'd be a target for the monster fish.

Captain Grosch hung there from a rope, fleetingly wondering if insurance was going to cover his vessel, or maybe it'd still be salvageable? Then he chastised himself for being so self-serving and not thinking about others first, his crewman who was God knew where right now, the dock worker who'd caught the line, and all of the other bystanders on the dock who'd been forced to run in panic. Grosch got to his knees, testing the stability of the floating platform. It seemed steady enough and like the worst of the water washing over it had subsided, so he rose unsteadily to his feet.

A line of people were wisely making their way along the long finger dock back to dry land. Grosch tried to see if the dock worker and Jairo were among them, but could see neither. He looked back to his boat, which was now truly sinking, only the prow above water. The water wasn't overly deep here, maybe twenty feet, so he knew it could be salvaged, but still, it would be expensive as hell and there would be tons of maintenance to do afterwards. Then there would be dealing with the insurance companies. This was absolutely terrible.

And yet it was about to get worse.

18

Miami Beach Lifeguard Headquarters

Mayor Cristobal ignored the questions from reporters while he jogged up the short concrete steps that led to the entrance to Miami's lifeguard central. What did they expect him to say? Obviously he was here for a meeting about the subject. Didn't it make so much more sense to ask him questions *after* the meeting? What could he say now?

"What are your thoughts on the marine predator plaguing our beaches?" *It sucks.*

"Have you heard there was another attack at the South Beach water taxi terminal this afternoon?" *What?! No. Must have just happened.*

One of his assistants addressed the press. "Mayor Cristobal will be available to answer questions following the meeting with lifeguard management. That's all for now." The mayor and his contingent breezed through the two-story building's front entrance and down a hallway on the first floor. His people knew what room in which the meeting was held, but Cristobal would have had no trouble finding it on his own because of the rowdy arguing emanating from the open door.

"You're not listening. It's not a shark, it's a sawfish!"

"It's not even *a* sawfish, there has to be more than one!"

Cristobal took a deep breath as he entered the room, a simple space with tables set up in a rectangle in the center, with damn near the entire Miami Beach lifeguarding staff sitting around them. The walls were occupied with whiteboards, maps and posters pertaining to everyday lifeguarding functions—personnel schedules, hazard warning signs including riptides, high surf and jellyfish, hotline phone numbers. One of Cristobal's people introduced the mayor, and the hubbub died down a bit but did not stop.

A man in his fifties of squat but fit build and graying hair with a gray mustache and trimmed beard stood from his place at the table. "Good afternoon, Mr. Mayor. I am Justin Rafferty, Director of Lifeguard Operations, Miami Beach. We're glad you could take the time. Please have a seat."

The mayor nodded and eased into one of the uncomfortable folding chairs that had been set up around the table. These people must not have very many meetings, he thought, or maybe it means they don't last that long. Could be a good thing. "Thank you, Director Rafferty. I'm aware that we have a problem at our beaches. Please fill me in."

Rafferty nodded and looked down at a tablet computer before continuing. "We sure do, Mayor. As of right now, my latest information has ten fatalities and fourteen victims with injuries requiring hospitalization."

Cristobal raised his hand to interrupt before Rafferty could go on. "When you say 'victims,' Mr. Rafferty, what exactly do you mean? Victims of what?" The mayor knew full well that the word "sawfish" was going to be in the answer, but he wanted to hear it from the man in charge, wanted to know that it wasn't a shark. Because to him, a shark would be even worse. The last thing he wanted was to live out a real-life *Jaws* scenario as the mayor of a beach town. He literally shuddered at the thought.

"While initial reports mentioned a shark of unknown species, and one of the Medical Examiner autopsy reports makes mention of a possible saltwater crocodile, later eyewitness sightings have conclusively identified a very large sawfish. A sawfish, though related to sharks, is actually a type of ray."

"Ray?" the mayor asked.

"As in stingray. Sharks and rays are closely related—they both have skeletons made of cartilage, but make no mistake about it— sawfish are rays, not sharks, even though they're sometimes called Carpenter Sharks."

A smile spread slowly over Cristobal's face. "So then we don't have a shark problem, especially if we refrain from calling them Carpenter Sharks." He cleared his throat as a warning.

Rafferty eyed him for a moment without expression before responding. "That is correct, Mr. Mayor, but make no mistake about it—that doesn't mean we don't have a serious problem. As I said, we have ten ocean users dead, more injured—"

The mayor held out a hand. "Yes, I heard you. A sawfish. Still, I'd rather have a sawfish than a killer shark, wouldn't you?"

Rafferty shrugged. "Killer shark, killer sawfish, jellyfish, red tides, whatever... With all due respect, Mr. Mayor, the net result is the same. We've got dead people on our beaches, making the national news."

Cristobal made prolonged eye contact with Rafferty. The mayor had always thought of lifeguards as sort of life-long beach boy types, not very serious people, fun to be around but not very smart. This guy seemed to be all business, though, more like a fireman or a cop. "So what are we going to do about it?"

Rafferty nodded enthusiastically and pecked at his tablet while a staffer flicked on a projector that lit up a pull-down wall screen. A satellite photograph of the miles-long stretch of sand comprising both Miami Beach and South Beach was displayed along with a series of colored marker points.

"In order to reopen the beaches, we propose implementing a system of human spotters drawn from both the pool of available lifeguards as well as City Fire, Police and Harbor Patrol." Rafferty looked to the mayor to gauge his reaction thus far, which was unreadable, so he continued.

"The blue circles you see on the beach represent proposed spotters on land—they would use binoculars to watch the water carefully. Upon sighting a potential threat, such as a large sawfish or shark..." Cristobal winced at the mention of a shark and Rafferty hurried on, "...these spotters would then radio their information to the nearest lifeguard on station so that he or she could evacuate swimmers from the water."

Cristobal nodded. "And the other colors?"

Rafferty aimed a laser pointer at the projection screen. "The yellow markers indicate water-based spotters who will be positioned on boats appropriated specifically for the purpose." He paused to let the financial implication sink in before continuing.

"And the green markers, here, indicate air spotters who will spot from helicopters."

"For how long will these spotters be in place?" the mayor wanted to know.

"I propose one month, after which time we'll evaluate the situation." Rafferty, along with the rest of the lifeguards, looked to Cristobal, eagerly awaiting his reaction. This was it, their best laid plans, about to get either the go-ahead or the axe.

One of Cristobal's assistants whispered something into his ear, and then the mayor spoke. "I assume that these additional resources are above and beyond your operational budget, and that you require supplementary funds in order to implement them, correct?"

Rafferty wasted no time in nodding. "That is correct, Mr. Mayor. We estimate that our normal operating budget would have to be increased by..." He leaned over to consult with the person sitting next to him, a middle-aged woman who handled administrative matters for the lifeguard division. He raised his eyebrows at her, she nodded, then he resumed talking to the mayor. "...by 125% for that single month."

An audible gasp escaped the mayor's lips. "That's more than double!"

"For one month only, and I'm sure it's much cheaper than the lawsuits the City will no doubt be faced with from the families of these victims. I doubt you want to add to that, but it's up to you, Mr. Mayor. The cheap solution, which we have already implemented in the meantime, is simply to keep the water off limits."

The mayor fumed. He was struggling to mentally calculate whether the lost revenue from closed, scary beaches would be greater than that of additional lawsuits and operational expenses, when a man strode into the room.

"Excuse me, sorry I'm late." The newcomer watched as those seated gradually took notice of his presence, then spoke again. "I apologize for interrupting, but I'm told that this meeting is to discuss the recent sawfish attacks?"

Some of those in attendance nodded. One of Rafferty's personnel demanded, "And you are?"

"My name is Dr. Mason Rayman. I'm an ichthyologist who happens to be an expert on sawfish, and Florida smalltooth sawfish in particular. I can help you get rid of these predators. No spotters needed. I'm talking fish gone, beaches safe once again. I can catch it. Or them, if there's more than one."

Rayman was met with stunned silence as everyone in the room exchanged surprised and confused glances. One of the mayor's assistants swiped through screens on a tablet until she squinted a bit and whispered something to him.

Cristobal addressed the newcomer. "I understand you were granted an appointment, Dr. Rayman, but I was told it was to be at *my* office, scheduled for later today. You weren't specifically invited to this meeting."

"That's true and I apologize for that, but in the news after the attack this morning they mentioned that you would be meeting with lifeguard management to discuss beach closures. So I decided to step forward and offer my services. Listen, spotters are only a Band-Aid. The dangerous fish will still be there, whether you see them coming or not. If you want to actually address the underlying issue, that is—get rid of them altogether—then I'm your man."

A beat of silence followed while everyone digested this. The mayor's people looked like they were about to call security, but the mayor himself looked to Rafferty and shrugged, saying, "Justin, do you mind? Maybe it would be good to hear from a marine biologist, right?"

The head lifeguard stared at Rayman, assessing him. At length, he said, "I suppose we can give him a couple minutes."

A seat was pulled out for Rayman, but he declined, opting instead to stand at the table. "Thank you for your time. I'll be brief. About sawfish...can we?" He held out a flash drive and pointed to the projector. "A picture is worth a thousand words, as they say, and my presentation aids, here, will speed things up, I assure you."

A technician took the drive from Rayman and inserted it into the projector. A slide appeared on the wall screen showing an underwater photograph of a sawfish over a sandy bottom, saw angled up toward the camera. Rayman nodded at the screen. "This is an adult smalltooth sawfish. As you may know, it's not a shark, but a ray." He paused, received no argument, and so continued.

"The saw is an extension of the rostrum, and is lined with twenty-five to twenty-nine teeth, which are not truly teeth in the biological sense, but which are a specialized type of hardened fish scale. They are not used for chewing, but for digging, slashing, tearing and incapacitating prey." Rayman clicked a remote and the slide advanced to an illustration depicting a sawfish drawn to scale next to an adult human male, about the same size.

"This is what the average adult smalltooth sawfish *should* look like. But I took a look at two of the victims at the morgue, and I can say with certainty that unfortunately, the animal that caused those injuries had to be substantially larger than this, possibly three-to-four times larger." He paused for effect and a wave of chatter spread around the table.

Rafferty held out a hand. "Did you say three-to-four times larger...so...twenty-four feet?"

Rayman looked at him, stone-faced, and nodded. "That's correct."

Rafferty looked to one of his lifeguards, a younger female. "Alyson, does that jibe with what you saw out on the sandbar?"

Rayman sucked in his breath a bit as he recognized the lifeguard from the television news that morning, but outwardly maintained a nonchalant appearance. Alyson nodded. "If anything, the one I saw was even longer than that."

Rayman reared back a bit, as if surprised. "It's quite possible. If someone were to ask me a week ago, can sawfish get this big—any species at all—I would have laughed them out the door. But obviously they can. The sea still holds many mysteries."

"But how?" Rafferty asked. "How is that possible?"

Rayman put on a thoughtful expression as he appeared to consider this. "The best I can come up with, without further study on the matter, is that some kind of inter-species breeding has occurred." Then he held up a hand. "But listen—I said I wouldn't waste your time, so let's not get bogged down in the details, shall we?"

The mayor's assistants were both whispering to him, one of them pointing to a tablet screen. He addressed Rayman. "Excuse me, but I'm looking at the Medical Examiner's report on the first two victims—a report which is signed by both the M.E. and by yourself, Dr. Rayman—"

Rayman began to flush as he realized the implications of what was about to come.

"—and it says here that the cause of death is listed as a *crocodile* attack. Not a sawfish, but a saltwater crocodile." Rayman flashed on his spot decision in the Medical Examiner's office to pretend it was a croc attack, when he was more worried about being discovered for releasing the sawfish than in finding a new job. But right now, he was the sawfish expert the City needed, and he had to convince them of that. The mayor looked up from the tablet at Rayman while his assistant angled the screen to show Rafferty, who had leaned over to get a look.

"Are you saying that there are both crocodiles *and* sawfish attacking our beachgoers? The first attacks were by a crocodile, and the later ones a sawfish?"

Rayman cleared his throat before answering. "My initial assessment of those first two victims was incorrect, and I will be revising my report with the Medical Examiner's office. At the time, although a little voice went off in my head, telling me that these don't really look like saltwater crocodile bite wounds, I couldn't reconcile the injuries with any other type of animal. Before I arrived, the Medical Examiner was ready to call it a boat propeller injury, and I knew that wasn't the case, so I told her it's definitely an animal attack. In order to at least get that much right, I called it a crocodile, for the sake of the report, although I did note this determination as tentative pending additional species identification work."

"And has that identification since been completed?" the mayor asked. Rayman shook his head. "Actually, I interrupted it to come here. I thought this was more important for the time being."

A mixture of frowns and nodding heads circulated around the table. After a pause, the mayor stood at the table and turned to Rayman. "Look, I don't have a lot of time. Can you fix this…marine predation problem we're having or not?"

"That's why I'm here, Mr. Mayor."

"Good. You're with the university, right? So just have your people contact my office and we'll set up a retainer…"

Rayman shifted uncomfortably in his seat. "Uh, one problem with that, sir. As of yesterday, I'm no longer employed at the university—research grant termination. I'm in between jobs right now, so you'd have to hire me on as a consultant. I will provide all my own equipment and resources, however, including boats, other equipment and personnel as needed."

This was met with silence and slightly confused looks as all eyes went to the mayor, who consulted briefly in hushed tones with his assistants before replying to Rayman. "I think we can work something out, Dr. Rayman, but the contract is to be results based. If you are unable to achieve results within one month's time, then the agreement will terminate. Is that acceptable?"

The prospect of being terminated yet again didn't sit well with Rayman, but with these fish he certainly had an edge. He had created them, after all, and he could destroy them.

"Not a problem at all."

19

Virginia Key, Ocean Sciences Institute

Elisa Gonzales dropped her purse onto the desk in her new office and slowly turned in a circle, taking in her surroundings. *My new office. Sorry, Dr. Rayman, looks like your loss is my gain.* But the mere thought of his name put a damper on her enthusiasm. *I probably shouldn't have blackmailed him. Why did I do that? Because you need the money, dumbass, and plus he's an arrogant asshole, he deserves it...*

The office looked as she had last seen it, so she decided to check out the wet lab, to see what kind of state Rayman had left it in. Not that she suspected him to be one of those types to vandalize the place out of spite, like the ousted owner on a foreclosed home ruining the place before they're kicked out, but if anything was topsy-turvy, she certainly didn't want to get blamed for it.

She exited the office and entered the lab, which still had its outer doors closed, indicating no one had likely been inside since Rayman vacated. The hum of air pumps and fizzing of bubbles from the tanks was the same as she remembered; the extra equipment stacked up against the walls—nets, aquaria gear, bottles of various chemicals, tools—all the same. She walked over to the nearest tank—#12, the label read—and had a look inside.

It was empty. She moved to its neighbor, finding it without occupants, too, and then checked all of them.

Each was full of water, but there were only animals in half of the tanks, six of them. And they were all normal size. *What happened to rest of the sawfish?*

She rested a hand on the edge of a tank as she thought about it hard. She'd seen Rayman toss the giant one over the pier. But that was only one. What about the other five normal ones? She didn't see how he'd have time to dispose of them, unless... *He came back here overnight and did something with the rest of the sawfish?*

She began to pace the lab, absentmindedly staring into the vacant round tanks while deep in thought. Rayman's reasoning for getting rid of the huge one was pretty obvious: he did something to it to make it grow that big, and he didn't want to share how he did it with his now ex-colleagues. That was as best as she could figure, anyway. At the same time, she knew he'd been concerned about being seen releasing it into the ocean, the way he'd been casting furtive glances in all directions? Why not just destroy it—kill it and then dump it. Wouldn't it be way easier to handle that way? He could have simply drained the water from the tank and let it asphyxiate. He must have wanted it to be alive for some reason. But why?

The simplest explanation is usually the correct one. Elisa wasn't exactly sure where she'd heard that, but it resonated with her now when she thought about the rogue fish scientist. Rayman is a vindictive jerk. He was just let go, and so what would his reaction be? To get back at the people who allowed him to be terminated, as he would think of it. Not in a dramatic shoot-'em-up fashion or anything completely crazy like that, but in some petty way that would make him happy by doing something he wasn't supposed to be doing.

She came to the last row of tanks and turned back around.

Such as dumping a giant sawfish—that he himself created—into Biscayne Bay where it would prey on people. Kind of like that, you think? She was sure enough of that as she walked down the line of aquaria. So what happened to the other sawfish? They were normal size—she'd seen them herself the day Rayman chucked the mega one. Those would be easy to get rid of, she reflected. But why? Perhaps he didn't dispose of them... Maybe he told a colleague he could have them to save himself the trouble of having them responsibly relocated or processed out, and that person came and took them. Maybe.

Or maybe...she flashed on the bevy of recent news reports, each highlighting a different fish attack, some occurring nearly at the same time some miles away. *No...oh my God... Could it be?* The possibility that Rayman had repeated whatever process he had used on the first fish...to do *five* more terrified her. That would mean that she herself could be implicated for not coming forward and saying something about what happened, couldn't it? But if she went public, then there goes her blackmail income, and even worse, the possibility that her little illicit scheme could come back to haunt her.

She exited the lab back into the office—her office, shutting the door to the lab, as if to close off what had happened there from her new world. Were it only that simple. What the hell had she been thinking? She had no idea what Rayman was up to. She'd blackmailed a monster, and now...and now what? She had no idea. She felt like she was in way over her head, and suddenly she wanted nothing more than to return her dull, pedestrian, administrative life back to the way it was before she had opened her stupid mouth to Dr. Asshole.

She eyed the computer on the desk. Time to log in and get to work. It was the same PC that Rayman had used, but she doubt he'd have left any clues or remnants of his lab work for anyone to find, especially since these days the university used a server system where the local desktop computers were used only to login to a private account, each with different access settings that determined what could or couldn't be seen. She logged in with her password, Rayman logged in with his, even though it was the same physical machine.

Still, she thought, noting the system was powered off and flipping it on, people had been known to put things on the local hard drive, either by mistake or because... A chill came over her as the implication hit...because they had something they wanted but didn't want people to see on the network, permissions or not. The IT people could see everything, the network could be hacked, mistakes and glitches happened. She decided to check the contents of the local hard drive to see if by chance Rayman may have put something there that he forgot to take off when he was forced to leave on relatively short notice. She examined the desktop and frowned. It looked factory fresh, as though it had been recently reformatted and the operating system reinstalled. Absolutely devoid of any personal touches or user files. Next she clicked on the drive C: icon and opened its contents. Nothing unusual there, either. Might as well open My Documents, which everyone was told by IT not to use, because they don't back that up, they back up the server. But just to see if by chance…

Elisa sucked in her breath as the folder's contents displayed on the screen. A few spreadsheet files, and some strange system files, too, lots of them. She didn't know for sure what they were yet, but it meant one thing: Rayman hadn't deleted his hard drive contents completely, hadn't reformatted, or if he did, he put something back on the drive afterwards. That seemed unlikely, but who knew? As she clicked through them, it became apparent that they meant nothing to her, other than the spreadsheets appeared to contain experimental data of some kind. She closed them, deciding that she had enough to worry about right now.

Perhaps these would come in handy later. Rayman would know, after all, that even though she might not be able to make heads nor tails of these files, his colleagues would.

20

Coconut Grove

Even though traffic was heavy as usual for a late afternoon, Rayman couldn't wipe the huge grin off his face. Unemployed no more. Sure, it was a contract gig, a temporary situation, but for now at least he was gainfully employed once again as an ichthyologist. Hopefully, it would lead to something more permanent. Time would tell, but for now he had something to focus on, and the pay wasn't bad either.

Only one thing stuck in his craw. Well, besides the small matter of actually doing something to contain the threat of half a dozen monstrously large sawfish now swimming loose in the ocean. But he had created them (not that the City needed to know that little tidbit), and he could destroy them.

But Elisa…she was another matter entirely. He couldn't exactly destroy her…or could he? No, he didn't see how. When she found out about his new gig, though, would she make more trouble for him? She must be moved into his old office by now. And that thought made him smile, because he had left a little present for her on the desktop computer, that bastion of micromanaged IT supervision.

He pulled into the parking lot for his condo and got out. Said "Hi" to one of his neighbors, an old lady he barely knew, on the way up the steps to his second floor unit. He keyed in, dumped his bag on an entranceway table and went straight to his laptop in the living room on a coffee table. He ignored the beautiful view of the marina out the window, boats going by, stand-up paddle boarders and kayakers in the mix. Rayman lit up his machine and brought up a remote viewer app that he'd installed some time earlier. He'd originally started using it as a way to log into and access files on his work computer without IT being any the wiser. Some of the early sawfish stuff was sensitive, and the later sawfish stuff, of course, was beyond sensitive.

When he realized bitchface blackmailer would be taking over his office, though, it occurred to him that she would be using the same physical computer, just with a different login. So he had left the remote access utility installed on it, figuring that it might allow him to see what she did on the computer.

The program opened and he pressed keys that would tell it to login to his old work PC. Rapidly scrolling characters whizzed by on the screen along with a weird series of screeches, hums and clicks as it made the connection.

There! He was in. Now to see if there'd been any activity on it since he left. He froze a hand over the keyboard, wondering if the presence of the utility could be noticed by someone using the computer; usually there was no one there when he used it. He thought he recalled his friend, the computer genius who had set him up with the app in the first place, saying how it ran in the background and only someone both looking for it and who knew what they were doing could detect any trace of its existence. He hoped that was the case now.

The first thing he did was to verify that someone new had logged in. It was her first day, after all, so it was possible she hadn't gotten around to the computer yet. He supposed she could be arranging furniture, moving papers and personal items like all the stupid family pictures she cluttered her too-small workspace with, but her job pretty much required her to sit at a computer so the odds were good she was using it. He navigated to a settings screen and verified who was logged in: Egonzales. *Gotcha. Now let's see what you've been up to...*

He didn't have the program configured to show past history of the users or to log keystrokes, but he had full run of the machine as though he were an invisible man running around a house where he wasn't supposed to be. He opened My Documents, that stupid folder no one was supposed to use because it had been replaced long ago by networked drives... *Ah, there's my little babies, still there, safe and sound; nothing else there.* That was good. She probably hadn't even looked in there yet. Hmmm, what are those spreadsheets?

Rayman cringed as he recognized his early sawfish experiment data sheets. He should not have left those there. He was about to delete them when he realized he could see if she'd opened them. He examined the file properties for one of the spreadsheets and looked at the metadata that showed when the file was last opened: *wow, only a couple hours ago!* That wasn't him, so it had to be Elisa. She wasn't wasting any time.

He stroked the stubble on his chin while he considered the ramifications. She'd seen some of the sawfish files. They were early attempts, nothing that would allow anyone to duplicate his work, but they did provide a proof of the direction he ended up taking. He deleted the spreadsheet files. It was also troubling that if she'd seen the work files that she'd also laid eyes on the remote access app files, but presumably they appeared to non-trained eyes like boring system files, not immediately recognizable, and if they were clicked on from that end, nothing would happen. Still, IT tended to give some attention to a system when a new user started, so time was of the essence in case the remote app files were deleted.

Let's see what else you've been up to, Elisa... Rayman knew what to look for since he was familiar with the university work environment and culture. Most everything was handled via email, and a lot of people also sent and received personal emails from their work computers, so this should be good. He navigated to the web browser, which he noted with satisfaction was open. Found her university webmail account, also already open. *Let's see, here...*

It became quickly apparent that Elisa was not one of those people who used her work email for personal messages. It was all work related. He glanced at a few subject lines, curious as to whether anything about him or his grants was there. He found one, a month old, but it was routine, about giving notice to all grant employees that the grant was terminating. Other messages about Elisa's upcoming office move, but they were all dry and straightforward. He gave up on the work email and checked her browser history. Hoping she wasn't one of those people who only used their phones for email these days, Rayman saw an entry less than a week old for a well-known free email account. He clicked it open and perused the message subject lines.

One entitled "this weekend" caught his eye. Opened it. Looks like it was from a friend, an invitation to meet her at the sailing club to go out on a sailboat this weekend....does Sunday work for you? Not very exciting stuff, Rayman thought, and then he froze, ramrod straight, on his couch. If she did get out on the water, that was his chance, wasn't it? Where was this sailing thing again? His gaze flicked back to the email. Leaving from Miami Marina, Biscayne Bay. Perfect. He looked at the Sent Mails folder to see if she had replied. *There it is…* He clicked it open, grinning like a Cheshire cat while hoping she had the itch to go sailing.

Janey,
Sure, love to! Sunday's good, be there at 10? I'll bring the wine.
-E

Rayman nodded slowly to himself and disconnected from the remote login, leaving no traces of his presence. He had what he needed. He would not be making another payment if he could help it.

21

Next day, Saturday, Biscayne Bay
Rayman was up with the sun. He'd promised results to the mayor and he was going to get them. He checked the weather report on his laptop—the general conditions looked good, no rain, light wind—but more importantly, the marine forecast called for calm seas. Should be a perfect day out on the water, which would be to his advantage when hunting giant saws.

He gathered up a backpack he'd loaded the night before with equipment and supplies for the outing. Then he placed a call on his smartphone to an old fishing buddy, Bobby Flannigan. He was the brother of an ex-girlfriend, and other than that he really didn't have much in common with the guy at all—he was a carpenter from a working class family—but he liked to fish, while Rayman was an ichthyologist who sometimes fished to collect specimens. Like today, he thought, listening to the phone ring while waiting for Bobby to answer. *C'mon, Flannigan, you said yesterday you'd be up for this.* He hoped he hadn't spent all night at one of those Miami strip clubs he blew his paychecks on and was sleeping off a king-size drunk.

Rayman would have preferred a far more technically inclined helper, such as one of his former lab assistants or colleagues, but part of what he needed to do wasn't exactly above board, so he wanted someone who wasn't too bright and wouldn't ask a lot of questions as long as he had a good time out on the water and maybe got a little bonus out of it. That was Bobby Flannigan to a tee. If he wasn't hung-over.

The ring was interrupted and a groggy-sounding male voice said, "Mason?"

"It's me, Bobby. You ready? I'll pick you up in thirty."

A long pause. Then, "You're paying me what we talked about, right?"

"Right. And I'll bring coffee and donuts."

#

Bobby Flannigan dropped a heavy crate into the eighteen-foot Carolina Skiff, the *Something's Fishy,* with a grunt. "What is all this crap, anyway?" he asked Rayman, who was busy flipping on and testing the electronics at the console—GPS, chart plotter, sonar, radar, marine radio, and the regular boat gauges.

"That one there's just got a bunch of rope, I think. With some lead sinkers."

"No wonder it's heavier than shit." He stood and then grabbed his coffee and a bag of gas station convenience store donuts from the dock. "That's everything. Here." He handed Rayman his car keys.

"You locked it, right?"

"Yeah. Believe me, I know this 'hood's not that great. So where are we headed today? Got plenty of gas, I see," he said, glancing at the two spare gas cans next to the standard one in the back. All three had been topped off this morning. "Offshore? Big game?" Visions of tuna, marlin and sailfish danced in his head, but Rayman shook his head.

"Sawfish."

Flannigan appeared confused. He had been about to plop down into the co-pilot chair but instead froze just over the seat, eyeing Rayman carefully. "Come again? Did you say sawfish?"

"That's what I said, yeah." Rayman revved the throttle, idling the outboard engine, warming it up for the day ahead.

"Normally those are catch and release only."

"Not today they're not."

Flannigan looked more puzzled than ever.

"C'mon, get the lines and I'll explain while we're underway."

Flannigan released the ropes from the cleats—T-shaped fixtures of metal that were bolted to the dock as well as on the boat—and cast them off while Rayman put the boat into gear. Once they had motored away from the dock and Rayman had maneuvered around a large sailboat, Flannigan took the co-pilot seat. "Sawfish. So does this have anything to do with those attacks?"

Rayman glanced his way. "Bingo."

His fishing buddy looked a little paler. "Aren't those things supposed to be huge, like forty feet long?"

Rayman shrugged as he pushed on the throttle and the boat picked up speed until it eased up on plane, gliding smoothly over the calm surface of the water. "I don't think anybody knows for sure, but we're going to try and find out."

"Why you want to catch one of those?"

"City of Miami hired me to." He explained his new contract position, without mentioning he no longer worked at the university.

"Wow." Flannigan rubbed his scalp through his ball cap.

"Keep it on the down low, will you, Bobby? I don't want a bunch of vigilantes following me around, trying to catch these things out from under me."

"No problem. Boss," he added, hinting that he was now a subcontractor for the City.

"I mean it, Bobby. No getting drunk and telling fish stories about this at the local pub—you got it?"

"Yeah, yeah, I got it! I'm just glad you picked me to go with you. I mean, I'm sure a big scientist like you has lots of people—"

"You're a good fisherman, Bobby. That's why I picked you. I just don't want word to get out where I'm looking, that's all, because then lots of people will look there, too. And I want us to be the ones who bring these things in first. Are you with me?"

"I'm with you, boss!" He gave him a fist bump and then Rayman turned the boat until the prow pointed to a distant mangrove shoreline.

"How do you know where to look?"

Rayman pointed to the thin green line that broke up the horizon. "Sawfish like shallow mudflat areas like the kind found next to mangroves. That coast over there is miles of nothing but mangroves, but it's not that far from where the attacks have been taking place. I also know that they're bottom feeders and they're nocturnal. That means they're most active at night, Bobby, but these are so big I'm thinking it might be easier to deal with them in the day when they're a little lethargic. I've caught regular size ones in the day before, so they will attack bait then. And people, as we've seen."

That seemed to satisfy Flannigan, and they made the rest of the way across the bay in silence, enjoying the day out on the water as if they were just a couple of buddies on a run-of-the-mill fishing trip. Sometime later, the water beneath the boat became shallower as they neared the mangrove coast and Rayman decelerated. The boat fell off plane and sunk back into the water, plowing through the waves rather than hydroplaning over them.

"Keep an eye on the bottom, would you, Bobby?" Rayman said, casting a worried glance over the side. "Depth finder says three feet here, but I want to get as close to the mangroves as possible.

Bobby hopped up onto the bow, where there was a flat platform ideal for fishing from. He stood there and scanned the water ahead for any sign that it would be too shallow for the boat's motor, which stuck down below the hull, as well as any potential obstructions like submerged logs, wrecked vessels, or even...giant sawfish.

A few minutes later, they had reached the thick line of mangrove trees, their tangled, reddish roots above the waterline. Rayman killed the engine.

"Okay, Bobby, drop the anchor. Let's get some chum out."

22

Biscayne Bay

"This ain't the same chum I normally get. Where'd you get this stuff?" Bobby Flannigan screwed up his nose in an expression of distaste as he poured a five gallon bucket full of the chunky, brownish slurry over the boat's rail into the water.

Rayman didn't look away from the binoculars he had glued to his eyes while he answered. "It's my own special home brew. Sheep, cow and chicken blood, with chunks of cut bait fish thrown in for good measure, a few shrimp."

"I think it's the sheep's blood that does it." Flannigan set the empty bucket on deck and hefted another full one.

"No, I'm pretty sure it's the fact that this stuff is a few years old, and during that time the freezer it was kept in occasionally lost power, so it's been thawed and re-frozen several times. Definitely don't eat any of it, you'd probably die."

Flannigan guffawed while dumping out another bucket. "Oh yeah, right, glad you told me. I was really getting the urge. I mean, those gas station donuts aren't anything to write home about, I know, but I'll take those any day over—"

"Hey, Bobby?"

Flannigan finished dumping the second bucket and turned around as he set it on deck. "Yeah?"

"Hold up on the fishing. We got a boat here, coming toward us."

Flannigan followed Rayman's point until he spotted a white flats boat—a small skiff designed for fishing in shallow water such as where they found themselves now. "Looks like they're slowing down. Probably going for bonefish. They're pretty far away—you really want to wait? Chum's already out."

"I guess we should get on with it. Just makes me nervous."

"Look, Mason, if we have to fish with nobody in sight on a beautiful day like today, we'll never get any fishing done. Might as well go at night."

"Also not a bad idea. Sawfish are nocturnal. But logistically it's a lot more difficult. Let's see how this goes first."

#

Three hours later

Bobby Flannigan was covered in blood. He'd been chumming almost non-stop since they'd started, and after hours' worth of a splash here and a spill there, he now looked like an extra in some B-movie zombie-fest. Rayman, for his part, was mostly still clean, though even he hadn't managed to avoid being splattered a little bit. But he was mostly using his eyes, while Flannigan was using his hands. While Flannigan rigged hooks, doled out chum, and poled the boat across the shallows, Rayman scanned the fish-finder monitor to keep tabs on what was below them, used binoculars to spy on nearby vessels as well as to watch the water for signs of large predators, and also spent a decent amount of time staring into the water. He also monitored the marine radio for fish reports, listening for anything that might clue him into the presence of a giant saw.

But so far he'd seen or heard nothing out of the ordinary. For all the promise this extraordinary little fishing sojourn held, it was turning out to be a typical trip—lots of waiting around punctuated by moments of excitement when they hooked something. Though they caught quite a few normal game fish—mangrove snappers, barracuda, snook, even a tarpon that Flannigan insisted Rayman snap a picture of him with—the object of their expedition had thus far remained elusive.

Now they had stopped in only two feet of water a few yards from the mangrove tree line, because Rayman spotted a large school of bait fish. Knowing these would be popular with sawfish, he observed them carefully, but after a few minutes concluded that nothing was chasing them. Flannigan declared it a good opportunity to stock up on live bait, and threw a cast net over the roiling ball of fish.

Rayman could see the resistance he was met with on the dragging the net back to the boat—it must be chock full of fish. Flannigan hauled the net in and actually had trouble hefting it into the boat, so laden it was with fresh, glistening bait. Laughing as he dumped them out into the boat, he asked Rayman if the school of baitfish was still nearby.

"Yeah, they're still there," Rayman returned, eyes scanning the water around them carefully. A sea bird called from above, starting to circle.

"One more net full and we'll be all set," Flannigan declared, stepping up onto the stern platform and gathering up his net. He untangled the line and threw the wet nylon webbing over one shoulder while eyeing the school of fish.

"It's almost too easy!" he said to Rayman, who now stared at a map he had made that pinpointed the known saw attacks on a marine chart, mumbling something about how this has to be the right area. "These fish are hardly moving, even after I netted them once. And it's shallow enough that they can't dive down to avoid the net. Here goes nothing…"

He wound up his arm a couple of times, then let the net fly, more toward the far side of the bait ball this time, away from the mangroves toward open water. He hoped to drag it through the entire school. The net opened midair in a perfect circle and gracefully fell on the water fully extended, exactly where he'd intended. He grinned as the ring of lead weights around the edge of the net immediately dragged it down on top of the fish.

"Look at that shot! Boy, I tell ya, I still got it. You see—"

Flannigan was violently jerked toward the net, the line for which he had wrapped around his left wrist. Rayman looked up from his chart when he heard the splash to see Flannigan not only in the water, but being dragged, fast, away from the shoreline. Rayman dropped the chart and pencil he'd been holding and bolted from the captain's chair over to the port side rail, where he scanned the water. Flannigan's baitfish streamed past the boat, flashing in the sun as they moved toward the shelter of the mangroves, an errant one of them landing in the boat itself.

Rayman looked just ahead of Flannigan into the water and felt the chill course over his body as he made out the immense, dark shape.

Flannigan was struggling to keep his head above water, gasping for breath when he could, one arm entangled with the net while the other sought to free himself. Rayman jumped back over to the console and fired up the engine. He threw it into gear and propelled the boat toward Flannigan, who was still being dragged by his unseen catch.

He reached his man-overboard crewmate in a few seconds, pulling up just ahead of him and shifting into neutral. He grabbed a life ring and ran to the port rail. "Bobby, grab this!" He hurled the white ring, connected to a yellow polypropylene line. It splashed down next to Flannigan, who used his free hand to snare it and then hook it in the crook of his elbow.

"What is it? Is it the saw?" From the sound of his voice, Flannigan was panicked far more than a seasoned fisherman would be who fell into the water casting a net. He knew something big was dragging him, afraid that it might be what they were fishing for.

And with good reason, Rayman noted. He couldn't be sure yet, but there was a widespread disturbance on the bottom, stirring up the muck that was prevalent near mangrove coasts. He knew from experience that it didn't take a gigantic fish to stir up this kind of bottom, and the water wasn't clear enough to see the creature Flannigan had netted. But to drag him like that...could be a bull shark, he mused. They inhabited these waters, and were very strong. But the next few seconds made it abundantly clear that it was no bull shark.

A pair of dorsal fins, one in front of the other and of equal height, broke the surface, and Rayman could tell from that alone.

Sawfish.

Along with the tail fin behind them, slightly higher, it appeared as three triangular fins protruding above the surface. The only thing was, although the proportions were the same, these fins were perhaps four times larger than those of a large adult sawfish. He had found one of his babies.

Is that you, number twelve? My, how you've grown. Even though Flannigan was still in trouble, he couldn't help wondering how big this sawfish would get. It was unbelievable—he'd always suspected his gigantism measures would have some kind of appreciable effect, but this was so unanticipated that he had difficulty reconciling this was the same fish he'd received in the lab all those months ago.

Flannigan's panicky voice broke him from his reverie. "Mason!"

Oh, right. How to save him without losing the saw?

Rayman pulled tentatively on the life ring line, to see if Flannigan would be dragged closer to the boat, or if he was still stuck to the net, which was also apparently snagged on some part of the sawfish. The fisherman was dragged about five feet closer to the boat when the water exploded around him in a furious thrashing. Luckily for Flannigan, the giant ray's namesake appendage was entangled in the netting, such that when it launched its formidable head out of the water to slam it back down, its movements were impeded enough to prevent its full range of motion. This caused its saw to weakly graze Flannigan's head, rather than the forceful blow it could have been.

Even a weak blow from what is essentially a large club studded with crocodile-like teeth is a serious issue when in water, though, and when he saw the blood on Flannigan's face, Rayman sprang into action. He grabbed a fishing knife from the console of his boat and leapt over the side. The water was shallow enough to stand, but the bottom had a spongy consistency that made it difficult to walk. He made his way in short order to Flannigan, who was semi-dazed but not fully panicking.

"Relax, Bobby, I'll cut the net." Rayman watched the water ahead of them as he spoke. He spotted the ginormous sawfish mere yards away. It had settled onto the bottom in a quasi-stupor, lulled into inaction by the cast net obstructing its mouth, wrapped around the base of its broad saw. Rayman had seen them act this way before, and he took advantage of the situation to leverage the behavior before it relapsed into spastic activity to free itself.

He reached out and grabbed Flannigan with one hand on a shoulder to steady him. Then he brought the knife up to the cast net line that had become hopelessly entwined around his left wrist. He sliced through the line easily and it fell away. "Let's go, Bobby, back up to the boat."

The two men shuffled backwards through the waist high water while keeping an eye on the torpid monster. Rayman whipped his head back a couple of times to gauge their progress toward the boat, and when he could he reached back and pulled it alongside of them. Flannigan was silent while they walked.

"Okay, Bobby, here we go. How's that arm, can you put pressure on it?"

Flannigan gingerly felt his left arm, which sported a patchwork of bleeding welts from wrist to elbow. "Not much."

"Let me get in first and I'll pull you up." Rayman climbed up the boat's swim ladder and threw first one leg and then the other into the boat. He glanced over to the sawfish, which still darkened the bottom where he'd rescued Flannigan. Then he turned and reached both hands over the boat to grip Flannigan by his good arm while the injured fisherman stepped onto the ladder. Rayman pulled him up and they both fell back into the boat, where Flannigan collapsed in a heap on deck, cradling his left arm while staring up at the cobalt blue sky.

But Rayman was all action, bustling about the boat, opening hatches, pulling out gear and putting it back, looking for something. In the midst of his whirlwind of activity, he found a first-aid kit and dropped it on the deck next to Flannigan, who pulled it toward him and said, "What're you doing?"

"I know I have another cast net on board somewhere...here it is!" He pulled a five-gallon bucket container from a hatch and peeled a lid off, revealing a net bunched up inside.

Flannigan propped himself up on his good elbow. "You're not really going to try and catch that thing, are you?"

23

"That's what we're here for, Bobby, isn't it?" Rayman began untangling the new net while keeping one eye on the beleaguered saw.

"You really think one more cast net's gonna do it?" Flannigan pulled himself to a sitting position, tenderly rubbing his elbow.

"No harm in trying. Well," he added, glancing at Flannigan's arm, "there might be some harm, but we knew that going into this, right? Don't want your hurt arm to be for nothing, do you?" Rayman had the net unfurled and began tying a rope to the end of its line to lengthen it.

Flannigan opened the first-aid kit and began digging through its contents while Rayman took his new net rig to the stern of the boat. He eyed the distance to the saw, which was stirring now, sending clouds of brownish mud radiating out from its body in all directions. Rayman dropped the net and picked up a long metal pole used to push the boat along in shallow waters without using the motor.

"Need to get a little closer to him, but I don't want to fire up the engine and possibly spook him." He dug one end of the pole into the bottom and pushed against it, sending the boat skimming toward the entangled sawfish. After three more pushes, he put the pole down and let the boat coast the rest of the way to the mega-beast. By now, Flannigan had regained his feet and was glaring at the sawfish.

Rayman wrapped one end of the net around a metal cleat on the stern rail. "This time, what do you say we let the boat hold the net?" He got no argument from Flannigan. Rayman gathered up the business-end of the net and stood on the transom in preparation to cast it. The water was calm, the wind laying down, no other boats were in sight, and the sawfish was still there. Everything was as good as it was going to get, so Rayman tossed the net. It opened like a flower in mid-flight and dropped down in a perfect ten-foot wide circle right on top of the giant saw's head.

The ichthyologist jumped down from the rail back into the boat, knowing that the huge fish would probably start to thrash when it felt the net, and he didn't want to get caught by the net line swinging one way or the other.

"There he goes!" Flannigan breathed. The mighty sawfish tumbled around beneath the surface, parts of its body becoming alternately exposed to the air.

"More lines, we need to get more lines on him!" Rayman scurried about the deck, gathering up ropes. He had been prepared to catch one of his monsters with heavy duty hook and line, not a net. But Flannigan's accidental discovery might be a boon after all, he thought. He fastened a grappling hook onto the end of a line and prepared to throw it. He told Flannigan to rig another one.

"If we get a couple of lines hooked on the net, maybe we can pull him to the boat."

But the sawfish had other ideas. It launched its tail out of the water, splashing them in the boat before submerging again. Rayman's hook found the net, though, and he tied it off to another cleat on the boat. It was Flannigan who noticed they were being dragged.

"He's pulling us!"

"I'll toss the anchor while you throw another hook." They'd been slow drifting in order to move with the chum when released, when they first came across the saw. Now that they were connected to it by the net, it weighed so much more than their boat that it was able to drag them around at will, even when constrained by the netting. Rayman, having no desire to go for a classic "Nantucket sleigh ride" of whaling lore days, moved to the bow and freed the anchor. He dropped it straight over the side and fed out the chain and rope to make sure it wouldn't snag on anything. Even though it was a soft bottom, he knew the anchor would provide plenty of drag, and with any luck, it would latch onto a patch of hard bottom.

Rayman moved back to the cockpit area of the boat, where Flannigan had just tossed a second grappling hook and now stood wincing in pain as he cradled his elbow. The hook found its mark on the sawfish's netting, though, and was already cleated off on the boat. The big saw was still thrashing, but the boat was no longer being dragged freely along, the anchor doing its job.

"Now what?" Flannigan asked.

Rayman watched the fish struggle for a few seconds before responding. "As long as all the lines are holding, we wait. Let him tire himself out."

"I can do that." Flannigan stood there and watched great fish churn the shallow water into white, frothy foam. Both men gasped when the sawtooth bill of the fish emerged from the water at a slant, toward the boat. Rayman instantly recognized the chip out of the tip of the saw blade. *It's you again, number eight.*

"It's like a ladder with teeth," Flannigan observed. "I don't know, Mason. This thing's like twice as long as our boat."

Rayman turned to him and grinned. "We're going to need a bigger boat, is that what you're saying?"

Flannigan eyed the thrashing animal with eyes full of doubt. "It wouldn't hurt, Mason. We could mark our position on the GPS and come back with more firepower."

Rayman shrugged. "Thing is, most boats that are bigger than this one also have a deeper draft—they can't operate in water this shallow. Might not be so easy to find a bigger boat on short notice that could get into this skinny water."

Flannigan had no immediate reply and so Rayman went on. "Not only that, but without us here, it's possible it could break loose and swim off. We've got him now, Bobby. Once we get him up to the side of the boat, we can lash him down and then motor back slow to the dock. We can do it."

Flannigan turned to look at him. "You're the boss. It's Miller time, you want one?"

He opened a cooler full of ice and took out a can of beer.

"No, thanks. Gonna try to stay sharp."

"Fine, I'll use yours as an ice pack." He opened one can and put the other on his bruised forearm. He took a long pull from the beer and nodded toward their quarry. "Looks like he's settling down some."

Rayman cast a glance at the saw and then rummaged around the boat, piling coils of rope on the deck. "We'll lash him along the side, especially the tail, where most of it propulsive power comes from."

"What could go wrong?" Flannigan took another pull from his beer.

24

Virginia Key

Elisa Gonzales opened a local news station's website on the browser of her new work computer. She was feeling drained from a busy day of moving into her new space and getting adjusted, and now it was time for a little break before responding to a new raft of emails requiring her urgent attention. She read the headlines, seeing the expected reports of the recent sawfish attacks, but there was a new headline now, too.

CITY OF MIAMI HIRES FISH EXPERT TO COMBAT KILLER SAWFISH

There was a photo of Rayman, dressed formally in a suit and tie. She recognized the picture as the same one he had used on the university faculty web page, taken about five years ago.

Bastard! Creates a bunch of monsters and then gets paid to stop them! That's Rayman for you—deliberately creating a dangerous situation so that he can be the hero putting an end to it. She clicked on the article which had quotes from the mayor declaring that the City would do everything in its power to make the beaches safe for people to enjoy this summer season. To that end, the mayor said, noted ichthyologist and sawfish expert, Dr. Mason Rayman, has been contracted by the City in order to lead the effort to capture and relocate the dangerous shark relatives.

Elisa was half inclined to pick up the desk phone and call the mayor's office right now to let them know what Rayman was doing, that it was him who had created and deliberately released these monsters in the first place. But then the reasoning part of her brain took over and she continued to sit there, staring at the screen without seeing it. After a time, she reached for her cell-phone instead of the desk phone. Not her real cell-phone, either, the one she used to keep in touch with family and friends and for work, too, but the cheap, disposable pay-as-you-go one she had purchased specifically for contacting Rayman. She powered it on and opened the text messages. Nothing new, as expected. She would do the initiating when it came to this relationship.

She typed in a new text message:

CONGRATS ON YOUR NEW JOB! YOU SHOULD BE ABLE TO AFFORD YOUR NEXT PAYMENT, WHICH IS DUE NOW. SAME AMOUNT.

She stared down at what she had written so far, deciding that this little game had to stop. This was it. She pecked some more on the tiny keys:

PLAY NICE AND THIS WILL BE THE LAST ONE. DON'T PLAY NICE AND I'LL SEND THE MAYOR MY LITTLE VID OF YOU PLAYING WITH YOUR FISH. DROP WILL BE TOMORROW, WILL SEND TIME & LOCATION LATER. BE GOOD.

She read the message over once, decided she was happy with it and then pressed Send.

25

Biscayne Bay

"Watch the tail, Bobby!" Rayman clutched two ends of a rope that he had managed, with a lot of trial and error, to sling around the sawfish's gargantuan head. He now had the upper portion of the fish's body up against the side of the boat, holding on with all his might to keep it there while it began to thrash its powerful tail.

"It came loose!" Flannigan held up one end of a line in frustration.

"Try again! Around the caudal peduncle."

"Around the *what*?"

"The base of the tail."

"Why don't you just say that, then, Professor." Inwardly Rayman cringed at the reference to a job title he no longer held, but at least Flannigan attempted to lasso the saw's scythe of a tail, passing the rope around the caudal fin where it joined the body.

"Now pull hard—pull!"

"Need help!" Flannigan struggled with his weakened arm to contain the saw's muscular powerhouse of propulsion against the side of the boat by a single rope.

"I can't leave now, Bobby, I've got the head." Even though the head was swaddled in netting, he still faced the saw blade, which made it a position that couldn't be abandoned. One slip, one lapse of attention, and Rayman knew that he could end up paralyzed or worse. "You can try and wrap one end around a cleat, then use your good arm to pull the other end. As soon as I get the saw lashed down, I'll move back there to help you."

Flannigan eyeballed the nearest cleat, bolted to the boat's stern rail. He pulled the rope toward it but there was still at least a foot gap between the end of the line and the cleat. Adding to the confusion, the boat's radio erupted in chatter, causing Rayman to perk up, but it was unrelated to them, something about a naked drunk man in a sailboat requiring assistance.

Rayman caught a lucky break when the big saw blade became wedged inside the Bimini top frame—a series of metal poles that held up a canvas sun shade. The teeth were interlocked with the one-inch diameter struts, effectively locking the saw blade in place. The ichthyologist wasted no time in grabbing another rope to secure the saw in place, lashing the fish's primary weapon fast to the Bimini top, then fortifying that with additional ropes from the netting around the head to a cleat on the opposite side of the boat.

He turned to see how Flannigan was doing, pleased to see that he'd somehow gotten one end of the line around the beast's tail tied off on a cleat. He held the other end in his hands, the huge fish still whipping its tail back and forth, slapping the side of the boat with loud thumps. Rayman leapt over and grabbed the free end of the line from his assistant. "I got this—you grab another line, we'll want more than one on the tail."

Flannigan moved to carry out the instruction while Rayman dealt with his number eight. He yanked the rope with both hands and took satisfaction in hearing the creature's tail slam against the boat. "C'mon, number eight. I remember when you were only five feet long, buddy. Come back to papa now…"

"What'd you say?" Flannigan, thinking that Rayman was talking to him, lifted his head back out of a storage compartment.

"Nothing, just talking to myself. Find that extra line!"

Bobby went back to the compartment while Rayman returned his full attention to the animal. He tied the rope he had around the fish off to a hand rail and then watched the sawfish carefully. It hugged the side of the boat, lashed there by ropes and netting, longer than the vessel by far, its saw sticking way past the bow and its tail protruding well past the stern. It wasn't completely immobilized, Rayman could see by the wiggling it did, nor was it able to swim away. He wasn't sure how long the gigantic sea beast was going to stay quiet for, but it was clear that for right now, anyway, they had it.

"Bobby, you got that other line?"

"Right here, boss." He pressed a coil of rope into Rayman's hand, no doubt glad not have to handle it himself and place more stress on his arm. He'd managed to patch it up some with the first aid kit, but the injury was significant. Rayman looked down at the trussed fish.

"It would be best if we could get this rope underneath the boat so we could tie him tight against the other side." Flannigan had to agree. As it was now, the mammoth animal was fastened only on one side of the boat, basically hanging there in a series of rope loops. A line under the boat that passed over the sawfish's midsection would pull the fish into the hull, giving it no room to move. Gauging the list that the boat now had, the last thing Rayman wanted was for his quarry to get a second wind once they were under way and start trying to move around again.

Rayman scrambled for a fishing tackle box and removed a lead weight from it. He quickly tied it onto one end of the rope. Flannigan watched with interest. "Sink it and pass the boat over it?"

Rayman nodded as he cinched his knot tight. "Then pick up the other end. Only way I can think of, other than swimming the line under the boat, and I'm sure neither of us want to try that." He looked up at Flannigan as he prepared to throw the rope. Flannigan nodded. "How about I drive the boat, you handle the rope."

Rayman agreed. The entire moment was so surreal to him—the fish on the side of his boat so goddamned huge that he could barely fathom it, it didn't seem real, like he was floating through some kind of action-filled dream. He snapped out of it when Flannigan started the motor up, revving it a couple of times in neutral.

"Let her rip," he told Rayman, who tossed the weighted end of the line over the sawfish and watched it sink to the bottom a few feet below. He let out the slack line as Flannigan eased the boat toward the rope.

"We're passing it...now! Hold position." Rayman picked up a boat hook—a long-handled grabbing tool usually used to snag ropes from docks or mooring buoys. He went to the opposite side of the boat and peered intently over the side, down through the water at the bottom, looking for the end of the rope that had to be down there somewhere. It took him a few seconds, during which he heard and felt the massive saw thumping into the boat, along with the vibrations of the boat engine as Flannigan made fine adjustments to hold them in position, but he found it.

He jabbed the boat hook underwater and hooked the line, bringing it up so that he could grab it with a hand. That done, he dropped the boat hook and pulled the rope until there was no more slack, feeling the sawfish stop struggling as it was pinned against the hull. Then he tied off the line and stepped back to admire his handiwork.

The sawfish was still moving, but could no longer slam any part of itself into the small craft. They had done it. The sawfish was under their control. "We got him, Bobby!"

Flannigan turned around in the pilot's seat to check on the fish. "Where to now, boss?"

"Back to the marina." Rayman knew that the public marina they'd left from would be very crowded this time of day, and even more so once he phoned in a media report on the way in. He was hoping for a media frenzy, with himself as the ringleader. Miami needed a hero and he was delivering. He would need to parlay this into an actual job at some point, but the first step was to deliver the goods and then make sure he got the credit for it. It wouldn't be easy, though. In fact, there was still work to do, as Flannigan reminded him in no uncertain terms.

"We're listing bad to one side, Mason. Means we're gonna have to go real slow. Take a while to get all the way back to the marina."

But nothing was going to dampen Rayman's high spirits now. He absolutely could not wait to personally deliver this fish to the mayor. "No problem, take it as slow as you need. I'll get on the horn and try to have the news cameras waiting for us when we get there."

Flannigan cautiously put the boat into gear while craning his head back to see if the sawfish would try to work itself loose once it felt the motion of the boat. "I'll watch him," Rayman said, eyeing the tied-down behemoth. "You just worry about the driving and I'll let you know if anything's happening with the fish."

At this, Flannigan cranked up the throttle a bit and the heavily laden boat began to slog its way across the bay. Rayman peered over the side and watched the saw as the boat leveled out at cruising speed, which was far from really cruising, but more like a laborious churning motion. Rayman noted that the saw's right side gills were mostly submerged underwater, while the left was totally out. He looked across the bay and wondered if it would possibly still be alive when they docked it.

He hoped so.

26

Miami Marina

"That's one down!" Rayman proclaimed triumphantly for the TV news cameras clustered in the marina parking lot. The sawfish had been hung from a crane and measured out at thirty-seven feet and three inches, weighing 2,214 pounds. A crowd of hundreds of onlookers was gathered in a circle around the spectacle, including seasoned commercial fishermen who had never seen anything like it.

"How many more do you think are still out there?" a reporter from a Miami television news station shouted. The crowd quieted as they waited to hear the answer.

Five, Rayman thought but could not say. "I can't be certain at this time, but judging from the time and location of the noted attacks, it seems likely there are more than one sawfish behind the attacks." A murmur of surprise and concern trickled through the crowd. Staring at the monster hanging from the crane, they were now able to visualize with crystal clarity exactly what they were sharing their local waters with.

Then another reporter made his voice heard above the crowd. He was accompanied by a cameraman who stood from a position so as to catch both the reporter and Rayman, who stood at the base of the sawfish next to Bobby Flannigan, who wore a long-sleeved sweatshirt to cover up his injured arm.

"Dr. Rayman, is it true that you were just let go from your Florida University position?"

The question was not one Rayman had anticipated. Here he was, an ichthyologist hired by the city to do something about a killer fish plaguing the beaches, and he had literally dragged one up into a parking lot, yet all this guy wanted to know about was his job? He gave the man a no-nonsense, but not overtly hostile stare before answering matter-of-factly. "I wasn't *let go*, per se, but the federal funding for the grant that paid for my position was cut. As you can see," he said, turning around to look at the frighteningly gigantic saw hanging behind him, "that was sort of a mistake."

The crowd erupted in laughter, and in the back of the crowd a new arrival frowned. Elisa Gonzales stared at Rayman across the sea of heads. Even she had been surprised by the directness of the reporter's question, in a good way, but Rayman had handled it well and now several reporters vied to have their new questions heard, and about the sawfish itself, not Rayman's career.

Still, that didn't mean Rayman was off the hook yet. A bear of a man followed by a woman wielding a boom microphone held up his arm and shouted into a lull of questions: "This is an Atlantic Smalltooth Sawfish, correct?"

Rayman nodded. "That is correct, sir. Scientifically known as *Pristis pectinata.* Although technically a type of ray, they are closely related to sharks." He beamed smugly, hoping the mention of the word *shark* in the same sentence would scare people into ponying up more funding for the eradication and relocation effort.

The same reporter followed up. "Why is this sawfish so large— that isn't typical for this kind of sawfish, is it?"

Indeed it was not. Rayman saw no way to sugarcoat this without letting the cat out of the bag as far as his own culpability. But he had to say something. He was the expert. "You're right, it's not typical at all. I can't say with any degree of certainty at this time what is responsible for the uncharacteristic growth. If I had to guess off the top of my head..." He made a show of scratching his head and shrugging, "I don't know...interspecies breeding? Like maybe the smalltooth sawfish cross-bred with a different variety and it resulted in this freakishly large specimen here?" He waved an arm at the hanging saw. "But really I'm not comfortable speculating at this time. That's why further research is required," he added, hinting at the importance of his cut position.

"What's your next move?" a female reporter called out from near the back of the crowd.

Rayman looked to Flannigan and patted him on the back. "We're headed back out to make sure the coast is clear, literally. Clear of giant sawfish."

27

Biscayne Bay

An hour later, after purchasing some additional gear from a boating store and topping off the bait and chum, Rayman and Flannigan were back on the water. At first, Bobby had suggested calling it a day—they had already been successful, after all—but Rayman had offered him more money and so off they went. They targeted a different part of the bay this time, almost twenty miles away from where they caught the first monster saw, but the same type of habitat—shallow mangrove flats. Rayman figured that large predators like the saws would need that kind of minimum distance apart to find sufficient food without competing.

Rayman was at the wheel while Flannigan took it easy, resting up his arm for the second bout of activity to come. A mild breeze had picked up, creating a light chop across the bay which made the boat ride bouncier. It didn't slow Rayman down, though. If anything, he was travelling even faster this time. He slowed only when they were about half a mile off the new remote mangrove shoreline. He picked up his binoculars and had a look. After scanning left and right a few times, then consulting the electronic marine chart displayed on the GPS unit, Rayman set a course toward an area of the coast.

He slowed as they approached the greenery, and they had a moment of excitement when a sizable animal darted away from their boat, spreading a cloud of mud in its wake, but it was nothing but a large spotted eagle ray. Flannigan threw the anchor and they settled in for another round of fishing. Far from being tedious, both men found the work energizing after such recent success. They had done it—captured a gigantic sawfish—and everyone knew about it.

Rayman wondered if the mayor himself had tried to contact him yet after hearing the news. It had been a while since he'd checked his messages, what with all the excitement on the water and then in the marina. The mayor hadn't been there to see the saw in person, but surely he'd heard of the catch by now.

While Flannigan started ladling out chum, Rayman pulled out his phone. He perked up on seeing that he had a new message, a text. It seemed odd to him that the mayor's office would send texts to contractors, but whatever, Rayman thought, as long as they could reach him to let him know how happy they were with the job he was doing. But as soon as he opened the text, it became plain as day that this communication was not from the mayor. He read the words on the small screen with mounting fury:

PLAY NICE AND THIS WILL BE THE LAST ONE. DON'T PLAY NICE AND I'LL SEND THE MAYOR MY LITTLE VID OF YOU PLAYING WITH YOUR FISH. DROP WILL BE TOMORROW, WILL SEND TIME & LOCATION LATER. BE GOOD.

The message had been received today, only a couple of hours ago, which meant that tomorrow he was expected to make another drop, probably another ten grand. That was about what he was making on his contract for the city. *Out here doing all this dangerous work just to give the fruit of it to this bitch...* He slammed his fist on the gunwale in frustration, causing Flannigan to look over at him from the stern deck where he'd just picked up another bucket of chum.

"Everything all right?"

Rayman dropped his phone into the console. "Bobby, if we catch us another big saw, everything's going to be just fine."

Flannigan nodded and proceeded to disperse the last of his chum. "This stuff's even smellier than the last stuff, if that's possible, so we might be okay."

Rayman stood and turned his attention to the fishing. He'd deal with that bitch, all right. But first, he needed a little luck out here, had to do things just the right way.

"This time we'll give the nets a rest and try rod and reel, okay?"

Flannigan laughed. "Not a problem, boss. I'm glad it worked the first time, but I'm not looking to go through that again. I'll get the rods rigged."

Rayman eyeballed the stretch of mangrove coast off their bow. They were anchored in a shallow cove, with a weak current running away from the bow that would carry the chum along the shoreline. The idea was to follow the chum drift and put out fishing lines rigged with chunks of bait, so that when the big saw was attracted by the chum, it would find a nice piece of meat to bite onto. Then they could reel him in.

There was another reason Rayman preferred to use a rod and reel, too, one that for now he was keeping to himself.

He dropped the binoculars around his neck and settled in at the helm for a long stretch of trolling—motoring along at slow speeds while the baited fishing lines trailed behind the boat. When Flannigan said he was ready, they pulled anchor and Rayman put the boat into gear. He drove parallel to the coast, perhaps fifty yards from the mangroves, up and back...up and back, like he was mowing the lawn.

While they plowed back and forth, Flannigan watched the lines, looking to see if they would go taut. Sawfish—the normal sized ones, anyway—weren't known to be big jumpers when hooked, and they were usually hooked by accident; they weren't target sport fish for the most part. But Rayman had caught a few before for collection purposes, and even Flannigan had landed one once inadvertently, so if anyone could deliberately boat a big sawfish, it was these two.

Flannigan reeled in one of the lines a bit—he had one in a rod holder on each corner of the boat's stern—to get a feel for the tension, and to pull it in line with the other rig. Call it obsessive compulsive, he was fond of telling his fishing buddies, but he liked both of his baits to be the exact distance from the boat at the same time. Easier to spot both of them quickly that way, is how he justified it, but really—and he was pretty sure he wasn't fooling anybody—he was just particular about it.

Then he grabbed another chum bucket and dribbled it out behind the boat, to leave a fresh scent around the baits, a chum slick. Flannigan pulled a buff up around his face to shield it from the sun, in addition to the hat and sunglasses he already wore. The reflection of the sun off the water was brutal, and he had learned from experience that this was the best way to avoid a serious sunburn. Rayman, who was shaded beneath the canopy top, wore sunglasses but did without the hat or bandana.

The ichthyologist glanced frequently at the rear view mirror he'd affixed to his windshield, hoping to see signs of a hook-up, of course, but also checking for other vessels. They'd had a lot of publicity, and he had been somewhat concerned that they might be followed back out by other fishermen hoping to hunt the monster saws. To combat this, he'd travelled fast, taking a couple of zigzag routes to throw anyone off who might have been following from a distance. He saw a couple of boats now, but they were far off, and through his binoculars, he could see that neither were fishing. One was pulling a water skier, while the other was a giant luxury yacht, almost a mega yacht, merely floating at anchor, doing whatever rich people did aboard such craft.

It was smooth going, but Rayman's eyes were busy as his gaze shifted constantly from the water ahead of them, to the rear view mirror, to the depth readout on the fish finder, the boat's dash controls, and back around again. When he reached a coastal point that jutted out into the bay, he turned the boat around in a wide arc and headed back in the direction from whence they came, back along the mangrove coast. All the while, Flannigan kept a close eye on the lines, carefully monitoring them for signs of activity, adjusting tension here, reeling in a bit here, letting more line out there.

He'd rigged the lines with very large hooks, so as to rule out strikes from typical game fish. The only thing that would be hitting these baits would be their intended targets, with the possible exception of extremely large sharks. So when one of the rods suddenly bent double, Flannigan knew he had something to worry about on the line. He pulled the lit cigarette from his mouth and tossed it overboard.

"Captain, we got a live one!"

Rayman glanced up at the rear view, saw the rod bending hard, and slowed the boat into idle mode. He then jumped down from the captain's chair and joined Flannigan out on deck, where the fisherman was stepping into a fishing rod harness, preparing for a big fight with an as yet unseen opponent.

Rayman studied the line, carefully observing the way it moved, how the rod tip jerked and pulled. "Slow, strong movements. It hasn't broke the surface yet, right?"

Flannigan shook his head as he cinched a strap tight on the harness.

Rayman nodded. "Not a game fish then, like a big marlin or a mako shark."

"He's slow but real, real strong. If he ain't a sawfish, I dunno— maybe the biggest grouper I ever seen in my life?" He looked up at Rayman and grinned before walking up to the left of the two rods. He looked back at Rayman and said, "Spot me," before placing two hands around the butt of the rod. This was a risky maneuver. He needed to lift the rod from the boat holder and into the harness around his waist, so that he could reel in the fish. But the fish was exerting a lot of force on the other end, and as soon as the rod was pulled free from the holder, the lack of support meant that it would want to go flying overboard. Flannigan didn't want to let out too much slack on the line, knowing he'd have to fight for every inch of it back, so he asked Rayman to add his hands to the rod while he fit it into his harness.

The operation worked, and when the butt of the rod was firmly in the holder mounted around his waist, Rayman resumed his position at the cockpit, ready to operate the boat as needed.

"Back 'er down a little!" Flannigan yelled, struggling to reel in more line. This called for Rayman to put the motor into reverse, and "back down" toward the fish, which would create slack in the line, enabling Flannigan to reel it in without resistance. They repeated this process a few times, Rayman putting the vessel into reverse for a few seconds, then Flannigan furiously reeling to take up the slack.

After the back-down operations, the fish stayed directly beneath the boat. Flannigan pulled hard on the line to no avail. "Maybe he dug into the bottom?" he gasped. It was common for bottom fish, when hooked, to seek the seafloor and wedge themselves into a cave, ledge or crevice, to prevent their bodies from being pulled upward without having to expend energy to fight. But Rayman voiced what even Flannigan knew all along.

"This critter's too big to dig himself in anywhere. But he's not pulling much anymore, either, so we must be tiring him out some. It's just sheer deadweight."

Flannigan kept working on the load, pulling up, up, with great effort, then reeling, reeling, reeling as he forced the rod downward, to quickly take up the slack he had fought for on the way up. After a few repetitions of this drill, a dark, hulking mass materialized out of the gloom.

"There it is!" Flannigan shouted, breathless. Even though he'd been working on the fish for a while now, actually seeing the fruit of his labor was energizing and caused him to double down on his reeling efforts with renewed vigor. Rayman began gathering the implements that would be needed once the fish—he was sure it had to be one of his saws, although without seeing it couldn't be positive—was brought alongside the boat. Normally, a gaff—a long pole with a stout hook on the end—would be used to pull the fish out of the water, to avoid the weight of it breaking the fishing line, but whatever was on the end of the line here was far too large for that. Same goes for a net. The standard gear to boat a fish was utterly useless with their quarry, so Rayman gathered what he had already had some success with: ropes.

"He's coming up!" Flannigan pulled hard on the rod. Rayman tossed two coils of thick rope on the deck and went back looking for more. Suddenly, they heard a high pitched clicky whine as the reel spooled off line against the drag.

"He's running!" Flannigan yelled. As was known to happen, when the fish got within sight of the boat, it became spooked and thrashed hard with a reserve of energy, running away from the vessel.

"Back it down, back it down!"

Rayman hopped up on the captain's chair and put the boat into reverse as fast as he dared. The line began to slacken.

"That's good!" Flannigan reeled again and then bent over to look into the water. "Holy crap...it's a sawfish, Mason, and this one's bigger than the last one! Holy..."

Flannigan was suddenly jerked hard toward the water, and went down on one knee, his head nearly hitting the transom. "Little help!"

Rayman ran back to his crewman and picked him up. Together, the pair of them hefted the rod, Rayman providing additional muscle while Flannigan frantically reeled. The mega-saw darkened the water below the boat, stubbornly rising with the reeled line.

"Something tells me he's not going to fit in the boat," Flannigan breathed.

Rayman jerked his head toward the pile of lines. "I'll lash him to the boat when you get him up, like we did the first one, but until I get that first line on him you're going to have to hold him up with the rod."

Flannigan had no response other than to continue pulling on the gargantuan fish. Rayman shook his head in wonder as the true scale of the beast became apparent—it was easily longer than the boat, not even counting the saw, and it was wider as well. Rayman slowly shook his head as he pondered the outlandish size of the creature—a sawfish, even a record length specimen of one— should be no longer than twenty-one feet, yet this one had to be twice that. *What have I created?*

An even more disturbing thought coursed through his brain. *Flannigan's right. This one is significantly larger than the one we caught earlier. Could they be still growing?* This was his first time observing the results of his induced gigantism, after all. Who could say for sure what the limits were? Not him, not anybody—not yet. Only time would tell, and for now, that time was filled with catching monster saws.

"Mason—head's up! Here he comes!"

Rayman snapped out of it and snatched up one of his ropes. He bent over the transom to get a look at what was on the line. A broad swath of sword blade slashed right at his head. He ducked it, feeling one of the teeth snag on his hair for a microsecond as it passed through. He rolled to the deck and heard the saw blade clatter on the transom as it slid back into the water. Flannigan cursed and wedged one of his feet against the boat as he doubled over on the rod.

"I got him as close as he can get, Mason!"

Rayman shot to his feet and approached his quarry again with a rope. He marveled at the sawfish's flexibility as it twisted and writhed on the line. It could touch the tip of its tail to the tip of the saw. He watched the wire leader come into contact with the rostrum teeth and was reminded they had limited time to do something with this fish. Even though they used heavy gauge wire, it wouldn't be long before those teeth sawed through it and they lost their bounty.

Rayman tossed one of his lines around the saw. He had to get that under control first. It snagged nicely and he was able to lash it against the boat to a cleat. Once the sawfish was tied the boat with two lines, Flannigan dropped the rod and helped Rayman with the ropes. Then, much like with the earlier quarry, they went to work with more lines on the tail, and then the body.

When it was done, they stood back and admired their handiwork. The gigantic sawfish was strapped alongside the vessel which now looked downright small in comparison. It had a pronounced tilt on the side with the captured fish, whose head and gills were underwater, keeping it alive. It struggled against the lines but they were lashed tight, preventing anywhere near a full range of motion.

Flannigan held up a hand to Rayman and they high-fived. Rayman reflected darkly that to Flannigan, this was almost just another fishing trip, good times to be had. For him, though, it was his livelihood and even more than that, a way out...

"So back to the marina?" Flannigan suggested. Rayman had already been thinking of next steps, too, but his were not the same as Flannigan's. He shook his head.

"Actually, Bobby, I'll handle this one myself in the morning." He glanced over toward the west, where the sky was perhaps barely beginning to redden. "It'll be sunset soon and it's probably better to have good daylight for the press. Besides, we already made a good showing today, let's leave it at that. I'll just drop you at the boat ramp, okay, and then I'll dock at my slip and deal with big boy here in the morning."

They both glanced at the thrashing sawfish. "Will you even fit in your slip with this thing tied alongside?"

It was a good point, but one Rayman had hoped Flannigan wouldn't bring up. Truth was, it wouldn't fit in his slip, not without attracting all kinds of attention anyway, sticking way out into the busy boat channel. But in fact he had no intention of leaving this fish tied up at his dock all night, or even of killing it at all.

28

Next day, Biscayne Bay

Elisa Gonzales tied her wavy hair back in a ponytail in an attempt to contain it against a persistent wind that made for a bad hair day but a great sailing day. Aboard a twenty-six foot sailboat with her friend Janey and their two kids, and Janey's boyfriend, Jim, a sailing club instructor, she looked forward to a fun-filled day out on the water.

A bottle of wine was opened and while the kids played and Jim minded the helm, the two women chatted and caught up. Elisa knew Janey not through work, but because they were neighbors and their kids went to the same school. When asked how her job was going, Elisa told her friend about her move to the new office, said everything was going great. Then she called over to Janey's boyfriend, "Hey, Jim, we going the usual route today or what?"

"Sounds good to me—that okay with you? Lunch at the island?"

Both women raised their glasses. "To the island!"

Neither of them knew the name of the small spit of windblown sand they had visited now and then on past sailing trips, but it was a regular stop for sailing club outings because it featured relatively deep water close to the island, somewhat of a rarity in Florida and needed for sailboats because of their long keels beneath the hull.

For now, they enjoyed the wind in their hair as the boat skimmed across the water, tipped up on its starboard side. The water below them was clear and dark in color, but gradually transitioned to a whiter hue as the bottom became sandier.

#

Rayman glanced at his watch again while he sat behind the wheel of his boat. He'd timed his trip so that he arrived about half an hour before Elisa would on her sailboat, if past trips of the sailing club were any indication. Rayman had colleagues—former colleagues, now, he reminded himself—in the club, and he'd been on the very route that Elisa was taking today. They'd depart from the Miami Marina around 10am, sail out across Biscayne, maybe tack back and forth a couple of times, then head for the sand spit for lunch. After that, they'd get back in the boat and sail the long way back to the marina.

But today, Rayman hoped, the trip would end at the island. He glanced down at the mega-saw still strapped to the side of his boat. Concerned that it would basically suffocate if immobilized for so long, he had placed a tube of seawater into its gill slits and used a live bait well pump to force it over its gills. The procedure had worked, because the big saw was still alive and kicking, straining to be let loose from its bonds.

"Almost time now, little buddy. Big buddy," Rayman corrected himself. In fact, he could swear the colossal fish was even larger today than when he'd caught it yesterday. It was ridiculous. When would it stop growing? Or were his tired eyes just playing tricks on him? But no, he thought, eyeballing the position of the saw's second dorsal fin relative to one of the registration numbers painted on the boat's hull—it had moved forward by a good two feet, he was certain of it. He told himself that maybe the ropes had worked loose after a night of the massive beast struggling against them, but when he placed a hand on the knots, they were exactly the same tightness as yesterday. There was no slack. In fact, if anything the ropes were even tighter against the fish's body, so much so it seemed they might be about to snap.

You've grown, haven't you? I'll be goddamned if you haven't grown two fucking feet overnight!

Where was the limit? How big would these saws get? He didn't know, but as he heard the rumble of a distant boat engine, reminding himself that this was not a private island and others would visit during the course of the day—he could be seen here— he told himself that he had work to do right now. Figuring out what exactly he had done to these sawfish would have to wait.

He picked up his binoculars and scanned the bay in the direction from which the sailboat would likely be arriving. Left to right...nothing yet...right to left...There! White sail atop a white sailboat, with a yellow stripe Rayman knew to be the club logo. *Gotcha.* He let the binoculars drop around his neck on the strap and grabbed a fishing knife.

"It's show time, buddy, you ready? You must be hungry after not eating all night, and still growing like that..." Wanting to be gone from the island before his boat could be seen by those on the sailboat, Rayman opted not to take the time to untie his knots in the ropes that held the sawfish to the side of the boat, and instead cut them free. He moved from one rope to the next, slicing and pulling, pausing now and then to glance up at the sailboat approaching in the distance. By the time he could see the white sail clearly without the aid of binoculars, the saw was undulating against the boat, testing its muscles, and only two lines remained to be severed.

Rayman did a visual check of his surroundings. No boats, no people he could see other than the still far away sailors. Looking into the water, he was pleased to see it was not crystal clear—the sand bottom had been stirred by currents and would obscure the big sawfish once it was released. He was banking on the fact that the saw would find itself very much at home here on this sandy bottom, and would still be here when the happy-go-lucky sailors arrived for their island stop.

"Goodbye again, old buddy." Rayman cut the last two ropes and the enormous ray drifted clear of the boat. It didn't immediately swim away, but floated there, causing Rayman concern that it had been seriously injured during its ordeal. He turned his head to gaze at the approaching sailboat—still on the way—and when he looked back at the saw again it was underwater, its tail swishing back and forth as it slanted down toward the submerged island sand.

He watched it until it settled on the bottom, wiggling around a bit until it was partially buried in sand.

Excellent.

"You should have visitors in your new home soon, number eight! Stay well!"

Rayman moved to the captain's chair and took the controls. It would have been nice to turn another monster sawfish over to the

City, but he had to do what he had to do. Who knows, he mused while putting the boat into gear, if he got really lucky the saw would do its job and would still be here later when he came back to check on it. Then he could capture it again and bring it in.

Rayman cast one more glance at the approaching sailboat, then circled around the island, heading away from it for some distance before turning back toward the mainland.

29

"Is that it?" Elisa Gonzales pointed from the deck of the sailboat to a small island off their bow.

The captain of the boat nodded. "Thar she blows!"

"You wish," Janey quipped.

Elisa laughed and shook her head. "Later, you two. So are we going to be able to get off the boat and walk on that beautiful beach?"

"You bet," Janey said, heading down into the boat's small cabin. "I'll grab the lunch stuff."

She emerged in a minute carrying a picnic basket and a small cooler, handing the latter up to Elisa. Jim, meanwhile, luffed the sails to slow the boat as it approached the island. "Where's my anchor girl?"

Elisa pointed at Janey. "I don't know what I'm doing."

"I got it." Janey left the basket on deck and walked around to the bow, where an anchor hung at the ready. She untied it so that it was free and held it, ready to drop. "Say when!"

The captain turned the wheel hard right, bringing the boat broadside to the spit of sand and slowing its progress toward the island even more. "Splash it!"

Janey tossed the anchor a few feet out from the boat, away from the island since they were already only feet away from it. She watched it drop through the water until she could no longer see it, but it looked like it landed on a darker patch of bottom. She hoped it meant she had found a rocky patch, because it would hold the anchor fast, but in the back of her mind she didn't recall this area ever being anything but sand. She was about to call out, "Anchor's down," when the entire bottom seemed to quake beneath them. She watched it for a moment, confused, thinking perhaps she was experiencing some sort of vertigo or seasickness from being on a moving boat and then suddenly staring down into the water, but...

No, something was definitely moving down there.

"Janey? Is it out?" Jim still manned the helm, waiting to hear that the anchor had been successfully deployed.

She turned her head from her kneeling stance on the bow. "I dropped it but—" She never got to finish her sentence, for at that moment the water exploded next to the boat. A saw blade the size of a length of railroad track crashed into the aluminum mast, and they heard the cracking and splintering of fiberglass as the base of the mast separated from its mount in the boat.

Elisa saw the freakishly large rostrum hitting the sailboat and felt her insides shrivel. "Kids, inside, now!" The kids looked up from their play on the deck, confused. Elisa ran to them, took them by the hand and led them into the cabin. She closed the hatch and went back out on deck, which was now enshrouded by torn sailcloth. Janey's boyfriend was trapped under a fallen sail, cursing and scrambling to get out from beneath it. Elisa whirled, looking for her friend.

"Janey? Janey, where are you?" Elisa whipped her head to and fro, looking up and down the length of the boat. She didn't see Janey anywhere. Had she already stepped off onto the island? But the strip of sand was bare. Then her blood curdled with the next logical place to look. She gazed down into the water between the boat and the island.

Janey floated face down, arms spread wide, unmoving. "Janey!" Elisa didn't think, only acted. She jumped overboard, a clumsy, awkward act, not the graceful swan dive so often depicted in the movies or on television, which in this case was a good thing since the water was shallow. She buckled to her knees on impact as she landed with a splash. She shot to her knees, riveted with fear while her eyes locked onto the inert body.

"Janey, I'm here!" She waded up to her friend and immediately pulled her head out of the water and flipped her onto her back. Her friend's eyes were closed and she saw no reaction, no coughing, nothing. She eyed the sandy beach of the island mere feet away. Conscious of both the fact that she needed to perform CPR and that the mega-predator could fall upon them at any moment, she hauled her friend up onto the wet sand of the beach.

"Janey, what happened?" She tilted her up on her side and water poured from her mouth. Her eyes fluttered, shut, then opened. Janey reached out a hand and gripped Elisa's shoulder. "Fell off...boat, hit head on side..."

"It's okay, Janey, not now, just—"

She heard Jim shout from the boat, "Look out!" at the same time as the massive shovel-like saw slid up onto the beach next to them. It slashed, but the wrong way, away from them. It started to bring its weapon back to the right, toward them, but it dug into the sand and the immense body of the sawfish twisted over on top of itself, rolling, part of its body on the island, the rest still submerged.

"C'mon, Janey, we've got to move!" She dragged her friend up to higher ground, of which the little island had precious little to offer. The top of the sand mound was perhaps two feet above sea level, in the very middle of the island. Elisa lay her friend down and slumped down next to her, exhausted. She saw the boyfriend standing on the edge of the boat, watching them.

"Huge sawfish!" he called, cupping his hands over his mouth. "Stay out of the water. I'll try to—"

Suddenly, the boat rocked toward the island as it was bashed hard from the opposite side by the monstrously large animal. The captain was pitched over the side into the water between the island and the sailboat. He immediately trudged on the wet sand toward the beach with a wide-eyed gaze toward the two women. He had just reached the exposed sand when the boat was pitched toward him violently, canting onto one side before righting itself. Jim hurried onto the island, barely avoiding being hit by the wayward boat. He ran to Janey's side and knelt next to her.

"You okay, babe?"

She looked at him with wide eyes, nodding.

Her boyfriend gripped Elisa's shoulder until she forced herself to turn away from the floundering sailboat and look him in the eyes. "Thank you for what you did. You saved her."

Elisa thought but did not say, *Least I can do since it's me who got us into this mess. Rayman, that sonofabitch...*

Janey looked all around the island, then to the rocking boat. "The kids! Where are they?"

"I told them to go down in the cabin." Elisa scanned the water around the boat, hoping like hell they hadn't fallen overboard.

Then she saw the sailboat, drifting away from the island. She pointed it out.

Janey's boyfriend looked beyond incredulous. "That huge thing—was it a sawfish?"

Elisa nodded.

"It must have dislodged the anchor and now the boat's adrift," Jim said.

Janey tried to stand upon hearing this, but she was still weak and in semi-shock, collapsing back onto the sand. "The kids are on the boat! We have to get them!"

The captain eyeballed his drifting boat. "Do you see the sawfish? I don't see it." He stood so as to gain a better vantage point from which to confirm this observation. Then his face brightened as he pulled something from his pocket. "I have my phone. I could make a call to the Coast Guard or Sea Tow or somebody."

Janey shook his head. "They're floating away right *now*! I don't even see the sawfish."

"The wind's blowing away from us, too," Elisa noted, holding a finger in the air.

Janey gripped her boyfriend hard on the shoulder. "Jim, we *have* to get the kids!"

He dropped his phone on the dry sand. "I'll swim out there and come back for you and Elisa." He stepped to the edge of the water, eyed the distance from the beach to the boat—perhaps thirty feet.

He stepped ankle deep into the ocean and then paused, surveying the stretch between him and the boat. With a final glance to the left and then right, the captain ran out into the water, opting for a fast approach rather than stealth. When he was waist deep, he dove in and began swimming a smooth crawl stroke, aiming for the back of the boat where the swim ladder was. Both women's gazes travelled back and forth, searching for signs of the humongous predator lurking somewhere nearby.

He was three quarters of the way there when both women began to scream at the same time

Elisa: "Sawfish behind the boat!"

Janey: "Get out of the water!"

He was already swimming as fast as he could, but he kept up the pace while lifting his head out of the water once to check that he was on track for the swim step, and of course to look for that horrible saw, imagining the broad blade coming down on his neck like a guillotine. But he kept swimming through the dark thoughts, and soon his wet fingers wrapped around the tubular steel rails of the swim step mounted on the rear of the boat. He planted a foot on the platform and yanked himself up and over the transom, where he landed on the deck with a thud.

"Kids! Hey, c'mon out!" He actually wanted to get on with the business of getting the boat under control again, but he had to make certain they were in fact still in the cabin. He shoved aside the mental reaction he started to picture of Janey should he have to yell over to her that the kids were not in the boat...so negative it was distracting...and then he heard two thin, small voices.

"We're here!"

"In here!"

"Okay, great." He opened the cabin hatch and looked in to make sure they were okay. The pair of youngsters was huddled together on a pile of beach towels and life jackets, looking plenty fearful but none the worse for wear. They started to get up, no doubt eager to leave the confines of the small cabin and see what was going on topside, but he waved them back down. With the big saw right outside, they were safer in here.

"Listen guys, I need for you to stay down here a few more minutes, okay? Can you do that?"

They asked if their mothers were okay.

"They're both fine," the captain said, omitting mention of the CPR on the beach. "They're on the island now, but it's time to go, and I need to bring the boat to them. So just stay put, and I'll tell you when it's safe to come out."

The kids complied and he stepped back out on deck. He looked to the island, clearly farther away now, where Janey was already shouting to ask if the kids were okay. He let them know they were fine and then followed Elisa's point past the boat, where three fins sliced through the water's surface like a trio of scythes.

He went to the anchor line and pulled, immediately feeling a lack of expected resistance. The anchor had been separated from its rope. He dropped it and then went to the keel, pulling up the centerboard that stuck down into the water so that he would be able to get very close to the beach. Then he moved back to the stern, stepping over mounds of fallen sailcloth on the way, past the cracked mast. There was no way he was going to get this scow under control by sail anytime soon, that was for damn sure. So he moved to the small "kicker" motor—a ten horsepower outboard used to motor the sailboat through marinas...or when there was something wrong with the sails or mast. It wouldn't get the boat going very fast, but it would move it. To get to the island, it was the perfect thing. After that, he'd worry about how to get back to the marina.

He pulled the starter cord on the old rusty workhorse three times before it cranked to life, cursing at it like the sailor he was until it did, then grinning ear to ear like a kid on Christmas morning. He'd get them all out of this jam yet! The captain glanced around quickly, checking for signs of the saw. He spotted a boil on the surface a few yards away and thought it might be the marauding monster, but couldn't be sure. He put the motor into gear and cranked up the throttle enough to start pushing the boat.

It faced away from the island so he had to turn it around. As he progressed through the turn, Elisa and Janey, watching his progress, walked down to the water at the edge of the beach in anticipation of his approach. He brought the sailboat closer to the island and then slid into a roundabout turn that brought the stern, and the swim step ladder, alongside the beach.

Janey was hesitant to even wade out into the foot or so of water the rear of the boat was in, but Elisa ran out first and climbed aboard. Seeing her success, Janey quickly followed, throwing herself into the boat as if Hell itself were on her heels. Both of them immediately ran past the captain, wanting to see their kids.

Jim called after them as they passed by, "Hey babe, you got my phone?"

"No!"

He looked and saw it on the high point of the island, laying on the sand. "Shit." He was ready to motor out of here, but on top of all that happened he didn't want to lose his phone, too, not to mention being able to call for assistance now would be good. He could use one of the girls' phones, he supposed, but he had the numbers for marine assistance in his contacts. He turned and faced away from the island, his gaze scouring the sea surface, looking for telltale signs of the elusive beast.

The water was quiet. He could hear the two women consoling the children down in the cabin. He turned back around and looked at the beach. His phone screen gleamed in the sun.

I got this.

The captain leapt over the side of the sailboat and down into the knee-deep water facing the island. He high-stepped it the few feet until he reached the island's wet sand, then trotted to the middle of the sand mound and picked up his phone. He almost decided to place a call for a marine tow right from here, but didn't want to alarm the girls when they emerged from the cabin and he wasn't on deck, so he decided to return to the boat first.

He waded out to knee-deep water before realizing that this time, unlike jumping off the boat almost directly onto the beach, he'd have to wade and swim out to the stern of the boat where the swim step was, which had drifted away from the island since the girls had boarded. It wasn't much farther, but having to keep the phone dry meant he needed to keep one hand above water, so swimming fast was out.

He began wading toward the ladder and soon was waist deep. He took longer strides, hopping from one foot to the next like a moonwalker, phone held high in one hand, and soon he rounded the back of the boat.

He reached the ladder and gripped it with one hand. He reached up and set the phone on the rail so that he'd have both hands free to climb. As he planted his right foot on the bottom step and started to swing the left leg up, the sawfish's blade erupted from the water to his left—the body almost thirty feet away, but the saw itself arcing towards him in a ferocious trajectory. He heard the splash from it breaking the surface and turned his head to look at it—the last mistake he would ever make, for the sight was so incredulous, so utterly transfixing—a gigantic, organic weapon slicing toward him through the air—that he couldn't help but simply gawk at it for two precious seconds. Seconds he should have used to move himself out of harm's way.

Instead, by the time he quit marveling at the size of the thing and scrambled to move up the ladder, his movements were too frenzied, too panicky, and he lost control, his right hand losing its grip on the ladder. He fell backwards into the water with a loud splash that sent the women running out on deck in time to see their captain impaled on the saw and flipped up out of the water. The sawfish had struck from below, swinging its blade upward, catching the man across his entire back.

He was paralyzed instantly, his spine severed by the forceful and decisive blow, and so his limbs did not flail as he was tossed through the air like a board shorts-wearing ragdoll. Worse, the back of his head slammed onto the edge of the transom on the way down, caving in his skull and leaving a copious amount of blood to drip into the back of the boat as his ruined body returned to the water.

The sawfish was there to greet it, greedily shoveling the prey into its waiting mouth.

30

Miami Marina

Dr. Mason Rayman slowed down his boat, partly because was nearing the marina and would soon have to do that anyway, but also because it made it easier to hear the marine radio. Some kind of report was coming in now over the distress channel...something about...boaters in trouble at a sandbar island...there was static, but then Rayman heard the telltale word: *sawfish,* followed by something even better: *fatality.*

Yes! Attaboy, old number eight, Rayman thought. He had done it—his baby, his creation—had eliminated that horrid bitch who had been ruining his life. He fairly beamed as he rode up to the dock in the pleasure boat marina. He navigated a little faster than he should, rocking the other boats in their slips, to his own space, where he nosed his boat in, hitting the bow against the dock but not caring. He jumped out of the boat onto the dock as soon as he was within reach and hastily tied only one rope off to a cleat. When he looked up from this rushed task, Bobby Flannigan was standing there, hands on his hips, looking at the empty boat with a confused look.

"Hey, how come you never showed off that second saw we got?"

Rayman straightened up, glanced at the empty boat and then back to Flannigan. "Oh, hey Bobby! Yeah, so I took a picture of it and sent it to the mayor and they said, great, but just to kill it and not make a big deal out of it this time. Something about seeing too many of them come up would scare people and make for bad publicity, so I just killed it and dumped it out in the bay." He waved his arm toward the water.

Flannigan shrugged. "Oh well. Long as they're happy, right?"

Rayman grinned. "You bet. Listen, you want to go out again? I really want to wrap this gig up, you know, show them I can get it done quick. I'll up your cut by ten percent."

Flannigan raised an eyebrow, as if considering it, but then agreed.

"Excellent." Rayman shook Flannigan's hand. "Let's get her gassed up and restocked for another run." Rayman said he would go to the marina chandlery shop and buy the fishing supplies while Flannigan took the boat (with Rayman's gas card) to top off the fuel tank.

#

Rayman was walking through the marina parking lot to the store when he felt his phone vibrate in his pocket. New text message coming in. He pulled out his phone and looked at the screen. His skin crawled when he recognized the number as belonging to his blackmailer. Funny how he thought of her that way now—she wasn't Elisa the Admin Assistant, she was His Blackmailer. Shaking his head, he paused on a parking lot island, standing on a bunch of woodchips while he read the message.

It's all over, Rayman. You're a killer now and you mess with my kid, you leave me no choice but to out you, turn over the video to the mayor. I know what you're doing. You're nothing but a fireman setting fires to be the hero putting them out.

Rayman kept shaking his head as he read the text. *Shit.* He had to deal with this right now. He thought furiously for a minute, running the fingers of one hand through his hair while holding the phone with the other. Then he began to poke at the virtual keys on his screen. When he had input his message, he read it back through once to make sure it was clear—or was it to give himself time to change his mind and not send it at all? He could ignore it, pretend he hadn't received it. No, he had to confront her. If he did nothing she would probably go right to the mayor and cause a stink. He read his message:

I have no idea what you're talking about. I had nothing to do with it other than the fact that they're my fish to start with.

Whoa. He decided he better not implicate himself in any way. There he was in black and white admitting they were his fish. *Careful, you idiot! She could forward that to the City.* Then again, a person had died, obviously someone on the boat with her, and not her kid. That was unfortunate, but he doubted he could actually be pinned for murder by releasing a dangerous fish into the ocean... He thought about it some more... Could he? *Maybe not murder, but manslaughter?* Not unlike if someone let their pit-bull off a leash and it mauled someone on the sidewalk... *Christ*, this was getting way out of hand.

He hit the Backspace key and deleted part of what he had written, looking up once at a family of four walking past him with a cart full of stuff, the kids eyeing him curiously as he feverishly pecked away at his device like a rat at some kind of stimulation reward contraption. He told himself to think about what Gonzales knew: He had experimented with the sawfish and released them from the pier on Virginia Key. That was basically it. She *suspected* he had not mentioned that to the City, but didn't know for sure. Maybe he should tell her they already know? That's why they hired him, he's the expert. But that could backfire, couldn't it? Yep. Also, it could possibly come out later that he was on his boat near the island, where a sawfish attack happened, but he doubted it or she would have mentioned already that she saw him there. So what did all that leave?

She wanted another payment to remain silent on the fish release; that's all she had on him, but it was just enough. He squeezed his phone in anger. Only one more...just one more...it would never stop unless he put an end to it. He was becoming like a source of income to her. The sawfish attack at the island was a nice try, but it came up short. He had to do something else. He closed his eyes as if he could shut out the marina and the store where he needed to go buy more supplies to be able to hunt down the monster fish he created, the people walking past and staring at him, and he pictured Biscayne Bay in his mind. All that beautiful, blue water, dotted with little islands here and there and lined by white sand beaches. He flew close over its waters as if on a magic carpet or a boat, seeing it from a few feet above the surface. Past the piers, the cruise ships, pleasure boats and out onto the flat bay proper. If he could lure her out there somehow...

He opened his eyes.

He began to type:

What do you say we make a deal that can end this? One more drop—2x the last one. Will that get you off my back FOR GOOD?

Rayman decided he'd stood in one spot for long enough and that he better move on before he attracted too much attention. He stepped off the island and strode across the lot to the storefront, which featured a shaded overhang in front of bulletin boards where flyers advertised used boats and marine services. He pretended to read the ads while he waited for his phone to beep. He didn't have long.

Acceptable. Same location. 10pm tomorrow.

Rayman shook his head. She sure did respond quickly to messages for someone who was supposed to be working a job. He always knew she barely did any work. That's the effect an extra twenty grand could have on people, he supposed. He pictured her sitting in his old office, running this lucrative side business while earning her regular paycheck. He looked up as someone exited the boating store, waited for him to pass by, and then resumed stabbing at his phone.

No. Not safe. Too many people saw me last time. I saw a cop, too. Different spot this time. I will send you coordinates. You will need to get to my location.

He thought of a location on the water, where she would need to take a boat to meet him. But then he stamped a foot in frustration as he realized how absurd that was. She'd just almost been killed on a boat, why would she volunteer to go out on the water again to meet him? No, he'd have to get her some other way. Best just to play ball for now. So he deleted what he had written and typed some more before hitting send:

Fine. Let's end this nonsense.

Rayman put his phone away and walked into the store.

31

Elliot Key, Biscayne Bay

Rayman and Flannigan dropped anchor along the far side of the bay, near a barrier island known as Elliot Key. A sandy cut ran through the isle that led to the open ocean side. Rayman explained that sawfish sometimes liked to sit on the sandy bottom right outside of the flow of water through the cut, which would often wash schools of baitfish through, making for easy pickings.

The area was also usually popular with boaters, and a sunny, hot day like today proved no exception. Dozens of power boats were rafted together in shallow water on the sand, people getting out and walking around, barbequing under umbrellas, many with drinks in hand.

The atmosphere was infectious to Flannigan, who reached into a cooler and opened a can of beer, which Rayman frowned at but said nothing about since he needed him. Flannigan offered him one, though, and Rayman shook his head, admonishing, "This isn't a pleasure trip, Bobby. We're supposed to be working."

Bobby gave him a concerned look that clearly said, *What the hell is wrong with you?* then shrugged and set the beer down in a drink holder. "Hey, third trip out to catch one of those damn monsters in two days? Forgive me if I don't want something to calm my nerves a little. I thought we were doing pretty good so far."

Rayman went back to his binoculars and scanning the coastline for activity, both human and animal. "I'm not telling you what to do. I just don't want one."

Flannigan said nothing, but opened a bucket of chum and peered inside, sniffing the air over it with flared nostrils as though he were a wine connoisseur evaluating a fine vintage. "This is good stuff. This'll do just fine. But hey, listen..." He eyed the group of boaters not far away, a couple of kids playing in the water, adults frolicking and splashing, too.

"What?"

"You think we should chum here? There's a lot of people around. Could attract sharks."

Rayman looked out across the boats. "If there's one of those monster saws around here, we're doing them all a huge favor. Plus, the wash-through in the cut will take it away from the sandbar. So let's get to work."

Rayman moved to the helm and consulted the marine chart displayed on the GPS monitor. The water was relatively deep here and he was trying to get a read on the bottom profile, whether it was hard bottom, sand, reef or what. He analyzed the contours and blips for a minute and then adjusted the boat's position accordingly by moving at low speed. A current ran strong through the area near the cut, and he had Flannigan drop the anchor.

He surveyed the area, eyeing the boats that were not far away. He moved to the stern and helped Flannigan dole out the chum, tossing it into the current so that it would flow past them and away from the boaters. He thought about his contract with the City while he chummed; it was going well, and at a certain point, maybe a little too well. How many monster sawfish would the City be expecting? How would he know to keep looking for them? He was pretty sure that if he brought in one more (which would be the second one the City knew about since he released the actual second one caught to get Elisa), that the mayor would be satisfied with his work. The City would have concrete, tangible results to show the public, and Dr. Mason Rayman would once again be established as a reputable ichthyologist that anyone would be pleased to hire.

He nodded to himself as he slopped some more blood and guts over the side. This was it. If they caught another one, whenever that was. If he couldn't catch another, though…what then? He didn't like to think about that, and there wasn't much he could do about it at any rate. He supposed the city would terminate his contract at some point, and then—

"Mason? Look over there." Rayman had been spacing out and quickly followed Flannigan's pointing finger toward the cut, which was like a river of ocean through two narrow islands, the Biscayne Bay on one side, the open Atlantic on the other.

"Yeah." He directed his gaze to the spot and immediately saw what had excited his deckhand. A thick, sizable school of fish was churning the water to a white, splashy boil as they jumped out of the water. They were both well aware that when fish did that it usually meant they were attempting to evade predators. Seabirds dove into the fray as well, adding to the likelihood that many fish waited beneath the surface.

Rayman cracked a smile. "Some of those are pretty big fish, too. Mackerel."

Flannigan agreed, shoveling out the last of the chum in the bucket he held before ditching it in favor of a stout fishing rod. "Let's get some lines out." He had pre-rigged the large hook with bait—a raw, whole chicken—on the way out, and now had only to cast, which involved first letting out line and then simply hurling the chicken overboard as far as he could toward the chum line. Rayman followed suit, but using a live mackerel as bait for variety. They repeated the process and soon they had four lines in the water near the fish boil. The lines were weighted such that they would drop down to the sand, where the monster bottom dweller would be.

The two men settled in to wait, Flannigan nursing his beer while Rayman alternately monitored the electronics and scoped through the binoculars. Their baits were large so they didn't need to worry about hooking the regular game fish which would no doubt be in the area. They were after only the largest of targets. After ninety minutes had passed without any real action, Flannigan hauled in his baits to change them out for fresh ones. When he got the chicken aboard, he could see that it had been nibbled on by the smaller fish, but had obviously not yet attracted a huge saw. He changed out the baits and got the lines back in the water.

No sooner had the last of the new baits splashed into the sea than the marine radio erupted in frenetic chatter. "…big fish on the Elliot Key sandbar…attacking people…help!"

Rayman and Flannigan locked eyes for a moment, knowing. Then Rayman jumped to the helm.

"Pull the anchor."

32

Elliot Key

After motoring through the cut and heading a short distance north, the sandbar lay before them, clearly in pandemonium. Rayman was stunned at how quickly the situation had developed. What had been a peaceful scene mere minutes earlier where the greatest disturbance was loud music from a boat or perhaps the revving of an engine or hollering of children, had been transformed into a scene of complete bedlam.

Two boats lay overturned while two others raced directly through the sandbar at unsafe speeds. The radio was a constant stream of emergency related racket—people requesting assistance, shouting for help, asking about what was going on... Rayman was there to help in only one way, though. He watched the area, looking for the saw. When he watched the canvas Bimini top of a smaller boat suddenly ripped away, he focused his binoculars and stared through the circular patterns. White foamy water, something dark...he adjusted the fine focus knob...

There!

He swallowed hard as he recognized the teeth, the neat rows of special scales along the bladed instrument of death.

Sawfish. His sawfish.

But as he dropped the glasses and watched the fish through his naked eyes, he could plainly see that something wasn't quite right. Besides the fact that a monstrous fish was attacking boats and people on a crowded sandbar, that is. Something else. It was just too big. He recognized the largest boat on the sandbar, one he knew to be forty-two feet in length, and this fish, from tail to tip of saw, was easily longer than that. It had to be about sixty feet long overall, Rayman judged. Impossible. Yet there it was. And it was all his doing. He told himself, while listening to the screams of the injured and those stricken with panic and shock, that he was here to undo it, that he alone would save these people from their horrible fates. He was being paid to save them. Never mind that he had caused the problem in the first place. He was here to fix it, and that's all that mattered.

Time was of the essence now. He knew that with all the distress calls going out it wouldn't be long before emergency responders arrived on scene. If he wanted to be the one to take down this monster saw, he needed to act fast. He eyeballed the contours and layout of the sandbar and made a snap judgment that he could get closer to the behemoth without running aground or making things worse by hitting anybody or anything. "Let's go back to the nets for this one, Bobby. Get them ready."

While Rayman skirted the sandbar in the boat, heading toward the flopping sawfish which had just taken down a small boat, Flannigan sorted the nets so that they were ready for deployment, untangling them, figuring out which was the largest. He had the most uneasy feeling he'd ever had about fishing—about anything, for that matter—but he was already here, he was getting paid to do a job and he was going to do his best to get it done. By the time he finished readying the nets, he felt the boat slow and he looked up at the sandbar.

The sawfish swam over the sand about 100 feet from them. Rayman brought the boat over the shallow water of the sandbar, so shallow he had to tilt the motor up to avoid hitting the bottom. Flannigan watched the distance between them and the positively monstrous fish grow shorter by the second. Rayman's boat had a flat bottom and would be able to coast all the way to the huge saw. He grew nervous as he realized he was out of his league here, way out of his league. Yes, he'd helped catch the other two, but they had been smaller than this one, and he still felt like it had been mostly luck that something hadn't gone horribly wrong. *Third time's a charm.* Did that work for bad things as well? He wasn't sure, but he felt off about the whole thing.

"Mason, this thing is too *huge*! I don't see how these nets are going to be enough."

Rayman's gaze didn't waver from the stretch of water in front of them between the boat and the sawfish. His hands were steady on the controls as he replied. "Get one on the saw—it'll snag real easy. I'll get on the horn for more nets."

Rayman picked up his radio transmitter and broadcast to the other boaters. "I'm a licensed City of Miami contractor here to capture this sawfish. Help us by giving me your fishing nets—bait nets, cast nets-any type of large net you have, but not the little ones with the handles!"

Meanwhile, the boat the sawfish had disabled flipped completely over, its occupants having already escaped by jumping out and running through the knee-high water to another boat. A few radio messages started coming back saying that people had nets, but were afraid to get in the water to bring them to Rayman's boat.

Flannigan tossed a net, one that seemed pitifully small in the face of the marine monster, but his aim was true and it landed perfectly across the base of the saw.

"Nice shot! It stuck. That should slow him down a bit." Rayman watched as the mega-sawfish thrashed back and forth, wiggling madly as it attempted to work the netting loose, but to no avail. After a minute, it settled down on the sand, gills flaring. Flannigan got ready to throw another net but Rayman stopped him.

"I need you to go to that boat over there and pick up another net. I'll throw the rest of the ones we have."

Flannigan followed Rayman's point to see a nineteen-foot powerboat with a yellow canvas top, two men aboard standing on deck. "Can't they bring it over?"

"They said they didn't want to. Scared I guess." Rayman looked at the sawfish, still for now except for the occasional swish of its tail.

Flannigan whipped around to look at his temporary boss. "Can't say as I blame them, Mason. I don't really want to get in the water, either." The two men stared at one another from behind their sunglasses.

"I'll give you a bonus, Flannigan, okay? It's in the opposite direction from the saw—just walk right over there, get the net and walk right back here. Don't run and splash, just walk calmly and you'll be fine."

"This bonus better be good."

"It'll be worth your while, I guarantee it."

Flannigan gazed over at the monster one more time. It still maintained a position in one place, mostly sedate. "It looks down but definitely not out." He glanced over to the boat again. The distance looked short. Under normal circumstances, hopping out of a boat into two feet of water and walking across the sandy bottom to another boat maybe forty feet away was routine, but with a sixty-foot leviathan about the same distance on the other side of the boat, it made the mind balk. But Flannigan picked up his can of beer and drained the last of it. Then he crunched up the can, dropped it on deck and declared, "I'll do it."

Rayman patted him on the back. "That's the team spirit. I'll have these nets, plus I think there's one more in storage, ready by the time you get back."

"Don't forget about that bonus."

Flannigan eased over the side of the boat, hanging from it and gently easing his feet down to the water rather than jumping in, which would create a splash that might cause the big saw to break from its stupor.

"Spot that thing for me, Mason. If it does anything, I want to know about it so I can bust a move."

Rayman nodded. "I'm watching." Then he cupped his hands and yelled over to the other boat. "Coming over." One of the men on board waved in response.

Flannigan did his best to walk without his feet breaking the surface, so as to be silent. When he was halfway across to the other boat, he called back to Rayman, "What's it doing?"

"Just sitting there. You're fine, keep going."

Flannigan didn't look back, only kept plodding on and soon the men from the other boat were holding up the net for him to see as he approached. It was good size and quality, Flannigan could see, and he was now glad he'd opted to make the trip. He reached the vessel and called up to the two men, both middle-aged Hispanics wearing nothing but Speedos, gold chains and suntan oil.

"You mind if I step aboard for a minute?"

They waved him toward the swim step at the rear of the boat. "Permission granted!"

Flannigan stepped into the boat. He turned around and waved to Rayman, who returned the gesture.

"You want to get a look at that sea monster before walking back across, don't you?" one of the boaters asked. Flannigan nodded.

"Exactly."

"He's still lying there, same place," the other man added, holding up the net.

"Here it is. You just going to throw this on top of him or what?"

"We got one on him already. Hopefully this will tangle him up some more."

"Guy over there's hurt real bad," the other boater said, pointing. Flannigan shook his head. "We're doing what we can."

"Hey, you want a shot of rum before you go?"

A bottle of dark liquid was held up. Flannigan glanced back at Rayman, who was watching the saw. "Don't mind if I do." He grabbed the bottle and took a long pull directly from it while his hosts looked on, grinning. "Now you're ready!"

Flannigan thanked them and handed the bottle back. Then he grabbed the net, folded it over his shoulder, and stepped off the boat.

33

Flannigan was halfway back to Rayman's boat when he saw the splash. Beyond their boat to the right, where the sawfish was. *He's waking up.* He swore under his breath and picked up the pace, sloshing his feet quickly through the water, still not creating big splashes, but rippling the water now. *Almost there. What are you going to spend that bonus on?* Anything to take his mind off the horror waiting on the other side of the boat.

Then Rayman's voice, laden with urgency, sliced through his thoughts. "He's moving, Bobby. Step on it!" Flannigan increased his pace but apparently it wasn't enough, which really scared him, because Rayman kept yelling, "C'mon, Bobby, *move!*"

The net was dragging in the water, hitting his legs, slowing him down. He adjusted it and then started high-stepping through the ocean, splashing a lot, no doubt making a ton of noise for all sea creatures anywhere near the sandbar to hear.

"Bobby!"

I'm moving faster, aren't I? he wanted to shout, but he didn't have the energy, didn't want to do anything that would divert his focus from the life-or-death race he now faced. Then he saw the reason for Rayman's incessant encouragement. A humongous dark shape came *fast* around the stern of their boat, right toward him, its dorsal surface protruding from the water like a submarine hull.

Jesus.

He tossed the net from his shoulder and started to sprint, but his right foot snagged on the edge of the netting and down he went, face-planting hard into fourteen inches of water. He pushed off the bottom with his arms, wasting not a second, got to his feet and bolted again toward the boat. He couldn't help but look to the right at the fish, though, and was stunned by its rapid progress. It was almost to him. Out of the corner of his eye, he saw Rayman hurling a net on it, still hollering.

He wanted to say something to Rayman, he wasn't exactly sure what, just something to the effect of, *Hey here I come, help me, get the boat ready, pull me up—anything!*—but all that came out of his mouth was a guttural, garbled scream. Then the tip of the saw was lancing over his head, the end of it missing Flannigan but the middle of it catching him in the side of the face as the fish turned.

Bobby Flannigan was felled instantly, dropped to the sandy seafloor, face up, watching Rayman throw another net from the boat while the water turned red around him.

#

"Bobby!" Rayman threw the last net at his disposal on top of the writhing sawfish as it seemed to ingest Flannigan's body head first. But his arms and legs were perfectly still and limp. No way would a man be consumed without so much as a twitch while still alive. Then the giant saw regurgitated its meal partway, and Flannigan's lower half washed back out of the mouth for an instant before being sucked back inside the cavernous gullet.

The scene on the sandbar was even more chaotic now, with some boats racing out of control to leave the area, running aground, crashing into each other, while still others threw objects like lead fishing weights at the monster from the relative safety of their boats. One man fired a flare gun at the beast, missing his target and sending the flare to fizzle into the water not far from Rayman's boat. Rayman urged them stop, but the radio was useless now, nothing but a constant wall of indecipherable chatter as everyone talked at once as news passed from boat to boat.

His nets, meanwhile, were impeding the motion of the fish, but not enough. It could still move sufficiently to scarf down Flannigan, that was for sure. Rayman eyed the large net Flannigan had lost his life trying to acquire, now floating a few feet past the bloody remnants of his eaten body. Rayman wasn't about to get in the water, but he thought he could bring the boat close enough to snag it with a boat hook. He put the boat in gear and idled slowly to the net, which wasn't all that far from the big saw, but the monstrosity was preoccupied with its meal as well as already being slowed somewhat by the existing nets.

Rayman put his craft into neutral and coasted the remaining distance to the drifting fishing net. The saw was thrashing more now, and in wider circles, but he quickly thrust a long-handled pole with a hook on the end into the water and dragged the net to the boat. *Thanks, Bobby, this ought to do it.*

Quickly, he hauled it in and untangled it, gaining a sense of what he was working with. It was high quality, no rips, ready to go. *Good work, Bobby.* He was close to the fish but wanted to be even closer, so he got back behind the wheel and idled the boat as close as he dared to the sawfish. Then he took the net and climbed on top of his boat's roof—the T-top, as it was known—a hard top that provided both a sun shade and supported fishing rod holders, antenna and lights. This gave him an excellent vantage point from which to toss the net, but was also less stable. The rocking of the boat was much more pronounced this high up.

The other boaters began shouting at him now, some encouraging him, others telling him to stop, but he tuned it all out. This was going to work. He could feel it in his crazy-ass bones. He eyeballed the other nets fluttering from the sawfish's rostrum and dorsal fin, and thought that from here he could lay this big net over the entire head and pectoral fins, impeding its forward motion. In theory, anyway.

He wound up to throw, sort of like a baseball pitcher on the mound. He held part of the net bunched up in his left hand, including a rope that would allow him to hold onto it once it was thrown. Then he heaved the mass of netting forward with his right hand, sending the assemblage of tied rope spinning through the air. He had good form, and the net unfurled in mid-flight like a blooming flower.

It landed exactly where the fish expert had hoped, spreading across the base of the saw, completely over the head and part of the fins. *Don't drop the line...* He needed to be able to hold onto that net, and if he let go of the rope connected to it, he could lose it. But he held on long enough to see that the animal grew irritated with the new entrapment and started to thrash wildly. It flipped over like an alligator once, a vicious thrust that almost caused the rope to be ripped out of Rayman's hand. He held on at the expense of a severe rope burn, blood sluicing down his palm onto the roof of the boat to drip into the water. *Great...excite it some more, just what you need.*

All too aware that one more sudden jerk like the last one could send him pitching into the drink, into the very maw of madness which he himself had spawned, Rayman quickly tied the rope off to a cleat on the T-top. Then he jumped down to the deck and wasted no time in fortifying his tie-down job on the tethered saw, cleating it off onto two more positions, fore and aft.

"Got you now...is that you, old number six? My how you've grown!" he was shouting at the fish like a crazy man, and didn't really care except for that fact that if he were heard referring to it as "number six" by a witness that might come back to haunt him, so he made a mental note to stop that.

The daunting process of actually securing the fish to the boat was up next, and Rayman studied the situation before proceeding. He was considering bringing the boat nearly alongside the great sawfish to create more slack without engaging in a tug of war with the animal when his entire craft was jolted hard. Rayman was pitched over the side and landed on his backside, somehow breaking right into a backwards crabwalk to evade the swinging stern of his own boat as the mighty sawfish pulled on the ropes.

Terrified at being in the same water which had produced Flannigan's fate, and now seeing his boat about to be pulled away from him, Rayman shot to his feet and reached out for the swim step ladder. He grabbed it and held on for dear life. Even if he survived being stranded on the sandbar without a boat, by making into someone else's boat, he did not need the negative publicity of losing control of his vessel to one of the sawfish he was supposed to catch or drive away. But the beast was so unfathomably huge, so powerful, he could hardly believe that using his boat to try and catch it was a sane thing to do.

Yet here he was. Rayman climbed back aboard and immediately ended up on his ass again as the boat was pulled into motion. He was lucky not have hit his head on the transom. It was such a swift, violent motion that for a fleeting second he wondered if somehow his boat had been put into gear, but no...he crawled over to the steering console and pulled himself into the captain's chair. Though running, the motor was locked in neutral, out of gear. But he was moving along, there was no doubt about it and at a decent clip now, too.

Rayman got a solid grip on both the steering wheel and a mounted handhold and then looked off the bow at the sawfish. The monster fish was heading toward the edge of the sandbar, to deeper water, dragging its captor's boat with it. *I'm going for a Nantucket Sleigh Ride after all,* Rayman thought. His radio still exploded with near constant chatter, and he heard something punch through about incoming Coast Guard assistance, but had no idea how far out it was. Not that he was going to sit around and wait for help, anyway. Seeing the ocean bottom turn color from the white of the sandbar sand to the green of the deeper water beyond it made him snap into action.

He slowly put the motor into reverse gear to counteract the saw's forward motion. The first few seconds of this had no effect, the boat continuing to plow through the ocean, bow coming dangerously close to nose diving, the boat taking on water. Rayman glanced over the side and saw that he was off the sandbar now, in deeper water where the giant fish could get a bit deeper, making it harder to see.

Bastard's towing me out to sea. Finally, the engine reverse began to take effect on the saw's progress…but not in a good way. The boat began screwballing backwards and sharply to the right, canting precariously. Rayman moved to put the throttle back in neutral, and the rampaging fish started dragging the boat behind it once again. He turned around to look back at the sandbar, shocked to see how far away from it he was now.

It made for a bumpy ride, the boat's hull slamming hard into the sea with every wave. Now and then Rayman would try a "test" pull, to imagine what it would be like to actually pull the fish in on his own. On one of these, when the huge saw decided to yank back, the rogue ichthyologist ended up pinned against the boat's chrome railing, shin bruised, the knuckles of his right hand bleeding as he was crushed against the metal. He let go, giving up the small amount of rope he had won, allowing the cleat to bear the brunt of the force. He began to worry that even that would not hold, that the cleat itself would be ripped right out of his boat.

The sawfish kept heading out to sea, towing the boat. Rayman looked back to see if anyone had witnessed what happened and decided to follow him. He didn't see anyone, and he couldn't blame them. There were still a lot of injured people at the sandbar who required medical, and probably psychological, assistance. He could put out a radio call to specifically request that someone help him—tying the beast off to two boats instead of one would surely help, but most of these amateurs were dangerous enough on the water as it was, Rayman reflected. Did he really want to depend on one for something as critical and dangerous as this? He pictured tow boats banging into each other while being pulled by the saw and abandoned the idea of radioing for assistance.

He looked back to the massive biological engine now towing his boat deep into Biscayne Bay. Surely this thing will tire itself out after a while, right? But how long would that take? He could be in the Bahamas by then. He chuckled to himself as he imagined the hubbub that would stir up, landing in Nassau, stringing up the gigantic sawfish on the crowded seaport, thanking the good people of the Bahamas for their graciousness while proclaiming to the Mayor of Miami that Dr. Mason Rayman had once again delivered as promised.

Then his opponent made a sharp turn to the left that at once broke him from the daydream and nearly overturned the boat, forcing Rayman to rethink his strategy of allowing the fish to tire itself out. If he couldn't actively take control of the situation, it was just a matter of time before the fish made some erratic move that would sink him. He didn't even want to dwell on the details of what would happen to him in that scenario, alone, miles from land with a sixty-foot, sword-bearing predator who just got dropped a snack after a lot of hard work...

He didn't have more nets, and had maybe one or two spare ropes. No guns, since he'd never thought about shooting a fish with a gun. Not even a flare gun, only the required hand flares. He had small knives for cutting bait, and a scuba diving knife. Hardly weapons worth mentioning against such a primal monstrosity. So what did he have? He looked all around the boat while he considered this. A gaff—the long pole with a stout, curved hook on one end used for snagging fish into the boat after they were reeled to the side. He prayed he never got close enough to the big saw to be able to use it.

He wiped a jet of water from his face that pelted him over the windshield. As he did, his gaze roved over the dashboard. He had that, didn't he? The boat. He tightened his grip on the throttle and the wheel as the revelation hit him. *The boat is your only weapon against this beast. Use it.*

He traced the ropes back from the sawfish to the boat. One of them was tied to the side of the vessel, and it was causing him to be towed at an angle, making things very unstable. He needed to move that rope to the front of the boat so he could be on a straight path. Once that was done, he could then accelerate toward the saw with some control.

Rayman accelerated as fast as he dared in order to gain some slack in the rope so that he could untie it. With the first burst of speed, the sawfish matched it, but he tried again and that time he closed the distance between him and his quarry. He then went to work on the line, untying it from the cleat and running it up to the bow of the boat to re-tie it there.

That done, he moved back to the steering wheel. Gripped the throttle and jammed it all the way forward. He was closing in on the sawfish.

34

Rayman felt the boat rise out of the water as it gained speed, hydroplaning over the ocean's surface. Exactly what he wanted. The gargantuan sawfish, no longer feeling tension on the ropes tethering it to the boat, turned toward the vessel while rising to the surface. Rayman knew what he had to do.

With small adjustments of the wheel born of experience, he turned the craft slightly to the left. It was all too easy to overshoot the turn and then have to correct, and he didn't have time for that. Salt spray peppered his glasses but he didn't dare lift a hand to wipe them off.

C'mon, you bastard. Stay up here with me. Rayman needed the fish at the surface to be able to hit it with the boat. If he could knock it senseless with the boat itself, great; cut it up with the prop, that would be fine, too. Either way, so long as he killed it or weakened it enough to be able to take it in.

But as he neared the monster-sized animal, he was dismayed to see it deftly disappear into the depths with a powerful slashing motion of its tail. It could only go so far because of the ropes, but it was deep enough to get underneath the bottom of the stalking vessel. Rayman would have to make another pass. Circled around again, throwing a tall sheet of spray out to the side of his boat. Lined up with where he knew the sawfish was and steadied his approach.

They say luck favors the prepared, and while Rayman would be the first to admit he got lucky when the giant sawfish loomed its fat head just above the ocean's surface, he had also put himself in that place, right there, right then. The prow of the boat collided with the side of the sawfish's head, impacting the soft gill silts as well as part of the top of the head. As for Rayman, he basically experienced the same kind of trauma one could expect who drove their car into a brick wall at thirty miles per hour. Not deadly force, but certainly not fun, and the marine biologist did not come away from it unscathed. He felt his chest glance off the steering wheel and then his nose cracked against the windshield. Even so, once he saw that fish laying stunned on the surface, he had a big smile on his face for the blood to run down.

We got him, Bobby, we got him!

Yet as Rayman idled up to the dazed monster, it quickly became all too clear that his moment of triumph might be short-lived indeed. The big saw was already beginning to stir, to splash at the water with its tail and saw. Apparently, whatever injuries it had sustained in the collision had not been all that serious. The window to take advantage of the situation was already closing fast.

Rayman idled the boat right up alongside the fish. He saw that all but one of his ropes was still attached to the beast. He began hauling them in, taking up the slack. If he could lash it alongside the boat as he did with the other two saws, he would then be able to transport it, be able to show off his mega-catch to the world. Trouble was, this one was three times as long as his boat, but if he motored slowly, he thought he might be able to get it back to the marina.

He proceeded to tie the monster animal down to the side of the boat with all available lines, ropes and netting. When he was done, he stepped back and appraised his work. Satisfied it was up to par, that it could hold the mind-bogglingly large creature even though his craft now listed precariously to one side, he then got behind the wheel again and fired up the engine. Immediately, he could feel the drag on his conquest in the water. He pushed the throttle almost halfway up, which should have sent his boat flying across the waves, but instead he was barely slogging through the water.

Turning into the direction in which the boat leaned was problematic, since it pushed water over the side into the boat. This meant that instead of turning directly toward shore, he would have to circle around the long way and then straighten out, which was fine. As long as he got there, he was in no particular hurry. But as he arced through the long turn, he began to have doubts that he would make it, even at a very slow speed. To make matters worse, the captured saw started exhibiting signs of life, its body whumping against the hull, booming like a bass drum. Were this fish to awake fully, Rayman wasn't certain that the rig he had fashioned for it would hold. Dead or at least inert—maybe. But alive and kicking? He didn't like the odds on that, not one bit.

He eyed his radio, now alive with the chatter of the wounded seeking help, the stranded looking for a ride off the sandbar. Again, he could request assistance himself to have another boat to work with, but that would take some of the limelight away from him, wouldn't it? Not only that, but it would put someone else at risk. He'd already gotten Bobby killed. At a certain point, the collateral damage would outweigh the good he was going. He made the decision to go it alone, for better or worse.

He motored on, the mainland coast seeming impossibly far away. He grew impatient and pushed the throttle back, coaxing more speed out of the overloaded boat. He enjoyed this increase in velocity for about four minutes until he saw water flooding over the side of the boat the sawfish was on. He eased up on the throttle, slowing the craft back to less than it was before. This wasn't going to work, that's all there was to it. He flipped on the pump to bail out the water. He wasn't sinking yet, but it was clear that he would have to cut the fish loose to make it back to the mainland. He had no doubt the big saw would take him down if he tried to make it all that way.

So what to do? He stood at the console and began turning 360 degrees to assess his situation. The mainland was pretty far away, farther than he thought he could get…the sandbar and unpopulated barrier island lay back in the direction from which he came…then there was straight out to sea all the way to the Bahamas and beyond…and…to the north, he saw a couple of structures protruding from the bay. Oil rigs? No, he knew there were no rigs here. Then he realized he knew what they were, he'd seen them before. What was that place? He had been there a couple of times, long ago, now.

Stiltsville. His eyes took on a new light as the name bounced around his brain.

An abandoned cluster of houses built…he wasn't sure how long ago, built a long time ago, probably close to a hundred years. Over the decades, hurricanes had claimed most of them but a handful were still standing. During the prohibition era, they used to serve as floating clubs, but nowadays they were owned by the National Park Service, listed on the National Register of Historic Places and closed to visitors except by special permit. No one lived on site and he was sure it was infrequently visited even by the park service.

He picked up his binoculars and stared at the nearest of the water houses while the great saw thrummed into the side of his boat, again and again. He focused on the wooden stilt house. It was doubtful he'd find any help there—he saw no signs of human activity, no boats, nothing—but he might be able to help himself there. It would give him a chance to get out of the water, for one thing, if his boat sank under the weight of this beastly creature.

Mind made up, Rayman put his vessel back into slow speed ahead and pointed the prow at the weathered wooden structure jutting up from the shallow flats.

35

Stiltsville

The sawfish was definitely waking up now. Rayman feared it would puncture the side of his boat with its insistent thrashing. Fortunately, he had arrived at the nearest of the four houses he had seen from a distance. Wooden posts held the house perhaps fifteen feet above the surface of the water. He spotted a ladder and a small dock underneath the structure and motored toward it at idle speed.

He asked himself if he was giving up, giving himself a way out, to just climb up into the house and let the big saw destroy his boat and escape. Perhaps he had met his match, after all. But as he glided beneath the house amid the framework of wooden support poles, a new idea came to him.

There was a lot of raw material to work with here. Poles, struts, a dock, various steel cables and ropes left behind. Perhaps he could use it, combined with what he had on the boat, to somehow tie the sawfish up here? If he could secure the animal here somehow, then he could take a picture to prove he had it, get back to land on his boat by himself and request assistance from the City. He'd still get the credit for capturing it, and it would actually be brought back to the marina for everyone to see.

The sawfish had other plans, though. When Rayman heard the sound of canvas tearing, he looked up to see the sun shade on his boat being shredded by the broad saw. He ducked behind the console just in time to avoid being decapitated. Knowing the oversized fish was about to break itself free, Rayman whirled into motion. Fortunately, the tail was still well wrapped; it was the head that needed to be secured the most. He threw on a pair of fishing gloves, no doubt not nearly heavy-duty enough for the task, but all he had. He was going to have to improvise here. He would deal with the head first since if that broke loose, he wouldn't be able to carry out the next part of his plan.

He rummaged through his fishing gear and picked up his largest hook, one he used for shark fishing. Any hook would be woefully small compared to a creature like this, but it was a good foot long at the shank, six inches across from the barb to the shank, and, as luck would have it—he had four of them. He rummaged through his spare tackle supplies until he found what he was looking for: heavy braided line, thin rope, really, that he also used for catching sharks. He added to this his heaviest gauge wire leaders—the run of wire closest to the hook that would feel the teeth of the fish. He rigged four, one for each hook, all the while praying that the big saw wouldn't rip free from its jury-rigged bindings.

When at last he had the rigs ready, he again took stock of the situation with respect to his extremely dangerous quarry. He needed to get that head under control, and soon, or it would break free. His only saving grace was that the tail was still mostly immobilized. *Stop putting it off and go for it*, he told himself.

He walked around the opposite rail of the boat from the saw, up to the small bow deck, which was a good fishing platform. From there, he stood and looked down on the sawfish's mighty, mighty head, the saw itself stretching far past the boat, but the actual mouth right beneath the boat's prow.

He didn't even want to take the time to rig the line onto a reel. His plan was to hook it by hand and then tie it off somewhere, probably to the boat. He was pretty sure that if he got all four hooks into the mouth he would be able to contain the creature's movements, but only time would tell. Looking up, he found that he had to be careful of the rafters that he was nearly head high with. He floated beneath the structure, with the floor of the house above his head. A rectangular hole was cut in the center of it, with a ladder leading up. Confident he could use these rafters to tie the lines off to, should he manage to hook the sawfish, Rayman set about hooking the beast.

Eye on the unforgiving saw blade, he moved to the broad base of the bow. He had the thick fishing line wrapped on a plastic spool held in his left hand, the huge hook dangling from a foot of line in his right. He compensated for the rocking of the boat, mostly due to the humongous fish beating its head into it and not the water, which was calm beneath the house. *C'mon, big guy, let me see that pretty mouth...open up...*

The sawfish rolled to its right to the extent its bonds allowed, exposing the head, and Rayman tossed his hook. He tensed as it dropped into the yawning jaws of the tethered beast, knowing he would have to set that hook lest the animal spit it out. When the saw's mouth closed and he could no longer see the hook, Rayman yanked hard on the line and was pleased to feel resistance immediately. The big hook had dug somewhere into the creature's gullet. This caused the sawfish to struggle, and Rayman carefully planted his feet for maximum stability as he pulled on the line again in the same direction. Confident the hook was set, he looked for a place to tie off the line so he would be free to work with another hook-and-line rig.

He eyed the multitude of wooden rafters above his head. It would be nice to get this thing off of the boat, to tie if off to something steady and come back for it with a bigger boat and some more help. He could barely touch one of the beams while standing with his arms outstretched. He didn't have a stepladder on board, so he got a five gallon bucket and turned it upside down on deck beneath the rafter. Balancing on that, he was able to loop the fishing line several times around the beam and then tie it off.

He turned his attention back to the sawfish, which showed a lot of signs of life. The single hook and line, combined with the other ropes, though, was restricting its movement some. Rayman grabbed another hook and tried again. He was able to repeat the process with a lot of failed attempts and dogged persistence, and after an hour or so, he had four fish hooks embedded in the monster's mouth and tied off to different support beams above.

Next were the ropes. One by one, he untilled them from the boat and fastened them instead to the underside of the house. It was far from easy and he sustained many minor cuts and bruises in the process, but he was tough in a stubborn, persistent kind of way and sometime later, he emerged through a haze of concentrated effort and pain to see a sixty-foot long fish effectively held captive in the water beneath the stilt house.

He was pleased with his work and impressed with himself, but at the same time had the discipline not to dwell on this milestone. He was about to leave when he spotted the ladder leading up to the house itself. He could only reach so high with his bucket stepstool, and so was limited in the beams he could use to tie off the beast. Seeing the ladder made him want to do an even better job, to hoist a rope over one of the higher level beams to more evenly distribute the load. The fish was powerful enough that, left here overnight, could possibly even snap the rafters, since only two main ones were bearing the brunt of the fish's applied force when it thrust its massive body downward to try to dive and escape.

Rayman moved his boat alongside the ladder, tied it off, and then ascended the rungs. They were weathered and cracked—years of salt air having taken their toll—and the lower ones were covered with barnacles and oysters because they were submerged at high tide. One of them was brittle and cracked under his weight but he moved off of it quickly enough, scampering up to the top, where he stepped onto an open air porch of sorts.

Three sides of the rectangular space were open to the air with commanding ocean views, while a closed door on one side led into the house itself. Looking down on the sawfish, Rayman tensed as he realized were he to fall from here, he'd land right on the toothed saw as it raged back and forth. He stepped back from the edge. Curiosity got the better of him and he walked to the door. He didn't bother knocking since he didn't see how anyone could be here—no boat was tied up, and if someone was here, surely they would have emerged upon hearing a boat approach. So he tried the handle, and to his surprise it was not locked.

He pushed the door open a little, until the wind took it and blew it back against the inside wall, as if beckoning him in. He called out, "Hello," in case someone was inside, but as expected he got no response. From the doorway, he could see through a short entrance hall which led into a wider space. He walked in and entered a living room, furnished simply with furniture unable to completely withstand the humid air over the years—a couch, a low table, and a bar. The floor was bare wood. To the right was a kitchen area, minus plumbing—no appliances or sink. He walked down another short hall to the left and found a small bedroom with a twin bed, a framed poster of a sailboat on the waves, and a nightstand.

Curiosity satisfied, Rayman exited the house and stood once again over the cutout in the elevated porch. The sawfish was as he had left it, swinging that perilous rostrum like a whipsaw while held in place. He very carefully backed down the ladder, testing each rung to be sure it would hold his weight before removing his grip on the upper rungs. Upon reaching the bottom, he jumped onto his boat and marked his position in his GPS so that he could easily return without having to guess which of the Stiltsville houses it was.

He untied the boat from the ladder and headed for shore.

36

Florida University, 6:55pm

Dr. Mason Rayman, once an esteemed member of the faculty at the very university on whose grounds he now found himself, squatted low in the bushes near the planned drop site. He was here almost three hours early by design, and a rather elaborate design at that. After sleeping in to recuperate from the previous day on the water wrestling the giant saw, he had devised a plan that involved making the drop so that he would see the bitch when she came to pick up the cash.

On the first drop, he suspected that she arrived early and hid somewhere to observe him leaving the cash. Because of this, if he wanted to catch her unawares, he needed to arrive even before she would get here. To be on the safe side, he opted to make it three hours early. He doubted she would have the stamina and fortitude to wait longer than that, not to mention that it was risky; the longer one hid around in the foliage, the greater the chance of being seen and questioned.

So here he was, lying deep inside a miniature bamboo garden situated diagonally across from the bench with the plaque and the clump of average-looking green bushes that served as the drop point. He was no professional spy, but he made sure to silence his phone and move as little as possible while lying in wait. He'd even worn a greenish outfit to help him blend in.

These steps were far from the height of his preparations, though. Parked nearby, inside a square of orange safety cones, was an electric work cart. The school used a large fleet of them as maintenance vehicles, so they were a common sight. This was not one of the little ones with an open back, but a somewhat less common full-size cart with a steel cabinet on the rear bed, like a micro-truck, used for hauling heavier supplies or expensive equipment that needed to be locked up when the vehicle was left unattended. Rayman knew from experience, having worked here, that the carts not in use during the day were left in a designated parking area behind a maintenance building, unattended unless someone happened to be getting in or out of one. He had simply walked up to one, got inside, pressed the button to start it, and drove it away down one of the many narrow, paved paths that criss-crossed the university grounds. He parked it there near the drop site, got out, and checked that the back would open. It did, and inside he found the orange cones that he set around it to make it look as though it was left here on purpose. After waiting a couple of minutes to be sure he wouldn't be observed, he slinked into the bushes.

Sure, there was a chance someone from maintenance would see it and take it, but he figured the odds were low, since someone could have used it for a service call at any number of nearby buildings and therefore be inside. He eyeballed the drop zone now, a little flustered that a guy parked his fat ass on the bench to make a phone call. *You're messing up a huge cash drop!* But then the dude started yelling into the phone, calling someone a liar, something about he was there, she wasn't...and then he got up from the bench and stalked off. The joys of college relationships, Rayman thought. Then he shifted positions to get more comfortable, moved a stone out from under his hip, unwrapped a banana-flavored Powerbar and settled in to wait.

#

Two hours later

Rayman had always thought of himself as a patient man, but being hunkered down in a shroud of landscaped greenery for hours was almost too much to bear. At once it was tedious, uncomfortable, demanding and risky. He was beginning to doubt he'd be able to tolerate another hour here, at least in an effective, watchful state, when the sound of soft footfalls walking on concrete reached his ears.

He tensed, directing his gaze to the widest expanse of walkway within his somewhat limited field of view. He saw the shoes first—brown loafers below dark brown slacks, definitely belonging to a female, and older, not a student. Work attire. He propped himself up a little higher on an elbow in order to see the upper half of her... Beige blouse, shoulder-length, wavy auburn hair....

Well, well, well, if it isn't Elisa Gonzales out for a little evening stroll on campus... Working late today, are we sweetie? Putting in that extra effort....good for you.

As she approached the bench, Rayman held his breath and watched as she slowed down a bit and turned her head to the right to look into the bushes behind the bench—exactly where the drop was last time. Then she stopped and actually sat on the bench—staring for a heart stopping moment directly into the foliage in which Rayman hid—but then her head turned and she focused once more on the drop zone.

She's scoping it out.

She looked into the bushes but then quickly away, shifting her gaze upward to the windows of the surrounding buildings, including Dr. Asura's lab. He wondered if she did this little ritual last time, too—got here an hour early so that she could watch for his arrival, check to make sure he didn't bring any cops with him, or any accomplices, or weapons. But now came the good part, Rayman thought. She obviously couldn't stay where she was for too much longer without fear of him seeing her. How could she know, after all, that he might not arrive a little early as well to recon the site, in order to feel comfortable dropping off the cash?

She couldn't, of course, which was why it was no surprise when she got up and walked over to the shrubs that made up the drop zone. He watched her stoop down and look under there. He supposed she was checking to see if he made the drop early. Couldn't blame her. Why sit around for another hour if the cash was already there? But it wasn't, and when she saw that, she walked over to the cart, the back of which was open, and peered inside. Rayman knew it to be empty. When she verified this for herself, she faced toward one of the buildings, trying to appear as though she were casually standing around, but Rayman knew she was checking out the windows to make sure no one was watching.

Rayman checked the windows, too, because the last thing he wanted was for anyone to see what he was about to do next. Doing his best not to snap any twigs or kick any rocks, he slid out from his hidey-hole in the bushes and rose to his feet. He was not wearing a disguise of any kind, other than a ball cap to hide his face a little bit, but she would recognize him instantly were she to look in his direction.

A quick snap of the head to the right and then left. No one else around. Then he started to move, gliding across the grass toward Elisa Gonzales. She turned her head to the right, but still faced away from him. Rayman's hands slipped into the front right pocket of his jeans and withdrew a zip tie and a bandana. He was about to cross a line from which there would be no going back, but she had left him no choice.

Rayman crept up on the unsuspecting blackmailer, his sneakered feet treading ever so lightly on the grass. When he was two feet away, he sprung, wrapping both arms around her shoulders in a smothering bear hug. He flung her and the work bag she held around in a circular motion, releasing her when she was even with the open storage locker of the cart. He shoved her inside, where she managed to place her bag between her head and the wall when she bashed into it. Knowing he would have to end this very soon or deal with a screaming Gonzales, Rayman leapt into the cart and pulled the door shut behind him.

Sure enough, Gonzales began to caterwaul, frightened with good reason for her very life.

"Quiet!" Rayman hissed. "I'm not going to hurt you." But this had absolutely zero effect on her. He came at her with the bandana in one hand. It was soaked with something, she could smell it.

"What is that? Something you stole from the lab! Don't kill me! Don't—" And then Rayman pounced on her, smothering her mouth and nose with the bandana, and she went limp. Wasting no time, Rayman bound her hands behind her back with the zip tie and lay her on the floor of the locker. Then he cracked open the door, peering out to see if anyone was nearby. Detecting no one, he exited the cart and closed the door. He had no way to lock it, planning instead to transport her to his rented van (no way could he risk taking his flashy Ferrari before she woke up).

Rayman got into the cart and drove toward the parking lot where he'd left his rental van.

37

Stiltsville, three hours later

Rayman slowed his boat to a stop and idled up to the same house he had visited yesterday. While he had seen some boats nearer to land, out here he was the only visitor once again. Which was definitely a good thing for him because in the seat next to him was Elisa Gonzales, hands still zip tied behind her back but now fully conscious and awake, if a bit groggy. He reached over and pulled the gag from her mouth, knowing there was no one to hear her scream.

"What are we doing here?" she demanded. Rather than answer, Rayman put on a show of intense concentration while he idled the boat beneath the structure.

"People will know it was you if you kill me out here! Let me go, Rayman. You're crazy as a loon!"

He glided the boat up to the ladder and tied up as before while Elisa turned around in the seat, watching his every move. Then Rayman moved back to the console and shut the engine off. In the silence that followed, they were able to hear the splashing. Both of them looked over to see the sawfish, still restrained in Rayman's bonds. Elisa eyed it with terror, afraid of what it meant for her, while Rayman saw it with relief, no longer having to wonder if it would still be here at all, much less here alive, after leaving it overnight.

But there it was, and still thrashing. Rayman guessed that it must have went dormant much of the time to preserve its energy, but that hearing the boat approach may have caused it to panic. That panic also extended in a cascade to Elisa—Rayman's other captive—whose eyes widened while she stared at the fish in horror.

"What's going on here, Dr. Rayman? I don't know what you're up to, but I want you to let me go right now, do you hear me? Let's forget any of this ever happened. All deals are off. Look—look what I—"

He reached over and tied the gag (a bandana, but not soaked with drugs) back into place around her mouth. "Sorry, Elisa, I can see I've made a mistake giving you a little freedom, so until you can learn that its don't speak unless spoken to, I'm going to have to leave this on."

Her muffled grunts in response may have been difficult to make out, but their overall meaning left no room for doubt. He pointed up the ladder. "Let's go inside for a while, shall we? We've got the place all to ourselves."

She grunted something in the negative and Rayman made a clucking sound while he wagged a finger in front of her face. "Would you rather stay in the boat? Just you and our friend here to keep you company?" He looked over at the sawfish. Its oversized rostrum, to Rayman, looked like it was even longer than yesterday. To Elisa, it was nothing but a hideous monster. She stared up at the cutout entrance to the house's porch and nodded her assent.

Rayman beamed. "Excellent! Here's the fun part: You won't be able to climb the ladder without using your hands, and I'm afraid you're a bit on the heavy side for me to lug all the way up there. We sure wouldn't want me to lose my balance on the way up so that both of us plunge into the water with our friend, here, now would we?"

Elisa glared at him in return while presenting her bound wrists. Rayman gripped her hard by the left bicep and used a bait knife to snap the zip tie. "Don't try anything silly, dear, unless you want it to be the last thing you do."

He marched her to the front of the boat, which was even with the ladder. "Ladies first."

She looked up but hesitated to start climbing, unsure of where it led.

"It goes up to a porch. Great view, you'll love it. Get on with it," Rayman said while slinging a coil of rope over one shoulder.

Elisa, still dressed in work attire with her work bag slung over her shoulders, gingerly climbed up the ladder. She tested each and every placement, slipping a couple of times, cursing often from behind the gag.

"Don't worry, I'm not enjoying the view," Rayman taunted, looking up at her while she climbed. "A little too much junk in the trunk."

He remained on the boat, concerned that she could deliberately fall on him to knock him off the ladder if he followed too closely behind. On the other hand, it made him nervous to let her get too far ahead of him, too. Her hands were untied, and so when she reached the top, she could hide inside the house. He didn't peg her for a fighter, but when a person had their back against the wall, there was no telling what they were capable of.

He split the difference of these two fears and started up the ladder when Elisa was halfway up. He climbed quietly, preferring she not know exactly where he was. He watched her reach the top and pause while she looked around, taking in her new surroundings while Rayman continued to climb. Then she scurried over the edge and was lost from sight. He climbed faster, his hand slipping off a rung once in his haste, but he recovered and soon was at the porch.

As he stuck his head through the opening, he felt a platform shoe smash into the side of his head.

Rayman was knocked to the left, off the ladder, but managed to grasp the edge of the porch with his left hand, a move that saved him from falling. He quickly added his right hand to the raw plywood, not caring about a nasty splinter that wedged deep into the side of his hand. His feet continued in motion away from the ladder and out over the water while his hands hung on. He could hear Elisa's shoes stomping on the wood above him as she moved to the other side of the opening.

He let his feet swing back until they caught on the rungs. He saw her shoe coming down fast on his hands and pushed off the edge of the platform toward the ladder. Her foot slammed the wood a split second after his hands had been there, and then he free-fell for about a second until his fingers came into contact with the ladder. He clutched, grabbed, hugged it until he somehow arrested his downward motion.

Then he bulled his way up the ladder, determined to get up there no matter what. He had thrown half of his upper body over the edge onto the porch when Elisa jumped on his back. She jammed the side of his face into the wood with one foot while dropping a knee hard into the small of his back. Rayman grunted in pain and rolled quickly to his left. The move knocked Elisa off balance just enough to let him reach up and grab one of her wrists. He yanked hard and she went sprawling toward the edge of the platform.

Rayman used the opportunity to get to his feet. He was in pain all over, bleeding from multiple cuts on his face and hands, but he knew this was his chance to regain the upper hand and so he acted immediately, forcing his battered body into motion once again. He bolted over to Elisa, whose eyes widened in abject fear with his rapid but uneven, dog-like approach.

She was lying on her back, propped up on her elbows, her work bag strapped across her chest like some kind of impromptu armor. She sat up and put her two hands up in self-defense as Rayman approached, but he descended on her in a fury, batting them away. She was still gagged, saying something unintelligible as Rayman shoved her toward the edge of the platform with one knee while keeping her down with his hands.

He kept pushing her until her upper body was over the wooden precipice. She twisted over to avoid injuring her back as she was bent over backwards. Rayman held her legs in place while her head, shoulders and torso dangled over the edge. She was no longer attempting to get words across, whether because of the gag or because a scream was all she could muster. But Rayman had words for both of them. He crawled up onto her lower legs and sat there, pinning her in place while her head dangled precariously over the side.

"What's that? I can't quite understand you. Oh, you want me to let you go. Very well, then." He started to get up and she yelped in fear, realizing that his weight was keeping her from sliding off into the ocean below. He stopped. "What's that? Right, I'm sure you want it all to be over now. You didn't want it to be over when you were blackmailing me, though, did you? You just wanted more and more money. I doubt this would have been the last time, either, would it? A month or so later, sometime when you're feeling like you need a little boost, you'd call me again, wouldn't you?" She was shaking her head no but he ignored her.

Looking down, he spotted the ginormous saw swinging back and forth as the beast tried to break its bonds. To and fro the organic blade swung like a machine, inches above the water. Then he took the rope he'd carried over his shoulder and tied Elisa's feet together with one end. "I want you to get a close-up look at my life's work—it's important to me, but I suppose to you it was nothing but another grant to process, a meal ticket for you, just as you came to see me as a meal ticket through your blackmail."

He paused while she shook her head rapidly back and forth, and then continued. "Now you will be the meal ticket, quite literally, for my friend down there."

He kicked her legs over with his foot and braced himself against the sudden pull on the rope. Elisa shrieked as she plummeted, not knowing what to expect, how far she might fall, but Rayman arrested her fall with the rope, controlling her descent. She hung there upside down, slowly twirling at the end of the line, her bag now dangling by the strap below her head.

"This might not be painless, but I promise you it will be quick," Rayman said, while the sawfish sliced through the water and air with its natural born weapon, a deadly pendulum, like some sort of eternal motion machine. Elisa cried wordlessly, legs tied and gagged. Her arms were free and as she got lower to the water she began trying to pull herself up in order to put two hands on the rope. But it was exhausting, she wasn't thinking clearly, and the image of that ungodly monstrosity waiting for her with a biological scythe was completely unhinging her.

Swish...swish... She was only about ten feet above the toothy blade. Rayman was lowering her right onto it so that it would swing into her head when she got low enough. Probably one hit would kill her, two at the most. Elisa became quiet as it dawned on her that unless she did something in the next handful of seconds, she would be decapitated by Rayman's lab experiment gone wild.

She began to undulate her body so that she set herself into a swinging motion. Rather than allow herself to be lowered straight down, she caused the rope to swing out and back, which made it a little harder for Rayman to handle. She heard the stomp of his shoe on the plywood as he repositioned his feet to adjust. Rayman looped the rope over a crossbar so that it had some support and was not held only by his hands.

"Accept your fate, Elisa. You're only delaying the inevitable."

She tried the sit-up motion again, arms reaching for the rope as she bent at the waist. Each time she missed, she had to start all over again, and with a little less energy. She was being splashed by the killer fish now, the tooth-studded bill passing through her dangling long hair, ripping some of it out. This was it. In the back of her mind, she knew there was no guarantee Rayman would lower her nice and easy to the fish, either. He could drop her at any time, either by accident or by design. All of these factors proved too much for her to take, and she redoubled her efforts to do something to change the situation.

Unable to lift herself up to grab the rope, she continued to swing, to increase the rope's arc. She was passing from below the porch entrance, over the saw, toward the boat.

"You're almost there!" Rayman called down. "Say goodbye."

She watched the bow rail of Rayman's boat draw near in her upside down field of vision. She outstretched her right arm and hand...almost...curled her fingertips and felt them brush over the cool stainless steel before slipping away, and then she was falling back again, passing over the saw. She pulled her head up to miss the teeth, barely able to do so. Blocked out Rayman's disgusting voice, his vile taunts, and told herself that she would get one more pass at it, as long as the fish didn't get her. One more chance.

She reached the apex of her arc and started to swing back. The giant saw sword swung toward her, and she strained her neck muscles to raise her head out enough to be missed by the fishy slasher. Seconds later, she was still thinking as the boat came closer, so she knew she had avoided the killer saw. She reached out a hand again in anticipation of grabbing the boat. The metal gleamed. She clutched at it, rejoicing when she felt her fingers curl around its smooth diameter.

Elisa tightened her fist around the metal bar, willing every fiber of her being not to loosen that grip. She heard Rayman barking something at her and blocked it out, concentrating only on adding her other hand to the railing. She found it and locked on. She felt the resistance on the rope right away. Both of her hands were curled around the boat railing while her feet slanted skyward at an angle, pulled by the rope that Rayman controlled. Just below her, the big saw attempted to get out of its own predicament, the massive saw blade still slashing back and forth.

She felt Rayman tugging hard on the line, and as her arms stretched to the breaking point, every muscle burning like a beach bonfire, she thought this must be what it's like to be on one of those medieval torture racks, pulled apart limb by limb. She wondered for a fleeting moment if she suddenly let go of the boat, if it would throw Rayman off balance enough to drop the rope, but she didn't give that scenario much hope.

She didn't know what she was going to do, but she needed real force, power…and then her eye caught the yellow keychain float in the console of the boat, directly below the railing she clutched. It was attached to the boat key, which was still in the engine ignition. Rayman had left the motor on, idling in neutral, probably so he could make a quick getaway after he murdered her.

She had observed him more on the way out here than he might have guessed. She mentally flashed on him now, putting the boat into gear, his hand wrapping around the gear shifter and shoving it forward, causing the boat to leap forward. *That's it…do it…*

"…see you in hell with Satan's little goldfish here…" Rayman blathered on.

And then Elisa's right hand darted out from the railing and reached for the gear shift. She stretched more than she thought humanly possible until she could wrap her hand around the shifter. She couldn't quite make it, her hand touching the top of the stick nut not able to grip it before falling away. The big saw swished beneath her, waiting for her to fail and fall, to be cut to pink ribbons of fish food and human chum.

But she tried again and this time, instead of grabbing the shifter, she balled up her fist and bashed it. The lever was rammed forward and the boat suddenly surged out of the water, its engine suddenly ordered to rev at wide open throttle while tethered to the house ladder.

One and a half tons of forward-moving vehicle reached the end of its rope, with Elisa still holding onto to the boat rail. She was feeling the pain of being pulled apart when she heard the sharp *crack* of wood snapping, followed shortly by the *plunk* of it splashing into the water somewhere behind her. Then suddenly the pain—not all of it, but the worst of it, at least—ceased to exist. As if a huge force had just been lifted from her.

Elisa held onto the boat's rail for dear life while behind her, the entire century-old house began to topple. Were it not for the fact that the boat ran headlong into an outer support piling, she would have been dragged out into the bay. But it hit the pole and stopped there long enough for her to swing a leg up into the boat and pull herself in. She shut the engine off and turned around to watch the house fall.

She was far enough away to not be hit by the falling debris. The porch, ladder, and house collapsed and fell mostly straight down, on top of the massive sawfish. In the midst of the chaos was Rayman, flailing his arms on the way down.

Something else was falling, too. Paper. Lots of it.

She looked down at her body and saw that her bag was missing. It had been torn from her body while being dragged by the boat. Inside it had been cash. Rayman's cash.

She had brought it to end this once and for all—but the right way. To return Rayman's money and tell him to put the whole thing behind them. She had planned to sit there on that campus bench, and when Rayman had shown up to leave the cash, she was going to hand him the bag with his money and tell him she was sorry, here's your cash back. Forget this ever happened. She had decided it wasn't worth it. She had her job, after all, and her kid; she didn't need the money that much. She had thought of the scheme as a way to get back at him in the heat of the moment, but now no longer felt the heat.

Hundred dollar bills fluttered in the wind over the destroyed house and drifted on the water...and there was Dr. Mason Rayman himself, in the middle of it all, floating on his back, unconscious, neck bent back at a terrible angle after the fall, rope wrapped around it. It must have caught on something on the way down when the house fell apart. Elisa put the boat into gear at low speed and idled it over to him. She leaned over the rail and felt for a pulse even though she could see he was gone. Nothing.

A green bill washed over his face, and she released him to the waves.

She glanced around looking for the sawfish. Even being in the boat was no great protection from it. But then she saw that the beams it had been tied to had broken off. Looking past the house, she spotted a trio of large fins—the tail and the two dorsals—cutting through the water before sinking lower until they disappeared beneath the waves.

Even though she feared the animal like nothing else, she felt empathy for the creature, that Rayman had put it through such a traumatic experience through no fault of its own. *Go! You're free now, too, free to be a fish and hunt and breed and live. You were made by a monster, but you are not one. Find the others of your kind that are still out there somewhere.* It occurred to Elisa that there must be five of them out there now, including the one now swimming away. Five monsters that would grow who knew how large.

Elisa Gonzales started the boat while staring out to sea. She gave Rayman's corpse one last glance before turning back around to focus on figuring out how to drive his boat. She couldn't help but think about the man, his lifetime dedicated to his lab work, his precious research, the strange files on his computer...

What else did you do, Rayman?

THE END

CPSIA information can be obtained
at www.ICGtesting.com
Printed in the USA
LVHW042156280623
751101LV00031B/419